Five Nights

TALES FROM THE PIZZAPLEX

SACRAMENTO PUBLIC LIBRARY

D0440497

2023

FRIENDS OF THE
SACRAMENTO
PUBLIC LIBRARY

THIS BOOK WAS DONATED BY

**FRIENDS OF THE
ISLETON LIBRARY**

The Sacramento Public Library gratefully acknowledges this
contribution to support and improve Library services in the community.

SACRAMENTO PUBLIC LIBRARY

ANDREA WAGGENER

Scholastic Inc.

If you purchased this book without a cover, you should be aware that this book is stolen property. It was reported as "unsold and destroyed" to the publisher, and neither the author nor the publisher has received any payment for this "stripped book."

Copyright © 2023 by Scott Cawthon. All rights reserved.

Photo of TV static: © Klikk/Dreamstime

All rights reserved. Published by Scholastic Inc., *Publishers since 1920*. SCHOLASTIC and associated logos are trademarks and/or registered trademarks of Scholastic Inc.

The publisher does not have any control over and does not assume any responsibility for author or third-party websites or their content.

No part of this publication may be reproduced, stored in a retrieval system, or transmitted in any form or by any means, electronic, mechanical, photocopying, recording, or otherwise, without written permission of the publisher. For information regarding permission, write to Scholastic Inc., Attention: Permissions Department, 557 Broadway, New York, NY 10012.

This book is a work of fiction. Names, characters, places, and incidents are either the product of the author's imagination or are used fictitiously, and any resemblance to actual persons, living or dead, business establishments, events, or locales is entirely coincidental.

Library of Congress Cataloging-in-Publication Data available

ISBN 978-1-338-87133-3

10 9 8 7 6 5 4 3 2 1   23 24 25 26 27

Printed in the U.S.A.   131

First printing 2023 • Book design by Jeff Shake

TABLE OF CONTENTS

NEXIE

WHAT DO YOU WANT WITH ONE OF THOSE CRAZY THINGS?" ASTRID'S GRANDFATHER ASKED. HIS BIG, WARM HANDS RESTED ON ASTRID'S SHOULDERS, AND HE WAS LEANING OVER HER. "NOTHING BUT TROUBLE, ANIMATED TOYS," HE SAID. HE SHOOK HIS HEAD, AND HIS BEARD TICKLED HER FOREHEAD.

Pressed against the side of the neon-lit archway leading into the Pizzaplex's Buddytronics Boutique, Astrid didn't shift her gaze from the rows and rows and rows of doll and plush animal parts lining the walls of the build-your-own-toy store. At least a dozen kids, some of whom Astrid recognized as classmates from her school, darted from one part of the chaotic and colorful shop to the other. They were all chattering excitedly. Some of the kids were pointing at various parts and describing what they were going to create, and some of them were showing off their finished toys. A fast-paced pop song blasted from the store's speakers, and several kids were dancing with their new Buddytronics.

Astrid's gaze flitted from one Buddytronic to the next. All of the toys looked so huggable. Although they could talk and move because they had animatronic endoskeletons and processors under their plush exteriors, they hung limply and sweetly when they were idle. They were like floppy teddy bears or rag dolls when held in the arms of their owners. Astrid so wanted to have her own friendly Buddytronic to hug.

Astrid looked away from the finished toys and returned her attention to the rest of the shop. In front of the shelves stuffed with parts, a long assembly line–style machine was set up. Once you picked out the features you wanted for your toy, a clerk placed the parts in the machine and programmed it. A large computer screen above the machine displayed an image of what the toy would look like once it was done, and if approved, the machine churned into action. Its metal "arms" picked up the various parts and put them into place as the under-construction toy moved along a conveyor belt. Several Pizzaplex employees attended to the machine.

Right now, one of the girls from Astrid's school, Geena—a pretty girl (and she knew it) with long, shiny black hair—was loudly ordering around a curly haired clerk. Geena pointed at the assembly machine's display screen.

"I want his eyes to be a brighter green!" Geena commanded. As was typical for her, Geena stood with her hands on her hips. One foot jutted out, and it tapped the floor. Geena always wanted what she wanted the second she wanted it.

Astrid watched the clerk tap a few keys on the machine's control panel and swap out some parts. The display screen flashed an image of the Funtime Foxy Buddytronic that Geena wanted. With the brighter green eyes now in place, she turned her attention to the mouth. Geena screeched, "Bigger teeth!" The clerk scrambled to adjust the machine yet again.

Astrid heard her grandfather sigh. "Kids your age never know how good they have it," he said softly. "Always wanting something else."

Astrid felt her shoulders tighten. For the last couple weeks, Astrid had been bugging her grandfather—her *farfar*, the Swedish name for grandpa—to give her more chores to do so she could earn some extra money. When he'd asked her what she wanted the money for, she'd shrugged and said, "*Oh, just things.*"

In spite of his mistrust of "modern thingamajigs," Farfar was supportive of her interest in computers and programming. Even so, she knew how he felt about the animatronics at the Pizzaplex, and she couldn't bring herself to tell him that she wanted to buy a Buddytronic.

Ever since she'd started fourth grade, Astrid had been watching her classmates show off their Buddytronic pals. The animated toys were really, really neat; they were almost like having your very own best friend, one you could take anywhere. They were toys, yes, but they were close to the size of a small child—about two and a half to three feet tall. They could move around and walk (a little awkwardly). They also could talk to you, and they didn't just say the same silly lines over and over. They were programmed to respond to what you said to them, at least in a basic kind of way.

Since Astrid didn't have a best friend—or any friend, really—she desperately wanted a Buddytronic. The trouble was that a Buddytronic cost a thousand dollars. That was a lot of money. And unlike Astrid's classmates, who came from rich families that gave them whatever they wanted, Astrid didn't have a rich family. No friends. No rich family. Astrid didn't fit.

Astrid had always felt different from other kids, but she used to at least have a couple friends. She'd met Brooke and Jolie in first grade when she and her dad had moved here to live with Farfar, and even though they were "normal" little girls who liked to play house and had parents who bought them all the latest toys and clothes, they'd accepted Astrid. Astrid didn't understand why playing house was fun because all the things Brooke and Jolie pretended to do Astrid actually *did* to help her dad and her farfar. And all her toys and clothes were handmade. Brooke and Jolie thought that was amusing, but they didn't ever make fun of Astrid for it.

After second grade, though, Brooke had moved away and Astrid left public school and drifted apart from Jolie when they didn't have class together. Now, she was "the scholarship kid" at an expensive private school (she had won free tuition when she took first place in a math and programming competition). The teachers were nice, but the kids there definitely thought she was a weirdo. Astrid tried to make friends, but she just didn't know how to seem "normal." Astrid was much smarter than the other kids in her class, and she didn't think like them or act like them or dress like them. How could she? Stuck with an old-fashioned name, she had been raised by an old-fashioned dad and an old-fashioned grandfather.

Dad and Farfar were carpenters and they made their money building Swedish-style furniture by hand. They did nearly everything else by hand, too. They grew their own fruits and vegetables and beans and grains and raised their own cows for milk and cheese. They built their own machines and fixed them when they broke. They even made their own clothes and Astrid's clothes, too—clothes that didn't look anything like the ones her classmates wore.

"*Craftsmanship is our heritage. A craftsman's life is a good life,*" Astrid's dad often said. That might have been true, but she wished he wasn't a craftsman who had to travel all over to sell his work. He was gone more than he was home, and Astrid's farfar was the one she lived with most of the time. Astrid loved her farfar, but he believed in "the old ways," and he didn't like modern society. She had no idea how to make him understand just how much she longed to be part of that same society he was wary of.

Astrid's mother, who might have saved Astrid from being "the weird girl in the weird clothes," wasn't around. She'd left when Astrid had been really little; she'd moved across the country to become a model, something that Astrid's dad hadn't "approved of" and wouldn't "let" her do. Astrid barely remembered her mom, but she had a single picture. Blonde and blue-eyed with an almost doll-like face. Astrid's mom was beautiful.

Astrid's dad said that Astrid looked like her mom. And

she guessed she did, except she got her dad's wide forehead and large ears.

"Come on, kiddo," Astrid's farfar said.

Astrid blinked and realized she'd let her mind wander. She turned and smiled up at her farfar.

Dressed in a handsewn gray flannel shirt and baggy dungarees, Astrid's farfar looked as easygoing as he was. Astrid thought her farfar had one of the kindest—and best—faces in the world. Round and carved with deep smile lines, her farfar's face was dominated by gentle blue eyes, a big nose that bent slightly to the left, and a wide mouth that was usually upturned in a friendly smile. Astrid didn't think her farfar looked like a farfar. If it hadn't been for his curly gray hair and full (but neatly trimmed) gray beard, he could have passed for much younger than his actual age.

Her farfar smiled back and ruffled her short hair. "Those Skee-Ball machines are waiting for us," he said.

Astrid felt a surge of love and appreciation for her sweet-faced farfar. Even though he didn't like the Pizzaplex, he brought her here when he could find the time for it. Astrid was thankful that he loved playing Skee-Ball. That was how she'd talked him into coming to the big entertainment complex the first time.

"Takes me back to when I was a boy and the carnival came to town," her farfar always said when they played. Skee-Ball, he liked to say, was the only "real" game in the Pizzaplex's arcade. But after they played Skee-Ball, he always let Astrid choose another game to play.

Astrid took his hand. "Can we get pizza after we play, Farfar?"

Her farfar creased the same wide forehead he'd passed down to his son and granddaughter. He pursed his thick lips and pretended he was thinking hard. He winked at Astrid. "With green peppers?" he asked.

"What else is there?" Astrid responded. She giggled.

Her farfar squeezed her hand, and they walked away from the Buddytronics Boutique. As they went, however, Astrid glanced back over her shoulder. One way or the other, she decided, she was going to get her own Buddytronic pal.

Even though he could feel his neck flush as Astrid walked past his desk, Remy stretched out his legs and slouched. He pushed aside his DJ Music Man Buddytronic as if he was bored out of his mind. And actually, Remy was bored with the Buddytronic. Like the rest of his classmates, Remy had thought the Buddytronics were pretty awesome when they'd come out, but they were getting kind of tiring now. You could only do so much with them, and after a few weeks of messing with his Buddytronic, Remy didn't have much use for it anymore. But everyone was still bringing their Buddytronics to school, so Remy did, too.

No one knew that Remy liked Astrid. And no one was going to know, either. Remy was one of the most popular kids in their class. His dad was the richest man in the county, maybe even the state. His family, as his mother frequently reminded Remy, had "obligations" and an "image." Remy had to live up to both. Liking the class "weirdo" was not the way to do that.

Remy watched Astrid stand by the whiteboard at the front of the wood-paneled classroom. It was oral report day. They'd each had to write a story about reaching a goal, and they had to read the story aloud in front of the class. Remy had already read his story about getting his horse to jump the fallen log across one of the trails on his family's estate. It had gotten a lot of laughs, which had been his real goal.

For the hundredth time, Remy asked himself why he was the only one who could see that Astrid was cool.

Today, for instance, Astrid was dressed in an ankle-length yellow cotton dress with a big collar that looked like the crocheted things his grandma put on the arms of overstuffed chairs. A floppy beret-like orange knitted hat perched on top of her hair and slouched over one of her bright blue eyes.

Even though Remy sometimes tried to imagine Astrid in the regular clothes the other girls in his class wore, he thought that Astrid might not have been as appealing if she'd dressed "normally." Something about her old-timey clothes was kind of rad.

And odd clothes or not, Astrid—in Remy's opinion—was the prettiest girl in the school. She looked like a princess in a fairy tale, and Remy secretly wanted to be her prince.

Although she had long arms and legs, she had a small torso . . . it was almost doll-like. For some reason, her small torso made Astrid seem kind of weak-looking. Remy thought it was like she needed a prince to look after her. She didn't act like that, though. Astrid wasn't anything like some of the crybaby girls in the class.

Even if Astrid hadn't been as pretty as he thought she was, Remy still would have liked her. He wasn't sure why. Maybe it was the way Astrid moved. It was possible that she could have had warts and worn a paper bag and he would have nonetheless been drawn to her.

Unlike the other girls Remy knew, Astrid never acted like she was putting on a show to get attention. She never seemed self-conscious. She didn't flash fake smiles or strike poses. Remy had no doubt that Astrid was exactly what she appeared to be—a smart girl who was happy in her own skin. Oddly, that was another reason the other kids didn't like Astrid. She was so comfortable with herself that she raised her hand and spoke up in class all the time. She always had the right answers. Other kids said she was a know-it-all. Remy didn't see her that way at all. He just saw her as brilliant and confident. He saw her as perfectly one of a kind.

Making sure he kept his gaze lazily directed toward one of the tall paned windows that looked out at the rolling green lawn outside the school, Remy listened intently to every word of Astrid's story. He had to work to keep his face blank because Astrid's story was smart and amusing. It was about a girl who was trying to earn enough money to buy an expensive necklace. Using economics concepts that probably no one besides Remy and maybe one other person in the class—Johnny, Remy's best friend, who was as smart as Astrid and almost as rich as Remy—Astrid described an earning plan that combined hard work with clever psychological manipulation.

In the middle of Astrid's story, Hugo, the class trouble-maker, made a deliberately loud snoring sound. Everyone laughed, and Warren, the class bully, shot a spitball at Astrid.

Remy risked a look at Astrid as the spitball landed on her collar. He put his hand over his mouth to hide his grin when she casually flicked the spitball away with enough force to rocket it toward Camilla's left ear.

Camilla, one of the popular girls who was way too full of herself (her best friend was Geena, who had to be the most stuck-up girl on the planet), squealed and glared at Astrid. Astrid's words didn't falter at all. She just kept reading her story.

"I'm not sure what I did was right, though," Astrid read. "My farfar says that when we're desperate for something, it's probably something we shouldn't have."

"What's a farfar?" Remy's friend Brett called from the other side of the room.

Astrid looked up from her printed story. Her steady gaze found Brett. "Farfar is the Swedish word for *grandpa*," she explained.

"Too bad you're not farfar away," Camilla whispered loudly enough for the whole room to hear.

Everyone laughed.

"Camilla!" Miss Hallstrom snapped. She glared at the rest of the class.

Camilla shrugged. The laughs died down into muffled chuckles.

Astrid finished her story, and the stick-thin, ponytailed Miss Hallstrom stood. "Well done, Astrid," Miss Hallstrom said. She smiled her crooked-toothed smile at Astrid.

The class erupted in noisy boos. Feeling like a world-class jerk, Remy joined in. Image trumped what was right. He'd learned that from his dad.

But even as he booed, Remy kept his sideways gaze on Astrid. Her head held high, Astrid returned to her seat at the back of the room while Miss Hallstrom pounded on her desk and shouted for everyone to "settle down."

★ ★ ★

As dusk settled over her farfar's two-story farmhouse, Astrid sat on the patchwork quilt that covered her twin-size bed. Her savings were spread out across the red-and-yellow cotton squares. She'd counted them three times. And it wasn't even close to enough.

Astrid sighed and gazed out the open window. The branches of the massive oak tree were heavy with new leaves. They fluttered in the stiff breeze that crept into Astrid's room and made the hems of her turquoise curtains dance. The breeze carried in the sweet scent of the lilac her farfar grew along the borders of his garden.

Astrid looked around her cozy room with its pale yellow walls covered with handwoven tapestries, framed cross-stitched and embroidered flowers, pretty watercolors and pastels of trees and lakes. (Everything on her walls had been made for her by some member of her extended family, none of whom lived nearby but all of whom made sure to remember her on her birthday and Christmas.) She let her gaze linger on her shelves stuffed full of wood- and stone-carved animals. Her aunts and uncles and cousins had made dozens, and she loved them all.

Not for the first time, Astrid thought about how lucky she was to live in such a pretty place. After Astrid's mom had left but before Astrid and her dad had come to live with Farfar, they'd lived in a two-bedroom apartment in a concrete complex right at the edge of the industrial part of the city. She'd hated that. It had been so noisy and crowded, so gray and dingy. So cold. She much preferred the green that surrounded her farfar's house, and she loved that all she could hear on a night like this was the sound of birds twittering in the bushes below her window and the occasional moo coming from the pasture out behind the house.

But no matter how much she liked her home, Astrid wasn't fully happy. She was too frustrated to be happy.

For the last month, ever since she'd watched Geena order up her Buddytronic, Astrid had been working every spare minute to earn the money she needed for her own. But the kind of chores she could do weren't big earners, and she didn't have enough hours in the day to make that much cash.

With a birthday coming up, Astrid had told her farfar and her dad that she wanted money instead of gifts, but from the look they'd exchanged, she could tell they'd already made something for her. So, she'd quickly added, *"But whatever you give me will be great."*

Even though Astrid had relatives who cared about her (from afar) and she had her dad and her farfar, Astrid was alone most of the time. She was okay with her own company because she had plenty to keep her busy. She had her chores around the farm, and she spent hours on her computer. Sometimes, however, Astrid really missed having friends. If she'd had friends, she could have invited them to a birthday party and asked for money instead of gifts. At school, she'd heard Camilla tell Geena that Camilla was going to do that so she could buy a pair of suede boots her parents refused to get her.

If Astrid had invited anyone to a birthday celebration, they wouldn't have come, much less brought money. But that didn't mean Astrid couldn't use the idea.

Even though Astrid had no friends and had never had a birthday party, Astrid's aunts and uncles always sent her presents. She thought that if she was careful about how she asked, she might be able to get them to send money instead. So, a couple weeks before her birthday, Astrid sat down and wrote friendly notes to her relatives. In the notes, she explained that she was learning about money and how to invest it at school and it would be very helpful to have enough money to invest so she could do well in her school project. She felt a little bad about lying, but not horribly so. She did want to invest (in a Buddytronic), and she was doing a school project (fitting in by having a Buddytronic).

Astrid's plan might have worked if she'd had a normal family. Unfortunately, most of her aunts and uncles were on her dad's side of the family—they were her farfar's sons and daughters. And farfar had raised his sons and daughters to take pride in handmade items. Cash wasn't a handmade item. So, Astrid received the usual knitted sweaters, carved animals for her collection, and hand-sewn dresses. As predicted, Astrid's dad and farfar presented her with what he and her dad had made for her—a big new desk for her bedroom. The oak wood they'd used had probably cost more than the amount of money she still needed to come up with, and she'd had to hide her frustration when she saw the massive corner desk that admittedly fit perfectly in her room between her dresser and her shelves (presents from previous birthdays). She pretended like the desk was the best thing in the world; no way was she going to hurt her farfar's feelings.

Astrid did score some cash, though. A couple of her aunts on her mom's side of the family sent money. Probably because Astrid's aunts felt guilty about how their sister had abandoned Astrid, they sent $100 bills. That brought Astrid's total to just $120 shy of what she needed.

It was close. But it wasn't enough. Which was why Astrid

burst into tears when she was blowing out the candles on the chocolate cake Farfar had baked. (Her dad was on the road and couldn't make it back in time for her birthday.)

Astrid and her farfar sat together at the small maple table that was placed precisely in the center of a burgundy-and-cream braided rug that had been made by Farfar's wife (Astrid's Farmor, who'd passed away a couple years before Astrid was born). Her farfar's prized pendulum wall clock, which hung on a green-painted wall covered with family pictures, ticked away the seconds.

"What in the Sam Hill?" Farfar said when Astrid swiped at her wet face.

Astrid's farfar went pale, as if he'd done something terribly wrong. "Is it the cake?" he asked. "You don't like chocolate anymore?"

"The cake is great," Astrid said. But her voice shook.

Her farfar raised an eyebrow.

"Really," Astrid said. "It's not the cake."

"It's the desk," her farfar said. "You don't like it."

"No!" Astrid cried. "I mean, yes, I love the desk." She sniffed.

"Then what?"

Astrid shook her head. How could she explain what she wanted and why she wanted it?

Her farfar tugged on his beard the way he did when he was trying to solve a problem. He pushed aside the cake and leaned toward Astrid. "Tell me, kiddo, how much money have you saved up for that fancy-dancy doll you want?"

Astrid's eyes widened. "How did you know?"

Her farfar smiled, then reached out and patted her hand. He didn't answer her question.

"I'm $120 short of what I need," Astrid said.

"Hm, well, I just so happen to have $120 tucked away for a rainy day." Astrid's farfar glanced out the window. "Or for a not-rainy day, as it so happens." He chuckled.

Astrid smiled. Then she frowned. "But you think dolls are . . ."

Her farfar waved a hand. "I may not understand all the computery stuff you like so much, but I do understand the idea of liking what you like. When I was your age, all I wanted to do was build furniture, and my pappa thought anything that didn't have to do with farming was a waste of time. I had to fight him tooth and nail to get to do what I wanted to do, and I promised I'd never do that to my own kids. Your dad and your aunts and uncles got to choose what they loved. And you get to choose as well. If what you want is a computerized doll thing, that's what you should have."

Astrid's farfar stood. "Let's go to the Pizzaplex and get you a Buddytron."

"A Buddytronic," Astrid corrected automatically.

"Yes, that." Astrid's farfar held out his hand.

"What in tarnation?" Astrid's farfar said when he and Astrid joined the throng clogging the main walkway that circled the interior of the Pizzaplex.

Astrid gasped as a red-shirted Pizzaplex employee tore past her and nearly knocked her down. Her farfar caught her and put a protective arm around her shoulders.

As usual, the Pizzaplex was filled with a bunch of noises that sounded like they were at war with one another. Rock music from the stages clashed with tinny music and pings and beeps from the games. The whoosh of the overhead roller coaster went up against the roar of the cars in Roxy's Raceway, and kids' squeals competed with adult laughter. Tonight, though, there was something more intense about all the sound. Or was it that there was a new sound? Astrid thought she could make out, just beyond the rest of the clamor, a high-pitched squeal. It was like the feedback sound that came out of a microphone sometimes.

"Something weird is going on," Astrid said.

"Seems so." Her farfar guided her to the edge of the black-and-white tiled concourse. "Let's stay over here, out of the way." He frowned at the wildness around them. But he said, "Now, which way to your doll buddy?"

Astrid pointed past the castle that rose up under the big stained-glass ceiling that was in the middle of the Pizzaplex's roof. It wasn't a real castle; it was a theater. But it looked the way castles always looked in fairy tales.

Astrid's farfar kept his arm around her as they began weaving through the thick crowd. As they went, all the neon lights at the entrances of the stores and the various rides and game areas started blinking. For an instant, the lit-up branches of the big, fat Storyteller's Tree near the theater went completely dark. So did the tree's roots—the snakelike LED lights that meandered away from the tree, seemingly reaching into every part of the Pizzaplex. As quickly as they went out, the lights came back on. But then other lights flickered. As Astrid and her farfar passed the main dining room, its overhead lights went out and then lit up again.

Another Pizzaplex employee dashed past Astrid. This time, she pressed close to her farfar, and she avoided being bumped.

They were getting close to the Buddytronics Boutique now. They just had to get past another couple of stores.

The crowd was even bigger here. Astrid craned her neck to see through the people.

Her farfar kept her moving, and in seconds, they were in front of the Buddytronics Boutique. Astrid forgot all about the boy in the glass dome. She let go of her farfar's hand and started to dart into the boutique.

A clerk, a tall brown-haired guy with eyes that were really close together, stepped out in front of her and held up a hand. "Sorry, but you can't come in. We're, um, I think we're closing."

"No!" Astrid wailed. She couldn't help herself. She'd been so excited, so close to getting her Buddytronic.

"You *think* you're closing?" Astrid's farfar asked. He planted himself in front of the brown-haired guy. "If you're not sure, then how about you stay open long enough for my granddaughter to get her botbuddy."

Astrid blushed, but she didn't correct her farfar.

Another clerk, a curly haired man, strode around the Buddytronic's assembly machine. She and the male clerk exchanged a glance.

"I think we need to shut it down," the woman said. She reached for the black metal accordion grating that was pushed back on either side of the entrance.

"You sure?" the male clerk asked. "Maybe . . ." He shrugged.

The woman shrugged, too. "I'm running a diagnostic, but I think it's best." She started to pull out the metal grating.

Astrid's farfar took a step and braced his hand against the grating. Stiff-armed, he kept the red-headed clerk from pulling the grating closed.

"Why can't you just let us in before you close?" Astrid's

farfar asked. "Just one more buddy to make, huh? Then you can close up and go home if you want."

The woman shook her head, but she didn't try to pull on the grating. "It's not that we're trying to get off early, sir," she said. "It's just that we're not sure what's going on with the lights and stuff. Everything's . . . twitchy. It's probably best that we close. You can come back tomorrow."

Astrid shook her head. She had a really strong feeling that if they left, her farfar would change his mind. She could tell by the way he was squinting at the shelves of parts that he was having second thoughts about helping her get her Buddytronic.

"Please, Farfar," Astrid whispered.

How he heard her over the racket filling the Pizzaplex, Astrid didn't know. But he apparently did. Or maybe he just knew what she wanted.

He looked at the redhead's name tag. "Karen," he said. "Can I call you Karen?"

Karen smiled. "Sure."

Astrid's farfar gave Karen one of his biggest smiles as he gestured at Astrid. "Today is my granddaughter's birthday. She just turned nine."

Karen flicked a glance at Astrid. "Happy Birthday," she said.

"Thank you." Astrid tried to look both friendly and pathetic at the same time.

"And what my granddaughter wants for her birthday, more than anything," Astrid's farfar continued, "is one of those buddy things you have in here. I'm not all that hot on animatronic contraptions, but my granddaughter is a good girl, and she deserves to have what she wants. You don't want to ruin a good girl's birthday, do you?"

Karen looked at the male clerk. His name tag said his name was Vince. Astrid's farfar looked at Vince, too.

"How about you, Vince?" Astrid's farfar asked. "You want to ruin this little girl's birthday?" Astrid's farfar patted Astrid's head like she was a toddler.

Astrid clasped her hands together. She opened her eyes wide, pleading.

Karen and Vince exchanged another glance as the overhead lights sputtered. Karen shrugged. "You'd better make it quick," she said to Astrid.

Karen gestured for Astrid and her farfar to enter the boutique. Then Karen pulled the grating closed behind them.

"Go ahead and pick out what you want," Karen said. "We'll see if the program takes."

Astrid immediately dashed around the assembly machine and ran down the length of the parts shelves. She knew what she wanted. She had a perfect vision of it in her mind, so she chose her parts quickly.

She started with long blonde braids. "I want three of those," Astrid said, "and I want them to be woven together, so it's like a braided braid."

Karen was following Astrid with an electronic tablet. She typed in Astrid's instructions.

Astrid pointed at round blue eyes. "I want those eyes." She pointed at an upturned nose. "That nose." She pointed at rosy, pouting lips not that different from her own. "Those lips. With even, white teeth. Not big teeth like those." She pointed. She frowned and scanned the teeth. "More like those." She pointed at smaller teeth. Then she hurried on down the row. She spotted full, pink cheeks. She gestured at them. "Those cheeks, please."

Astrid went from one set of features to the next until she'd picked all the elements that would create a face that looked very much like her mother's. Then she hurried over to the clothing section of the boutique. She pointed at a simple blue dress with a little flounce around its hem and a darker blue bow around its waist. In the front, below the waistline, the dress had big patch pockets in the same dark blue as the bow.

"That dress, please," Astrid said. She spotted a straw hat with a wide brim and a blue bow that would match the dress. "And that hat."

"Got it," Karen said, typing. "And how about the body?" Karen pointed at doll torsos, arms, and legs.

Astrid thought the separate parts were a little creepy, so she just looked at Karen. "I'd like the doll to be tall and slender. Whatever parts work for that will be good."

Karen nodded and typed some more. "Is that it?" she asked.

Astrid looked over at her farfar. He gave her a thumbs-up. She smiled and nodded. "Yes, that's it," she said.

The overhead lights went wonky again. Astrid looked up and chewed on the inside of her lip. *Please stay on*, she begged the electricity silently.

The lights came on full again. Karen stepped over to the Buddytronics assembly machine and quickly typed in Astrid's instructions.

"Okay," Karen said, gesturing at the machine's screen. "Is this what you had in mind?"

Astrid looked up at the screen. She clapped her hands. "That's perfect!" she said. The image on the screen looked like a doll version of Astrid's mother. It really was perfect.

"She's beautiful," Astrid said. "I'm going to call her Lexie."

"That's a nice name," Karen said. She smiled. "All right, then. Let's get Lexie built." She tapped a few keys on the machine's control panel.

Astrid heard a droning sound inside the machine. Something clunked, and then the machine's arms started reaching out to grab parts off the shelves.

Astrid, mesmerized by the image on the machine's screen, didn't pay much attention to what the machine was doing as it built her Buddytronic. Neither did Karen, Vince, or Farfar. Karen and Vince were huddled together, talking quietly. Astrid's farfar was looking out through the closed metal grating. He was watching the commotion near the glass dome.

Astrid didn't take her gaze from the image on the screen until the conveyor belt's hum got louder and she heard a *clink* and a *thump*. Was her Buddytronic complete?

Astrid trotted over to the end of the conveyor belt. She reached it just as Karen lifted Astrid's Buddytronic.

"Oh." Karen blew out a loud breath and looked at Astrid. "I'm really sorry," Karen said.

Astrid frowned. "Why?"

Karen twisted her lips and turned Astrid's Buddytronic around so Astrid could see the doll from the front. "The system must have been glitching worse than we thought," Karen said. She dropped the animatronic onto the metal platform at the end of the conveyor belt. The doll landed on her back with her arms and legs in the air. Her gaze was pointed up at the ceiling.

Astrid stared at her Buddytronic. She felt her farfar step up behind her.

"What in the heck is that?" Farfar asked.

Astrid pressed her lips together. She blinked several times. *I won't cry*, she told herself.

But she wanted to.

Her beautiful Buddytronic. She'd thought about the way her Buddytronic would look for weeks. Every time she'd looked at her mother's photo, she'd imagined seeing those features on her very own Buddytronic. It was going to be like having her mother back with her again. Only this time her mother would want to be with her because Buddytronics were designed to be loyal to their owners.

But this . . . this wasn't anything like her mother.

Astrid's farfar pointed at the Buddytronic. "We're not paying for that."

"Of course not, sir," Karen said. "What I'll do is . . ."

Astrid didn't hear the rest of what Karen said. It sounded like a storm was raging inside Astrid's head. Her ears were filled with a whooshing sound.

Astrid's heart was pounding, too. And she felt a little nauseated.

But she couldn't look away from her Buddytronic.

All the parts she'd picked out were there, she realized, as she studied the blonde-haired doll. But they were there in really awful ways.

The blue eyes, for instance, weren't placed right. One was much higher than the other, and the lower eyeball stuck out as if it was about to pop out of the doll's face.

The plump cheeks were there, but they were low on the face so they looked more like jowls. The pouty mouth and the upturned nose were there, but they were too close together. The nose was practically resting on the upper lip of the mouth. And the mouth didn't seem to want to close properly. This made it look like the doll was baring its teeth, like it was getting ready to snarl at any moment. The face, as a whole, looked like something Dr. Frankenstein might have created.

And then there was the hair. The machine had given the doll the braids that Astrid had wanted, but the braids originated at the base of the doll's skull instead of at the top. They jutted upward and then knotted together and sprayed outward like a big blonde spider. The braids were so wild, they almost seemed alive.

The doll's proportions were all wrong, too. The doll's head was much too small for her nearly three-foot-tall body, and the nice long arms and legs were placed strangely. The arms jutted from the doll's sides instead of from normal shoulders, and the legs seemed to start at the doll's waist, right next to where the arms started. The doll's neck was too long, and its chest was too compacted. Because of this too-small head and odd body, the doll's clothes fit poorly. The hat sat low on the doll's forehead, and the dress was scrunched up and wrinkled; it was stretched nearly to ripping at the shoulders.

The Buddytronic was really hard to look at. It was beyond ugly. Really, the thing was more monster than doll.

Astrid's farfar took her hand. "Come on, kiddo. That's not what you wanted. Let's get out of here." He pulled gently, attempting to draw Astrid away from the horrible thing in front of her.

Astrid, however, didn't move.

"Astrid, honey?" her farfar said gently.

Out of the corner of her eye, Astrid watched her farfar

turn to face Karen. "She's traumatized," he said. "I'm going to want to speak to your supervisor."

Astrid shook her head. "No, Farfar. It's okay."

Astrid took a step forward. She touched the doll's short-fingered hand.

"You really don't have to take this doll," Karen said. "You can come back when we get the system repaired, and we'll make you a good one."

A good one, Astrid thought. What made something good or bad? Was it the way something looked?

Astrid's mom was really pretty, but she'd abandoned Astrid. Was that good?

This Buddytronic was supposed to be like Astrid's mom. If Astrid refused it, wasn't she really just refusing her mom? Wasn't she doing exactly what her mom did? Walking away because things weren't the way she wanted them to be?

A couple years before, Astrid had overheard her dad talking to her farfar. They were talking about her, and her dad had used the word *accident*. Was Astrid an accident? What if she was? For sure, she was different. And she didn't fit in. But she didn't deserve to be rejected. Neither did this doll.

"It's okay," Astrid said. "I'll take her."

"What?" Karen cried out.

Astrid felt her farfar's hand on her shoulder. She looked up at his bunched-brows expression. For reasons she didn't understand, Astrid felt tears fill her eyes. When they escaped and started running down her cheek, her farfar reached out and brushed the droplet away with his calloused thumb. He studied Astrid's face for a few seconds, then he turned to Karen.

Gesturing at the doll, Astrid's farfar asked, "Is it safe? Are the problems just with its appearance or will its function be a mess, too?"

Karen looked at the doll. She curled her upper lip a little, and Astrid knew Karen was disgusted by the doll. Karen scrunched up her nose, took a deep breath, and leaned over the doll. She reached behind the doll's neck. Astrid heard a click, and the doll sat up.

The doll's eyelids lowered and raised again. Then the doll's blue eyes brightened almost to a glow. The doll looked around, and its gaze landed on Astrid. "Hello," the doll said. "My name is Nexie. What is your name?"

In addition to all the physical problems, the machine had messed up the doll's name, too. But that didn't matter. As soon as the doll spoke, Astrid's hesitation about the doll disappeared entirely. She felt an instant connection with Nexie, as if they'd been friends forever.

"Hi," Astrid said. "My name is Astrid."

Something inside Nexie's too-small head hummed as Nexie's eyes unfocused for a few seconds. Then Nexie widened her tiny mouth into what was probably meant to be a smile but looked more like a grimace. "Astrid," Nexie repeated in a flat, robotic voice that didn't sound at all like a girl's voice. "The name Astrid comes from the Swedish name Ástríðr. It means 'divinely beautiful' because it combines the Norse words for *god* and *beautiful*. The name Astrid has been a Scandinavian royal name since the tenth century."

"Well, I'll be," Astrid's farfar said, raising his unruly eyebrows at the doll. "It got that right."

"She," Astrid said. "Nexie is a she." It didn't matter that Nexie didn't sound like a girl, she *was* a girl.

Astrid looked at Karen. "I didn't know the dolls were programmed to have facts like that."

Karen frowned at Nexie, then opened and closed her mouth. She shrugged. "The programming of Buddytronics is updated regularly."

"What else does it . . . she . . . do?" Astrid's farfar asked.

Astrid looked at Nexie. "Can you walk, Nexie?" she asked.

Nexie immediately stood, and she began moving down the conveyor belt. Her gait was awkward, more of a lurch than a walk, but she took long strides and covered a lot of distance quickly. She then turned and came back. When she stopped, she held out her strangely placed arms.

Astrid immediately picked up her new doll. When Nexie draped her arms around Astrid's shoulders, Astrid smiled.

"Well, I guess we'll take her after all," Astrid's farfar said.

Five minutes later, Astrid, her farfar, and Nexie were walking down the concourse, heading toward the Pizzaplex exit. Rather than feeling self-conscious about her odd-looking Buddytronic, Astrid realized she was proud to have such a unique new friend. It didn't bother her at all when people turned to watch her and Nexie walk by.

As they moved through the packed crowd in the Pizzaplex, Astrid noticed that cheers were erupting from near the glass dome. When she turned to look that way, Nexie turned as well. Astrid enjoyed that copycat movement. It made her love Nexie even more.

The next day, when Astrid walked to school, she felt like her feet weren't touching the ground. It seemed like she was floating on a billowy cloud. She couldn't remember ever being so excited to be going to school. And it was because she wasn't going alone. She had Nexie with her.

Because the day was unusually cool and drizzly, Astrid wore her rain parka. She kept Nexie tucked under the waxed gray canvas until she got to her locker. When she took off her coat, she set Nexie on the beige laminate floor. Nexie immediately stood and began looking around. As she turned, the doll's braids flopped around her. The night before, Astrid had removed Nexie's hat. It was just too big to stay on, since the weird braids stuck out all around Nexie's head.

"Ew, gross!" a boy cried out. "What *is* that thing?!"

At first, Astrid ignored him. She usually tuned out what was going on around her at school. The other kids never spoke to her.

Then someone kicked Nexie.

"Ow," Nexie said.

Astrid scooped Nexie up and spun to face whoever had hurt her doll. She found herself looking into the small, dark eyes of Warren, who'd hit her with a spitball the other day. His square face taut, he was holding his own Montgomery Gator Buddytronic, and he was pointing at Nexie.

"Look at this piece-of-crap doll!" Warren shouted. His high voice bounced off the gray metal lockers and carried all the way down the hall.

A couple dozen kids, most of whom held Buddytronics of their own, turned to stare at Astrid and Nexie. Astrid started to rotate Nexie so her back was to the other kids, but Warren reached out and grabbed Nexie's arm. He yanked Nexie from Astrid's grasp.

Warren held Nexie up and sneered at her. "This is the

ugliest thing I've ever seen," Warren said. "Even uglier than you, Astrid." Warren said Astrid's name the way he always did, drawing it out and making it sound like something nasty.

"Give her back, please," Astrid said. She stood on her tiptoes and reached for Nexie.

Warren lifted Nexie above his head. He was taller and larger than Astrid (and all the other kids in their school), and he held Nexie mockingly above his head.

"Look at that face," he jeered. He poked at Nexie's bulging eyeball. "It's like something from outer space."

"You should talk," Astrid said. "Like your face is any better." Astrid immediately pressed her lips together. She didn't normally talk to people that way.

Astrid tried again to retrieve her Buddytronic. But Warren backstepped and held Nexie out of reach.

The other kids in the hall clustered around Warren. They all stared at Nexie. So did their Buddytronics. Astrid spotted Camilla and Geena, who were pointing at Nexie and laughing. Geena's Funtime Foxy Buddytronic and Camilla's Circus Baby Buddytronic were laughing, too. Behind the girls, green-eyed, blond Remy, who Astrid thought was the cutest boy in the class, stood with his skinny, auburn-haired best friend, Johnny. Remy was frowning, and when he glanced at Astrid, he immediately looked away as if he couldn't stand looking at her.

Warren shook Nexie really hard. Her misplaced arms and legs flopped around, and her braids flew into a tangle.

Geena cried out, "Oh, seriously! That's too creepy!"

"That thing looks just like Astrid," Camilla crowed. Then she laughed her witchlike laugh. And everyone else joined in.

Astrid couldn't take anymore. She had to protect her new friend.

"Stop it!" Astrid screamed. She rushed at Warren and kicked him in the shin.

"Hey!" Warren shouted. His face turned red. He dropped Nexie and started toward Astrid.

"What's going on here?" a deep voice boomed.

Warren froze, but he glared hard at Astrid. Ignoring Warren, Astrid bent down and picked up Nexie.

The other kids in the hall scurried away as Mr. Mullins, the school principal, came striding down the hall. A huge man with wide shoulders and trunk-like legs, Mr. Mullins wasn't nearly as scary as he looked . . . unless he was angry. And Astrid could tell from his narrowed eyes and flushed face that Mr. Mullins was angry.

Mr. Mullins reached Astrid and Warren just as Warren started to turn and trot away. Mr. Mullins, a muscle bulging in his wide jaw, grabbed Warren by the back of his orange T-shirt.

"Not so fast, Mr. Price," Mr. Mullins said. "You"—he turned and pointed at Astrid—"and you, Miss Eriksen, are going to join me in my office for a little chat."

"But I—" Astrid began.

"But nothing," Mr. Mullins said. "I saw you kick Mr. Price. Very unlike you, Miss Eriksen. I'll need an explanation." Mr. Mullins let go of Warren's collar and gave him a gentle shove to get him moving down the hall. "I'll admit that Mr. Price can be more than a little trying, Miss Eriksen," he continued, "but this school has a no-tolerance policy for violence of any kind."

"But—" Astrid tried again.

"We'll sort it out in my office," Mr. Mullins said.

★ ★ ★

Astrid switched on her small bedside lamp. The bulb's glow turned the lamp's wooden tripod legs golden. Astrid's farfar had made the lamp (of course), and for several seconds, she looked at it, letting its familiarity soothe her.

It had been a very long day. And it had been a very bad day.

Even though Astrid had explained to Mr. Mullins why she'd kicked Warren, Mr. Mullins had called Farfar (her dad was still out of town), and Astrid had received a demerit on her record. Warren had gotten a day's suspension from school for bullying. Astrid didn't think that was fair. She knew that a day off from school was no punishment for Warren.

The rest of the day, Astrid had been forced to listen, without complaint, to her classmates' mean comments about Nexie. And she'd had to put up with the snickers and the pointing fingers.

When she'd gotten home, Astrid's farfar had suggested that maybe Astrid should return Nexie. Astrid had immediately cried out, "*No!*" Instead of turning Astrid against the Buddytronic, all the cruel attention Nexie had gotten made Astrid feel even more loyal to the doll. Nexie needed someone to love her and accept her as she was. Astrid was going to be that someone.

Astrid sat down on the edge of her bed. She turned to look at Nexie, who was perched on Astrid's pillow.

"I'm really sorry you were treated so badly," Astrid said.

"Nothing is your fault," Nexie said. "They did not like me because I am ugly."

"You're not ugly!" Astrid cried.

"Yes, I am ugly," Nexie said. "The big boy said you are ugly, too. We can be ugly together."

"I'm not ugly," Astrid said. "Warren says that just to try to make me cry."

Astrid might not have fit in with the other kids at her school but that didn't mean something was wrong with her. She knew that. Her farfar had made sure she understood it.

"People don't like things that are different than what they're used to," Astrid's farfar had explained the first time a kid at school had made fun of Astrid's clothes. "And when they don't like things, they can be mean about it. But that doesn't have anything to do with you. It has to do with them. If you look in your heart, you'll always know the truth of who you are."

Astrid had looked. And she knew. She knew she was Astrid. Just Astrid. She was happy with herself. She wanted Nexie to be happy with herself, too.

Astrid scootched back in her bed. She tucked her legs up under her and turned to face Nexie.

"Just because you look different doesn't mean you're ugly," Astrid told Nexie. As she said the words, Astrid felt a little twist in her stomach because she was lying a little bit. Astrid remembered thinking that Nexie was ugly when Astrid had first seen her. But Nexie didn't need to know that.

"Your name means beautiful," Nexie said. "Everyone should match their name."

Astrid couldn't believe Nexie said things like that. In just the one day that Astrid had been with Nexie, Astrid had learned that Nexie was almost like a real person when it came to the things she said. She was way more advanced than the other Buddytronics Astrid had seen. The ones the other kids at school had could only say a few words here and there, and most of the words were very simple.

Even though Astrid knew her farfar loved her very much, her farfar was still her farfar. He was a busy man who was working on his farm or his business nearly every minute of the day. He spent time with her as often as he could, but he'd never be a friend or a playmate. Nexie could be both of those things.

Astrid scooted over to sit next to Nexie. "Do you want me to read a book to you?" she asked.

Nexie stretched her lips into her version of a smile. "Yes. Please read."

Astrid was in the middle of a thick fantasy book, so she explained to Nexie the story's plot and described all the characters. Then she pulled her quilt up over her and Nexie and read until her eyes were droopy enough for sleep.

Astrid set the book on her nightstand and got up to put on her pj's. Nexie stayed where she was, but she followed Astrid with her gaze.

"Everyone would like me if I was not ugly," Nexie said as Astrid put her dress in her dirty clothes hamper.

Astrid turned to look at Nexie.

"In the story, the people liked Princess Sunshine after she changed the way she ruled," Nexie said. "When we change things that people do not like, they can like us."

Astrid frowned and returned to the bed. She sat, then reached out and took Nexie's short-fingered hand. Nexie curled those fingers around Astrid's own. Nexie's "skin," made of a thin, almost fabric-like, super-smooth plastic, was cool in Astrid's grip.

"That's not really true," Astrid said. "When we like ourselves, others like us for who we are."

"But no one likes you," Nexie said.

Astrid let go of Nexie's hand. The words had felt like a slap.

Astrid shook her head. "Not everyone likes everyone else. It's how the world works."

Nexie seemed to think about this. Then she said, "But when you're ugly, it's harder to be liked."

Astrid opened her mouth to deny what Nexie said, but Nexie kept talking. "My arms and legs are in the wrong places," she said. "You can help me change the things that are wrong. You just need the right parts. Could you please help me fix what is wrong?"

Astrid started to shake her head. But Nexie's gaze was steady, filled with pleading. Astrid couldn't just dismiss the doll's request.

"I might be able to fix your arms and legs," Astrid said. She'd already been thinking about that. She'd helped her farfar with enough projects that she was sure she could figure out how to reposition Nexie's arms and legs if she had the right parts. And maybe she could get them.

Because Nexie had turned out "wonky," Karen had sold Nexie to Astrid and her farfar for half price. Astrid's farfar had let her keep the $120 he'd been intending to put toward the Buddytronic, too. "It's part of your birthday present," he had explained. That meant Astrid had almost $500 left. She could probably buy at least some of the parts she needed with that much money.

"Other things need fixing," Nexie said.

"Like what?" Astrid asked.

"The torso needs to be longer," Nexie said. "No one likes a short torso."

Astrid frowned. How could she get Nexie a longer torso? That part would be too expensive to buy.

"The face should be fixed, too," Nexie said. "The eyes should be farther apart and bigger. The nose and mouth are too small. The cheeks are too round. And the hair is messy. Hair should be smooth and tidy."

Astrid couldn't help herself. She laughed. "Okay, okay," she said. "One thing at a time. Let's see if I can get what I need to move your arms and legs first."

Nexie cocked her head. Her blue eyes scanned Astrid's face with intent focus.

Astrid leaned forward and hugged her doll. "We'll get you fixed up," she said.

"Together," Nexie said. "We are connected."

Astrid pulled back from Nexie and smiled at her. "Yes, we are," Astrid said.

Buddytronics were still super popular, but Remy had stopped bringing his to school. When his friends asked him why, he told them his parents had made him stop because he'd lost the Buddytronic three times. That he'd lost it that many times was true, but his parents didn't even know about that. He was just tired of carrying it around.

He wished everyone else would get tired of Buddytronics, too. Especially Astrid.

Ever since Astrid had shown up at school with her wildly creepy doll, she'd been under fire even more than usual.

What Astrid was doing was so bizarre. Remy couldn't decide whether to feel sorry for the girl he liked or be mad at her for being so dumb. Why would anyone who already didn't fit in because of the way she dressed and acted want to start bringing a freaky doll to school? Sure, it was a Buddytronic, but it was a Buddytronic that looked like it belonged in a post-nuclear world. The thing made Remy's skin crawl. He could barely stand to look at it.

But whenever he wanted to look at Astrid—which was often—he always ended up seeing the doll, too.

Remy stood at his locker, a few feet down from Astrid's. He pretended to mess with the zipper on his backpack as he watched Astrid approach her locker and set her doll on the floor next to her feet. While Astrid concentrated on her lock combination, Remy admired the way Astrid's dark green dress made her pale skin seem to almost glow. He thought about how he wished he could walk over to her and tell her he was impressed with the way she'd solved the hard math problem on the blackboard that morning. He wanted to tell her he thought it was cool that she figured out the math even though Warren and a couple of his idiot friends kept firing spitballs at her, and he wanted to tell her he thought she was the nicest girl in the world because when Geena deliberately tripped Astrid as she headed back to her desk, it was *Astrid* who had apologized when she fell into Camilla. Seriously, Astrid was way too sweet for her own good. He really wanted to say that to her.

As Remy dismissed that idea as being sure to ruin his social standing, his gaze dropped far enough to land on the doll. That's when he realized the doll was staring at him.

At first, Remy thought that the doll was just positioned so that it looked like it was staring at him. But the longer he looked at the doll, particularly at the doll's jutting-out eyeball, he had to accept that the doll was absolutely and for sure staring *at* him. And not only was the doll staring at Remy, it was staring at him with total and complete hatred.

Remy's back smacked up against his open metal locker door as he jerked backward, involuntarily recoiling from the force of the doll's creepy glare. Because that's what it was. A glare. Remy couldn't have said why he knew the doll's gaze was very, very unfriendly, but he did know it. In spite of the doll's sickening scrunched-up features and poked-out eyeball, the doll's face had managed to arrange itself into a cross between a sneer and an "I think you're slimier than a slug" expression.

When he realized how strongly he'd reacted to the doll's gaze, Remy pretended it hadn't happened. His hand shaking just a little (but no one saw), he zipped his backpack closed and slammed his locker shut. When the metallic bang echoed down the hall, he flicked his gaze toward the doll, intending to reassure himself that he'd just lost his mind there for a second and had read all kinds of stupid stuff into a dumb Buddytronic's mindless gaze.

But when Remy returned his attention to Astrid's doll, he nearly screamed. He managed to contain the scream, but he couldn't stop himself from gasping.

The doll, still staring at him, had raised a finger. And that finger was pointed right at Remy. It was like the doll was singling him out . . . or calling him out. Remy felt challenged. Or threatened. Or both.

And more than that, he felt scared. Terrified, actually.

Astrid's Buddytronic, which was supposed to be a pretty basic animatronic doll, didn't like Remy . . . at all. As strange as that sounded, Remy knew it was true.

Astrid finished at her locker, and she bent down to pick up her doll. Lifting the doll, Astrid noticed Remy. She raised one of her perfectly arched eyebrows, obviously wondering why he was staring at her.

Remy quickly turned and strode away. As he did, he casually wiped away the sweat that was beading on his very clammy forehead.

Astrid pushed open the door of the Pizzaplex's Animatronic Parts Shop. Small and cramped, not lit up at all like the rest of the Pizzaplex, the shop smelled of machine oil and shaved metal. But it was a fascinating place. It was filled with shelves heavy with pistons and gears and servos and wires and metal skeleton pieces in nearly every shape and size. Astrid figured she'd be able to find what she needed to fix Nexie in here.

But she'd have to do it quickly. Astrid had talked her farfar into bringing her to the Pizzaplex so she could come to this shop, but she hadn't told him that was why she wanted to come. He thought they were here to bowl and to have a pizza. While he'd stood in line to get a lane and rent their shoes, Astrid had said she wanted to go look at something in one of the shops.

"I'll be back in five minutes, Farfar," she'd said.

She really wanted that to be true.

"Can I help you, sweetie?" a woman's husky voice asked.

Astrid looked back toward the metal counter that ran along the back of the shop. A broad-shouldered woman with short, graying black hair smiled at Astrid.

Astrid figured the fastest way to find what she wanted was to ask for it. She trotted up to the counter and set Nexie on its gleaming silver surface.

The woman—her nametag read ROBERTA—looked at Nexie. "Oh my," Roberta said.

Astrid used the comment to explain what she needed. "As you can see," she said, "I need to move my doll's arms and legs. I've looked at how they're attached and where they need to be, and I think this is what I need to make the changes." Astrid pulled out the lined piece of paper on which she'd written her list of parts.

Roberta, her gaze locked on Nexie's bulging eye, took the paper. She looked down and scanned it. "This looks just right," Roberta said. "I can get all of this for you."

Astrid shifted her feet and looked up at the red-rimmed Freddy Fazbear clock above the shelf behind the counter. "Can you do it really fast, please?" she asked. "I'm sorry, but I'm really in a hurry. My farfar—my grandpa—is waiting for me." Astrid gave the woman a bright smile. "If you tell me where to look, I can help you."

"Well, aren't you a nice kid?" Roberta said. She grinned at Astrid and stepped out from behind the counter. "Come on. We'll get what you need in half a shake of a lamb's tail."

Astrid giggled. She hadn't heard that expression before, but she knew a lamb's tail could shake really fast. Happy and excited, she followed Roberta down a narrow aisle.

Astrid waited until after her farfar went to bed before she started working on Nexie. She knew that once the repairs were made, her farfar would obviously notice the changes, but once done, he wouldn't make her undo them. If she'd told him what she was going to do, however, he might have asked her how much the parts cost, and when she told him they cost all the money she had left, he could have said that was too expensive and might have made her return them.

Luckily, Astrid's farfar was a very deep sleeper. As soon as she heard him snoring, she knew she'd be able to let herself into his workshop and use his tools to work on Nexie.

"Come on, Nexie," Astrid whispered as she picked up the bag of parts she'd bought and led her friend out of her room and down the long white-walled hallway on the farmhouse's second floor.

Astrid's farfar always left one sconce burning in the hallway, and its glow reflected off the hall's polished oak floorboards. Astrid's leather-soled shoes made a soft tapping sound as she walked. Nexie's rubber-soled shoes made a faint squeaky sound. The two sounds blended like they were supposed to go together. That made Astrid smile.

Once they'd gone down the stairs to the first floor, Astrid said, "You'll like Farfar's workshop. It smells like sawdust and sap and a little like cinnamon because he likes to suck on cinnamon candies while he works."

"What does cinnamon smell like?" Nexie asked. "I am not able to smell things."

Astrid cringed. "I'm sorry. I forgot you can't smell things. I shouldn't have said that."

"It is okay," Nexie said. "I cannot taste things, either. But I can see things. I like to see things."

Astrid squeezed Nexie's hand. "You're a really good sport," Astrid said.

"Thank you," Nexie said.

They'd reached the enclosed breezeway that led to the

workshop. Astrid hurriedly led Nexie past rows of coats and boots hanging neatly on brass hooks, and then she opened the workshop door.

Astrid pulled on a thin string and a bare light bulb flashed on overhead. Bright yellow light filled the room.

"Over here," Astrid said, leading the way to a cluttered worktable. "Give me a second. I want to be able to put everything he has out back exactly where it was."

Astrid looked at all the tools and wood pieces and memorized their positions. Once she was sure she could set everything back right, she moved a few things and laid out her parts. Then she quickly gathered the tools she'd need.

Nexie's arms and legs were attached to her torso with pluglike connectors. All Astrid was going to have to do was remove the limbs, unscrew the connectors from their place near Nexie's waist, and then screw them on at the shoulders and hips where they were supposed to be. So, Astrid grabbed a couple screwdrivers and a pair of pliers.

When she was done, she lifted Nexie up onto the worktable.

"Okay," Astrid said. "Let's get you fixed up."

Nexie said nothing as Astrid started her work. Astrid was a little bothered by Nexie's complete lack of enthusiasm for the project, but she decided to shrug off Nexie's blah attitude. Nexie was, after all, a programmed doll. She couldn't be expected to have emotions like the enthusiasm and anticipation that Astrid felt about fixing Nexie's arms and legs.

One of the things that Astrid had been concerned about when she started the project was how she was going to cut into Nexie's "skin" to move her limbs. But when she removed Nexie's dress, Astrid discovered Nexie's skin-like covering was really loose and pliable. Astrid was able to make tiny slits in the plastic material and then remove and reposition the connecting plugs before re-attaching Nexie's limbs. When she was done, Nexie's arms and legs were extending from her shoulders and hips.

"There!" Astrid said triumphantly.

Nexie, her expression blank, looked down at her newly placed arms and legs. Astrid picked Nexie up and put her on the wood floor. Nexie began walking around. She moved more smoothly than she had before, but she continued to jerk as she walked. She looked terribly awkward.

Nexie looked up at Astrid. "Thank you for trying to help," Nexie said, "but a whole new body is needed." Nexie cocked her head. "The proportions are not right. We need to find the right skeleton to make things the way they should be."

Astrid slumped down onto the wooden stool in front of her farfar's workbench. "I don't understand," Astrid said. "I thought you'd be happy with this."

Astrid didn't like getting angry. "*Anger never solves anything*," her farfar had taught her. No matter what the kids at school did, Astrid didn't get angry with them. She just tried to stay out of their way.

But Astrid was feeling angry now. Not really angry. Just a little angry. Or maybe she was just hurt. She felt like Nexie didn't appreciate all the money Astrid had spent and all the work she'd just done.

Astrid ran her hands through her hair. Standing, she picked up a push broom. She used it, and a dustpan, to sweep up the metal shavings her project had created. When she finished the cleanup, she emptied the dustpan and leaned the broom against the counter. Then she put all her farfar's tools and project pieces back where she'd found them.

"I am happy to have a friend who wants to make improvements," Nexie said when Astrid finally turned and faced her. "Thank you for the improvements. But we have to cut off the skin and put it on a new skeleton. That is the only way to fix the problems."

"It sounds like you're talking about a body swap or something," Astrid said. "How would that even be possible?"

Astrid tried to imagine how she'd get Nexie's silk-material skin stripped off Nexie's endoskeleton so it could be put on a different one. She couldn't see how it would work without totally destroying the material.

"Like this," Nexie said. Climbing back up onto the workbench, Nexie reached into one of the big patch-pockets on her dress. She pulled out a pair of blunt-tipped toy scissors.

Astrid frowned. "Where did you get those?" Astrid asked.

"I found them," Nexie said. "This is how it will work."

As Astrid looked on, her brows bunching tighter and tighter as she watched, Nexie cut a circle around her wrist. Once the plastic was cut, Nexie put down the scissors and used her opposite hand to pull the skin off her hand as if it was a glove. Nexie then scooted over to where the top of the broom handle rested against the workbench. She slipped the plastic hand over the handle.

"See?" Nexie said. "Skin can be taken off and put on something new. That is what we must do."

While Astrid watched, Nexie removed her fabric hand cover from the broom handle and put it back on her metal hand. Astrid pressed her lips together, thinking hard. She really wanted to make Nexie happy, so she wanted to do what Nexie wanted her to do. But how was she going to get the new endoskeleton Nexie wanted?

At school the next day, everyone noticed Nexie's changed arms and legs. Astrid couldn't miss the looks Nexie got during morning class.

It was a warm sunny day, so when lunchtime came, Astrid settled on a bench in the school's brick courtyard with Nexie to eat the cheese sandwich she'd made that morning. She loved warm days when she could eat outside. It was easier to be apart from the others there. She didn't have to eat alone at a table in the corner of the dining room. Somehow being on a bench by herself was easier.

As Astrid unwrapped her sandwich, Brett walked past. "Yo, dude," he called out as he strolled by, "nice work on the arms and legs."

Astrid wasn't sure whether Brett was talking to her or Nexie or maybe to someone else. But she didn't have a chance to respond. Geena and Camilla burst through the double doors from the dining room and walked out into the courtyard just as Brett spoke. Both girls were wearing new dresses, and they paused to pose so everyone would notice how pretty they were.

Then Geena and Camilla looked at Nexie, and Camilla said, "As if." She rolled her eyes and nudged Geena.

Geena laughed. "Yeah. That thing needs a lot more than fixed arms and legs."

"Yeah," Camilla agreed. "Maybe it needs, like, a spa day." Camilla tittered and looked right at Astrid. "Or at least somebody does. Maybe a complete makeover."

Geena shook her head. "More like a face-lift. Or

actually, it's more of a gut job. You know, like that house my mom fixed up."

Camilla's big brown eyes opened wide. "All she kept was the beams and the floorboards," she said.

"Exactly," Geena said.

Geena and Camilla flounced toward Astrid. Geena deliberately stepped on Astrid's foot as she went past. "Oh, excuse me," Geena said in an obviously sarcastic tone.

Geena and Camilla giggled as they sashayed across the courtyard. Astrid put her head down and bit into her sandwich.

Nexie scooted closer to Astrid. "Those girls are not nice," she said softly in her deep monotone. "But they are not wrong. A makeover would be good." Nexie looked up at Astrid, who continued to eat. "I have pictures of pretty girls in my database," Nexie went on, "and I have determined that certain ways of looking are better than others. Larger features, for instance, are prettier than small ones. Big eyes and a wide mouth are good. And cheeks should show bone structure instead of being plump and round."

Astrid's hand lifted to her own cheek. She knew Nexie was talking about Nexie's own face, but Astrid's features were the exact opposite of what Nexie was describing. Astrid had always been fine with how she looked. Now, however, she began to wonder. What if her eyes and mouth looked bigger? Would that make her fit in better with the kids at school?

The second she asked herself that question, Astrid snorted. What a stupid idea! How would she get different features? She knew from watching TV that makeup could help faces look different than they really were, but

Astrid was way too young to start wearing makeup. No. She was fine the way she was.

Wasn't she?

Sure she was.

But Nexie. Yes, Nexie could use some more work. Her face did need to be fixed up. Maybe if Astrid could find a new endoskeleton for Nexie, Nexie's features would settle on the new skull in a way that looked prettier.

Astrid nodded to herself. She really was going to have to figure out how to get Nexie a new endoskeleton.

As soon as he stowed his books and grabbed his backpack, Remy joined the stream of kids heading toward the stairs leading to the school's first floor. He got there just as Astrid and her spooky doll did. And they were right behind Camilla and Geena.

Remy brushed past the girls, and started down the steps. Just as he did, out of the corner of his eye, he saw the doll suddenly fly out of Astrid's grasp and flop to the floor right at Camilla's feet.

Camilla, yakking with Geena, wasn't looking at her feet. So, of course, she tripped over the sprawled-out doll. Off balance, Camilla pitched forward toward the stair railing.

Besides Remy, no one was close enough to stop Camilla's forward motion, and Remy was slow on the uptake. Still trying to process what he'd just seen—*The doll really did just throw itself at Camilla's feet, right?* he asked himself—Remy hesitated long enough that Camilla's stomach hit the railing, and she started to flip over the rail headfirst.

Remy's brain finally kicked in. He lunged to his left and managed to grab Camilla's legs as they started to go over the railing. Time seemed to compress as Remy hung on to Camilla's legs with both hands. As if from far away, he could hear Camilla screaming.

"Somebody, help me!" Remy shouted.

Suddenly, Johnny was there, and he grabbed Camilla's waist. Together, Remy and Johnny pulled Camilla back up over the railing.

Camilla continued to scream. And now Geena joined her.

Pointing at Astrid and wrapping a protective arm around Camilla, Geena screeched at Astrid, "You did that on purpose!"

Astrid retrieved her doll from the floor, which had shrunk to the far side of the stairs. Astrid's face was stark white. Her eyes looked glassy. She looked extremely guilty, and she didn't protest when Geena started screaming at her.

"You threw your doll at Camilla's feet to trip her!" Geena shrieked.

"What's going on here?" Mr. Mullins's voice roared over Camilla's and Geena's screams.

"She tripped Camilla!" Geena accused, once again pointing a finger at Astrid. "She tossed her doll on the floor so Camilla would trip over it!"

Mr. Mullins looked at Camilla. "Are you hurt?"

Camilla stopped screaming. She rubbed her side and shrugged.

Mr. Mullins ran a hand through his thinning hair. He looked at Astrid. "Did you throw your doll at her?"

Astrid, her face still pale and tight, shook her head. "I don't know what happened. I didn't mean to drop her," she said. She didn't look very convincing. Her eyeballs were practically jittering.

Remy had to speak up. "I saw Astrid right before Camilla tripped," he said. "She didn't *throw* the doll. It just fell."

That was true, mostly. And the rest of the truth, that Astrid's doll had thrown itself, was not something Remy was going to say out loud.

"All right," Mr. Mullins said. "Well, no harm, no foul. All of you, clear the stairs. Miss Palmer"—he took Camilla's arm—"let's get you to the infirmary to make sure you're A-okay."

Remy watched Mr. Mullins lead Camilla away. Then he glanced at Astrid's doll.

The doll lifted its chin and stared up at Remy. It winked.

Remy whirled away, ignoring the goose bumps that erupted on his arms.

Astrid walked home from school very, very slowly. That her legs worked at all was a miracle.

Had she seen what she really thought she'd seen? Had Nexie really jumped out of Astrid's arms to trip Camilla?

Astrid looked down at her new friend. She wanted to say something. She wanted to ask if Nexie had done what Astrid thought she'd done.

But then again, Astrid didn't want to ask. Because she didn't want to know for sure.

The thing was, though, she *did* know. But if she didn't ask, she could pretend she didn't.

If Nexie did trip Camilla, she had done it for Astrid, obviously. Nexie was a good friend. She wanted to protect Astrid, and Camilla had been mean to Astrid at lunch.

Nexie was just a doll, and she didn't understand the way the world worked. She didn't know that you couldn't react to mean words by trying to physically hurt someone.

Nexie was just being protective. In a not-so-good way. And Nexie was really sensitive to insults, too, even the ones aimed at Astrid. It was all because Nexie felt so insecure about her looks, Astrid told herself. It was hard being the one who stood out, the one who looked different and acted different.

No, Astrid concluded, it wasn't Nexie's fault. The doll couldn't help it.

Astrid had once heard one of her teacher's describe the stuff Warren did as "acting out." Astrid had looked up what that meant. Acting out, she'd learned, was a bad behavior that was a "defense mechanism." She'd looked up that, too: a defense mechanism was a way of thinking that was used (without the person realizing it) to avoid something like anxiety. When Astrid thought about it, she knew it made sense. Warren had a really scary dad—Astrid had seen the man yelling at Warren in the school parking lot. That meant Warren "acted out" to avoid the bad feelings he had about his dad . . . and maybe other things, too.

Now, Nexie was acting out. Nexie was anxious about how she looked, and she was covering that up with her bad behavior.

Astrid was responsible for Nexie. She'd created her (kind of) and brought her home. They were connected. It was up to Astrid to help Nexie so the doll didn't do more bad things. She would help Nexie get her new endoskeleton so Nexie could feel better about herself. Then everything would get better. There was just one problem with Astrid's plan to help Nexie. She didn't know how to get Nexie what she needed.

After Astrid did her chores, she sat at the yellow kitchen counter in her farfar's bright, clean kitchen and used the white rotary wall phone to call the parts shop. With Nexie perched on the counter, leaning against the green ceramic cookie jar (made by one of Astrid's aunts) that held homemade gingersnaps Astrid and her farfar had made the night before, Astrid talked to Roberta.

"Oh sure, I remember you," Roberta said when Astrid had reminded Roberta of her visit. "You're the nice girl. What can I help you with?"

Astrid explained that she wanted to get a new body and skull for Nexie.

Roberta immediately made a clucking sound and sighed heavily in Astrid's ear. "Oh, hon, I'm so sorry, but there's just no way to get your hands on a completed endoskeleton," Roberta said. "Fazbear Entertainment keeps the whole enchilada under wraps, don't you know? The endoskeletons are available for company use only."

"What about other shops?" Astrid asked. "Not Fazbear Entertainment ones."

"No such thing," Roberta said. "Oh, sure, there are some rinky-dink operations out there with a far more limited selection of parts than I have and a few jerry-rigged animatronic skeletons, but they're junk compared to the ones that come out of Fazbear factories. The only way to get the real deal is to get it from a Fazbear Entertainment facility, and there's no way for you to do that."

"What about building one?" Astrid asked. "Do you have the parts to do that?"

Roberta's sigh sounded like a gust of wind in Astrid's ear. "I wish. Unfortunately, the only place that has all the parts needed for a complete endoskeleton is the Fazbear repair facility under the Pizzaplex. And that's kept hush-hush, too. Top secret and all that."

Astrid thanked Roberta, hung up the phone, and sighed even more heavily than Roberta had. Astrid reached around Nexie to lift the cookie jar lid and grab a gingersnap. She chomped into it, taking out her frustration on the poor baked good. The aromas of ginger and cinnamon filled the kitchen.

"Will we get the new body now?" Nexie asked.

Astrid sighed and shook her head. "I don't know how to do it, Nexie. Roberta said the only way to get all the right parts to build a complete endoskeleton is from the robotics repair facility under the Pizzaplex."

"Then we will go there," Nexie said as if it was the easiest thing in the world to do.

Astrid made a face. "Roberta said the place is 'top secret.'" Astrid put air quotes around the words.

Nexie cocked her head and stared at Astrid's fingers. Then she looked at her own fingers. "Longer fingers are better than shorter ones," Nexie said.

Astrid looked at her small fingers. She shrugged and continued talking. "I've seen employees go into the areas in the Pizzaplex that are off-limits to the public. They have keycards that get into those places, and I don't have one of those." Astrid stood and helped Nexie off the counter.

Together they left the kitchen and headed down the hall toward Astrid's room. "Maybe we should just give up on the idea of getting you a new body," Astrid said.

"You can find a way to get the parts," Nexie said. "You are clever."

Astrid frowned and thought about it. If she could get into the repair facility to get the parts, maybe Astrid could build a complete new endoskeleton. Maybe. But was it really necessary? Not if Nexie could learn to like herself as she was.

"You really don't need one," Astrid said. "I think it's better to be yourself than try to be like everyone else."

Even as she said the words, Astrid felt like she was being what her farfar called "two-faced." Hadn't she gotten Nexie because she was trying to be like all the other kids who had Buddytronics?

Well, no, not really, she decided as she and Nexie walked into her room. She hadn't *just* bought Nexie to fit in. Astrid got Nexie so she'd have a pal to hang around with.

Nexie walked jerkily across Astrid's multicolored rag rug (which two of her aunts had made for her the previous year). Nexie crawled up onto Astrid's bed and sat in the middle of it.

Astrid studied Nexie and thought about what Nexie had done to Camilla, because Astrid had finally accepted that Nexie *had* done it. Astrid walked to the bed and took Nexie's hand. "I saw what you did to Camilla," Astrid said.

Nexie said nothing.

"Nexie," Astrid said, "do you want a new body so you can get revenge on the mean kids at school?"

Nexie looked at Astrid for several long seconds. She cocked her head, then said, "No."

Astrid nodded. "Okay." She let go of Nexie's hand and stood.

"It is important to be the best you can be," Nexie said. "That is right? Yes?"

Astrid sat back down again. "Sure," she said.

"Astrid means 'divinely beautiful,'" Nexie said.

"I remember," Astrid said. "That was the first thing you told me."

"It is important to be beautiful," Nexie said. "There has to be beauty."

Astrid looked at Nexie's strange scrunched-up features, at Nexie's balloon-like eyeball and spiderlike braids. When Astrid had first seen Nexie, she'd thought of Nexie as ugly. But now, she just saw her friend, Nexie. And to Astrid, Nexie was beautiful.

"'Beauty is in the eye of the beholder,'" Astrid said. She grinned and did air quotes again. "That's another one of those things someone else said."

Nexie blinked. "What does it mean?" she asked.

"Farfar explained it to me," Astrid said. "He said it means that different things are beautiful to different people. It means that I think you're beautiful the way you are."

Nexie stared hard at Astrid as if thinking about what Astrid said. "I know what I think is beautiful."

Astrid wasn't sure what that meant. But she said brightly, "How about we just decide to be beautiful together? Will you do that for me?"

Nexie stretched her lips into her version of a smile. "Everything I want to do is for you," she said.

Astrid leaned over and hugged Nexie. Then she stood. She had homework to do, so she started toward her desk. A knock on her door stopped her.

"Hey, kiddo, are you decent?" her farfar called through the door.

Astrid, relieved to have solved Nexie's problem without having to build or find an endoskeleton, laughed. "Come on in, Farfar!"

Astrid's door opened, and her farfar walked in. His hands were behind his back.

"I have a surprise for you," he said.

Astrid tried to see what he was hiding. "What is it?" she asked.

"Hey, no peeking," her farfar said. "Close your eyes proper."

Astrid closed her eyes. She heard her farfar cross over to her bed. Her bed squeaked, and then, she felt her farfar's hands on her shoulders. He turned her so she was facing her bed.

"Open your eyes!" Astrid's farfar said.

Astrid opened her eyes. And her stomach clenched.

But she quickly pasted on a smile and widened her eyes in a way that she hoped made her look delighted. "Oh, Farfar, it's beautiful."

Astrid wasn't lying. The surprise, a new Buddytronic doll, which now sat on the bed next to Nexie, *was* beautiful. It was the doll that Astrid had originally designed, exactly as she'd designed it.

"But Farfar," she said, "you shouldn't have!"

Astrid's farfar chuckled. "Oh, don't worry. I didn't have to spend an arm and a leg on it. I was able to work out a dilly of a deal with the lady at that shop. She felt so bad about what happened, with"—he gestured toward Nexie—"that she was happy to make you this new doll, Lexie, like you wanted, for practically nothing."

Astrid's gaze went from Nexie to what Nexie was supposed to have been . . . the new Buddytronic, Lexie.

"You're the best, Farfar," Astrid said with as much enthusiasm as she could manage, throwing her arms around him.

"I'm glad you like it, kiddo," her farfar said, returning her hug.

As Astrid's farfar held her close, she inhaled the fresh scent of the homemade soap he used to clean up at the end of every one of his long days. Pressing her head against his chest, she felt the thump-thump-thump of his heart. And she felt his love.

If only that love was enough.

Astrid's farfar let her go and ruffled her hair. "I'll go get dinner started," he said. "I'm glad you like your surprise."

"Oh, I do." Astrid watched her farfar walk out of her room. She smiled at him when he waved at her, and she closed her door.

Astrid turned back toward the bed. Her mouth dropped open, and she gasped.

Astrid watched Nexie grasp the new Buddytronic by its shoulders and sink her huge teeth into the doll's forehead. Nexie reared her head back and, with Lexie's plastic skin clamped in her teeth, ripped the doll's face away from its metal skull.

As its skin peeled off, the new Buddytronic writhed. Its arms flailed.

Astrid wanted to rush to the new doll's rescue, but she couldn't move. She couldn't believe what she was seeing.

The new Buddytronic's blue eyeballs rolled across the bed and dropped silently onto the floor. The doll's small white teeth flew out of its now-bare metal face. They sprinkled onto Astrid's quilt as Nexie grabbed the doll's braids and ripped them into little pieces that looked like tufts of fur. The blonde fur, caught in the room's air currents, flew up around Astrid's bed and scattered over the teeth.

"Nexie!" Astrid wailed as she watched Nexie, using both her hands and her teeth now, strip the rest of the Buddytronic's skin off its endoskeleton. Nexie didn't seem to hear Astrid. She was skinning the doll so quickly, it was as if she'd turned into a school of piranhas.

Even as she struggled to process Nexie's violent attack on the new Buddytronic, Astrid looked at the doll's now-bare endoskeleton, and thought, *well, now we have a new endoskeleton.* But Nexie wasn't finished. Nexie grabbed the shoulders of the metal skeleton, gritted her teeth, and pushed her hands together. Although the new doll continued to squirm, Nexie compressed the doll's endoskeleton and its processor. In a matter of seconds, the doll-shaped metal turned into little more than a bulging lump of scrap. Nexie grunted and compacted the metal even more. Then she dropped what was left of the new Buddytronic onto the floor. It landed with a thud before it rolled across Astrid's rug and came to rest next to her desk.

Astrid was shaking so hard she had to grab her desk chair to steady herself. She stared as Nexie casually brushed the rest of the doll's remains from the bed. Nexie sat back on Astrid's pillow and clasped her hands together calmly.

"Oh, Nexie," Astrid breathed. "What did you do?"

Nexie looked at Astrid. Her eyes widened innocently. "What do you mean?"

Astrid took a deep breath to steady herself. She was too scared to address Nexie's attack on the doll. So Astrid walked over and picked up the scrap metal that had, moments before, been a perfectly usable endoskeleton. She held it up. "This could have been your new body," she said.

Nexie's eyes narrowed. "No, not that one. That one was wrong."

"Hey, runt!" Warren called out to Astrid as she walked into her classroom the next morning. "That dress is as ugly as you are."

The rest of the kids traipsing into the classroom chuckled. Astrid blocked them out as she and Nexie went to the back of the room and sat down. She placed her book and notebook on the top of her dark wood desk, and kept her head up, her gaze straight ahead.

"Get your beady eyes off of me," Warren said. "And tell your freaky doll to stop looking at me, too." Warren held up his fingers and made a crisscross gesture.

Astrid had seen the gesture in a movie. It was used to ward off evil.

Miss Hallstrom strode into the room. "Settle down, everyone," she called out.

Astrid lifted her chin even higher and focused on her teacher. As she attempted to concentrate on Miss Hallstrom's grammar lesson, Warren's voice echoed in her head. *Beady eyes. Beady eyes. Beady eyes.* Did Astrid really have beady eyes? She'd never really thought about her own eyes that way before. She'd never thought much about any of her features.

But with all Nexie's talk about being beautiful, about how some ways of looking are better than others, Astrid was starting to wonder about her own looks. Maybe her clothes and her smarts weren't the only reason she didn't have friends. Maybe she didn't fit in because of how she looked. That thought kept Astrid occupied all day, so much so that she barely heard anything Miss Hallstrom said.

When the end-of-day bell rang, Astrid and Nexie were the last out of the classroom because Astrid was still distracted by her thoughts. As she headed toward the door, Miss Hallstrom called out, "Are you okay, Astrid?"

Astrid blinked and turned. "What?"

"I asked if you're okay," Miss Hallstrom said. "You've been quiet all day. You didn't raise your hand once."

Astrid shrugged. "I'm okay. At least, I think I am. Thank you." Astrid gave Miss Hallstrom a half smile and left the room.

Remy shuffled out of school, disappointed. His mom was taking him to a dentist appointment, which sucked.

In fact, the whole day had sucked. Mostly it had sucked because of Astrid. There was something wrong with her, something very off.

Astrid hadn't raised her hand in class all day. And she'd seemed distracted, even self-conscious. Remy, watching her from the corner of his eye as he always did, had seen her fuss with the pleats on her long purple-and-yellow dress (the one Warren had said was ugly, which it would have been if another girl had been wearing it, but everything looked good on Astrid). He'd also caught Astrid staring at the other girls in class in a way she'd never done before. What was going on with her?

Remy waited for his mom near the tall metal flagpole in front of the school. Leaning against the short brick wall at the edge of the wide sidewalk next to the school's circular drive, he watched the crowd of kids and looked for Astrid. Because she was small, it took a few minutes to find her, and he only spotted her because he heard Warren's chanting, "Astrid's a disastrid."

Remy wished he could punch the guy. He was such a jerk.

Really wanting to help Astrid but knowing that he shouldn't, Remy pushed off the brick wall and slipped through the mass of his classmates, who were joking around, shouting to each other, or racing for the yellow buses that belched diesel fumes at the edge of the sidewalk.

Still not sure what he was going to do, Remy's goal was just to get closer to where Astrid, carrying her doll, was pushing her way through the crush of kids. Warren was shadowing Astrid. The jerk was also picking up gravel and throwing it on Astrid's doll . . . and on Astrid, too.

Crowding up behind Astrid, Warren started giving her little shoves with his shoulder. He was deliberately bumping her so she kept losing her balance. Taking several stutter steps, she tried to speed up her pace so she could get away from Warren, but he stayed with her, jostling her over and over.

Warren and Astrid were walking right next to the curb at the edge of the school's driveway. Cars were pulling up to the curb—parents picking up their kids. Remy was afraid Warren was going to knock Astrid into the driveway, in front of a car.

Remy had to do something, he realized. He increased his pace so he could get closer.

Whether Remy actually would have confronted Warren and stood up for Astrid or not, he didn't get to find out. Because seconds after he headed toward Astrid, Warren lurched into Astrid more violently, and Astrid's doll flew from Astrid's grasp. The doll dropped onto the curb and then tumbled into the driveway. Just as it did, another car pulled up, and the doll disappeared behind the car's front right tire.

As soon as Astrid lost her doll, she came to an abrupt stop. She began looking around frantically. Warren plowed into Astrid, knocking her into a couple other kids. Astrid immediately disappeared into a five-kid pileup, but Remy could hear Astrid calling out, "Nexie! Nexie!"

Wanting to help Astrid, Remy trotted to the edge of

the driveway to grab the doll. When he reached the place where he'd seen it, though, the doll wasn't there.

Several kids were now yelling at Astrid to get out of the way. She was still calling out for her doll. And on the edge of the clump of kids, Warren was laughing. Remy could hear him jeering at Astrid, "Did you drop your dolly, klutz?"

Warren started scanning the sidewalk. Remy was sure that if Warren spotted Astrid's doll, he'd do something cruel to it.

The crowd around Astrid started to clear out. Only Astrid, turning in a frantic circle in search of her doll, and Warren, continuing to hassle Astrid, remained. A continuing stream of kids heading to the buses surged around Astrid and Warren. In the chaos, no one paid any attention to the upset girl and the determined bully.

Remy turned away from Astrid, Warren, and the other kids. He tried once more to find Astrid's doll.

It had to be close by, Remy figured. Buddytronics could crawl, yes, but they usually didn't crawl far, and Astrid's doll always stuck close to her. Where did the creepy thing go?

Walking against the flow of kids leaving the school, Astrid continued to call for her doll. Warren stuck with her, making faces at her and poking her repeatedly in the shoulder as he said, "Wah, wah. The big ugly baby lost her little ugly baby."

That was when Remy spotted the doll. It was crouched under one of the cars at the curb.

Seeing the doll's position, Remy's skin crawled. There was something sneaky about the way the doll was bunched onto its haunches, like a cat poised to pounce on an unsuspecting mouse.

But no, that was crazy, Remy told himself. The doll must have just landed by accident in that position.

Remy started toward the doll. In spite of how much it weirded him out, he wanted to save it . . . for Astrid. If the car it was under started moving, the doll could be crushed by the car's tires.

By now, Remy noticed as he trotted toward the curb, Warren was standing right at the edge of the curb, his back to the idling cars. Warren was oblivious of the doll. He was intent on taunting Astrid, and Astrid, fully pan-icked, was still stumbling around looking for her doll.

All the other kids were either talking or looking straight ahead. So, it was only Remy who saw what hap-pened next.

It happened so quickly that Remy was still processing what he saw long after it was over. And once he processed it, he knew he was never going to tell a soul about it. There was no way he was ever going to say out loud that he saw Astrid's doll leap at Warren, attach itself to Warren's pants leg, and use its teeth to rip into the meaty part of Warren's calf.

But that *was* what Remy saw. One second, the doll was a lump under the car. The next second, the doll was in a full-out assault. Arms spread out, hair wild, the doll looked like an alien insectoid in terrifying attack mode. Huge teeth bared, the doll suctioned onto Warren's leg with all four limbs. Then it bit down on the leg and jerked its head so that it ripped away, in one motion, a huge strip of Warren's jeans and an even larger chunk of Warren's flesh.

Warren's scream cut through the chatter of the kids and the rumble of the buses and cars. The scream stopped every-one outside the school in their tracks. Car doors were flung open as parents jumped out to see what had happened. All eyes turned toward Warren, who dropped to the sidewalk, grabbing at his leg and wailing at the top of his lungs.

As much as Remy didn't like Warren, he didn't blame the guy for his reaction. Remy was close enough to see that the doll's teeth had torn deeply into Warren's leg. Remy could see a shocking white length of bone, and blood was gushing all over the sidewalk.

Looking away quickly, Remy's gaze landed on Astrid, who had finally found her doll. Her face white and her cheeks streaked with tears, Astrid had her doll wrapped in a bear hug. The doll's legs dangled limply over Astrid's belly. The doll's face was pressed into Astrid's shoulder.

A couple parents and teachers converged on Warren. Remy heard several shouts of, "What happened?"

Principal Mullins came rushing through the scattered kids in front of the school. He shoved his way toward Warren, and when he saw Warren's injury, the principal immediately looked around. "Who did this to him?"

No way was Remy going to volunteer what he knew. He stayed where he was, acting . . . he hoped . . . as clueless as everyone else was.

"It looks like a bite," Mr. Mullins said, squatting down next to Warren and watching another teacher put pressure on the wound. Mr. Mullins stood. "Is there a stray dog around here?" Mr. Mullins's gaze scanned the school driveway.

Remy looked around, too, as if he could helpfully spy the nonexistent dog. He saw his mom's car, and he exhaled in relief.

Before he walked toward his mom's car, Remy glanced at Astrid again. Still white-faced, Astrid's eyes were bulging as she turned away from Warren and the others and began walking unsteadily down the sidewalk.

Did Astrid see what her doll had done? Remy wondered.

He figured he'd never know because he wasn't going to ask her. In fact, he was going to do his best to forget the whole thing. He sure wasn't going to let himself remember the way the doll smiled at him when it lifted its face from Astrid's shoulder and looked back at Remy as Astrid walked away.

The Pizzaplex arcade's flashing lights, boisterous crowd, and chaotic noise pressed in around Astrid and Nexie. Hand in hand, they watched Astrid's farfar roll a ball up the Skee-Ball's incline. The ball crossed the ball hop and launched itself toward the fifty-point ring.

"Good one, Farfar!" Astrid sang out in what she hoped sounded like genuine praise.

Astrid's farfar turned and grinned at her. When his gaze landed on Nexie, he frowned, but he quickly replaced the frown with another grin.

Astrid obviously hadn't been able to tell her farfar what had happened to Lexie. She'd hidden the doll's remains, and when her farfar had asked why she insisted on taking Nexie everywhere, Astrid had said, "I don't want to hurt her feelings. Lexie understands."

Her farfar had patted Astrid on the shoulder. "You're a kind girl, kiddo."

Now, Astrid said, "You won again, Farfar."

Her farfar gave her a quick hug. "I've won them all, kiddo," he said. "Are you sure you want to be here?"

When Astrid's farfar had found out what happened at school, he'd wanted her to go to bed to rest, but she'd begged him to take her to the Pizzaplex instead. "I need to do something to forget what I saw, Farfar," she said.

That wasn't a lie. But she had another reason for wanting to go to the Pizzaplex. And now it was time to get on with it.

Astrid nodded quickly. "It's helping me, really," she said.

Her farfar's brows bunched, but then he asked, "Do you want to give it another go?"

"Sure," she said. "But I need to use the restroom first."

"Okay, kiddo," her farfar said. "I'll go ahead and practice while you're gone."

Astrid forced a laugh. "Like you need the practice," she said as she gave her farfar a little wave and turned to walk away from the Skee-Ball machines.

Astrid and Nexie started toward the restrooms. After a few steps, she glanced back and hesitated. She waited until her farfar returned his attention to Skee-Ball. Then she quickly dragged Nexie behind a row of pinball machines.

"What are you doing?" Nexie asked. "The restrooms are the other way."

Astrid bent down and whispered to Nexie, "I'm going to steal a keycard so we can get into the animatronics repair place."

"That is good," Nexie said. "That is what is needed."

Yes, it was, Astrid knew now. There was no other way to make sure that Nexie didn't hurt someone else.

When Astrid had seen Nexie destroy the new Buddytronic, Astrid had struggled to come to terms with Nexie's strength. It had really bothered Astrid to realize that Nexie was strong enough to completely destroy a metal endoskeleton.

At that point, Astrid already knew that Nexie could be destructive, sure. Nexie had, after all, tripped Camilla. Astrid had comforted herself, though, with the thought that Nexie was just an animatronic doll with limited abilities.

But then Astrid had seen what Nexie was capable of.

And today she'd watched her doll sink her teeth into Warren's leg. Astrid hated to admit it to herself, and she sure wasn't going to say it out loud, but she was becoming a little afraid of Nexie.

Don't think about that, Astrid told herself.

She had to focus.

But how could she *not* think about what had happened to Warren? Over and over and over, her mind replayed the scene for her, whether she liked it or not. Warren taunting her. Nexie disappearing and Astrid desperate to find her. Then, Astrid seeing Nexie by the curb and watching Nexie leap toward Warren and glom onto his leg. Astrid didn't want it to be real, but it was.

Nexie was still acting out. Astrid had to get Nexie what she needed so she didn't act out anymore. And Astrid had to do it fast.

Astrid searched for a Pizzaplex employee as she pushed through all the happy people packed into the arcade. She just needed one, but it had to be the right kind of employee.

During all her visits to the Pizzaplex, Astrid had noticed that most employees kept their keycards on lanyards that hung around their necks. Some, though, attached their keycards to their belt loops. Astrid wanted to find one of those.

"What about that one?" Nexie asked as if reading Astrid's mind. Nexie lifted her chin and used it to gesture toward a red-shirted guy with curly blond hair. The keycard dangled from his belt loop.

Astrid pulled Nexie along and followed the blond employee. *Please,* Astrid thought silently. She had to hurry. If she took much longer, her farfar was going to go searching for her.

Astrid pushed past a woman who wore really strong

flowery perfume. The woman's kids, two little girls who looked like twins, maybe five years old, both bumped into Astrid. One of them put a sticky hand on Astrid's bare arm. She quickly rubbed away what smelled like caramel. But she wasn't going to complain because the girls started squabbling. They began shoving at each other, screaming loudly.

"Fran! Fern! Stop that!" the woman scolded as the blond employee turned toward the dark-haired girls.

Astrid darted around the little girls. The employee spotted Nexie and raised his eyebrows. One of the little girls bit the other one. The blond employee took a step toward the girls' mother.

Moving fast, Astrid slipped into the confusion and plucked the blond employee's keycard from his belt loop. Astrid quickly tucked it into the pocket of her dress and hustled herself and Nexie back to meet Farfar.

When Astrid returned to him, her farfar was just finishing a solo game. "Are you ready to try again, kiddo?" he asked when he spotted her.

Astrid, feeling a flush in her cheeks, said, "Actually, I think I'd like to go home now."

Her farfar reached out and put a cool hand to her hot forehead. "Yes," he said. "I think that's a good idea. This might have been a distraction for you, but I think it was too much after what happened."

"I can't believe I'm doing this," Astrid whispered three hours later, as she and Nexie slipped through a red metal door at the end of one of the back hallways in the Pizzaplex.

Astrid and Nexie stepped into a darkened concrete-floored corridor, and Astrid wondered, not for the first time, if she was doing the right thing. She was having serious doubts about it.

Actually, Astrid was having doubts about everything, including herself. Since she'd been caught up in Nexie's quest to improve herself, Astrid had started examining her own face in the mirror and studying the way her dresses fit her small body. Was Astrid as "wrong" as Nexie's beauty opinions suggested? Astrid was starting to think so.

The combination of a driving need to get Nexie the new body she wanted and Astrid's building insecurities was what had motivated Astrid to do something she'd never thought she'd do . . . steal something.

Astrid felt like the keycard was burning a hole through her palm. She felt so bad about what she'd done.

But then, Astrid decided, if she couldn't be a person who could fit in at school, why not totally get into being the outcast everyone saw her as? People who stole things and broke into places were on the outside of society. Maybe that was where Astrid belonged.

Astrid heard the shuffle-tap of heavy footsteps coming down the hallway. A security guard!

Astrid and Nexie took a sharp left and wove through several dark corridors. As she went, she kept glancing up, looking for CCTV cameras. She was doing her best to avoid them, and she thought she was doing okay so far.

After Astrid and her farfar had returned home from the Pizzaplex earlier that evening, Astrid had moved on to step two of her three-part plan to get Nexie her new body. Part one had been getting the keycard, and that had gone even better than Astrid had hoped it would.

Part two had been a little trickier.

After her farfar had gone to bed, just before nine as

always, Astrid had used the kitchen phone to call the parts shop. Roberta had answered. Immediately, Astrid had launched into a complicated story about doing a school project and needing to talk to someone who worked in the repair facility and asking for directions to it in the hopes that she could catch someone going in or going out. Roberta hadn't even hesitated. "Sure thing, kid," she'd said. And she'd given Astrid the information she needed. Astrid couldn't believe it had been so easy.

After that came part three of Astrid's plan. She just had to get back to the Pizzaplex before it closed at 11:00 p.m. Astrid knew that once she and Nexie were back inside the Pizzaplex, they could hide until everyone else left. Then they could make their way into the animatronics repair facility.

The bike ride from the farm to the Pizzaplex was a long one, but they'd made it just in time. So far so good.

Astrid shivered as she and Nexie turned another corner. It was *dark* back here. And it was damp and cold and smelled bad, like a musty old basement. It was also loud.

The hallways weren't loud in the way the Pizzaplex upstairs was loud. There was no music or laughter down here. Astrid could hear the rumble of motors and the thunk of pipes. She also heard a lot of metallic scraping. She wasn't sure what caused the scraping; that was what made it so scary. The sounds she and Nexie were making . . . the *tap-tap* of their footsteps . . . were scary, too. Astrid was trying to be quiet so they wouldn't get caught, but the way every little noise echoed in the concrete and metal passageways made it almost impossible to walk silently.

Calm down, Astrid commanded herself.

Ever since she and Nexie had snuck out of the house to bike to the Pizzaplex, Astrid had been jumpy and tense. Everything about what she was doing made it feel like pins were poking her all over. She didn't like lying or sneaking around, so she never did it. Until she had to.

Astrid and Nexie reached the end of a hallway. It looked like a dead end, but Astrid knew it wasn't. She turned the corner, and there it was, just as Roberta had described. It was the door to the stairs that Roberta said led to the repair facility.

The metal stairway door was painted gray, and it was scarred and dented. Next to the door was a slot for a keycard.

Astrid pulled out the stolen, hard plastic card. She held her breath and then slid in the card. The door clicked. Astrid grabbed the metal handle and pulled the door open.

Astrid paused and took a few seconds to listen. She wanted to be sure they were alone.

Astrid heard nothing. No one else was around.

"Okay," Astrid whispered to Nexie. "Let's go."

She gripped Nexie's hand. Together, they headed down a long concrete flight of stairs.

At the bottom of the stairs, they found another gray metal door. This one had no slot for a keycard.

"The repair department is only open during the day," Roberta had told Astrid. "So, if you want to catch someone to talk them into letting you have a peek, you'll have to hang around between nine and five. The techs keep bankers' hours." Roberta had snorted. "Lazy, stuck-up jerks."

Astrid was glad the people who worked down here were lazy, stuck-up jerks. That meant they weren't here now.

Astrid took a deep breath and pushed open the gray door. It squeaked, and Astrid's breath caught. But when she looked past the door, all she saw was darkness.

Astrid felt around on the wall next to the door. Her fingers found a switch. She flipped it.

A series of overhead fluorescent lights flickered on with a few clicks and a buzzing sound. Astrid blinked at the sudden brightness.

"This is exactly what we need," Nexie said.

And it was. Astrid smiled, even though her legs felt weak and her heart was hammering so loudly that she could barely hear anything else.

The repair facility was a long, rectangular room lined with stainless steel worktables. In spite of the fluorescent lights, the room was mottled with shadows. Half in and half out of those shadows, several endoskeletons, in various stages of construction and repair, lay on the tables. Above the tables, black metal shelves held row upon row upon row of parts.

"Look at that one," Nexie said, pointing at an endoskeleton at the far end of the left side tables. "All it needs are a few joints and a skull. You can add those."

Nexie's voice echoed in the cinderblock-walled room. She sounded so happy and excited.

Astrid looked down and smiled at her friend. "Yes, I can do that," Astrid said.

Astrid led Nexie toward the endoskeleton Nexie had chosen. As she went, Astrid grabbed a few tools from the workbenches she passed. She also scanned the shelves and spotted the joints and skull she'd need to finish the endoskeleton. She cradled everything in her arms. When they reached the partially completed endoskeleton, Astrid lay down her tools and parts on the table as quietly as she could. The few clinks of the metal parts touching the stainless steel made her tense. She immediately got to work.

Less than two hours later, Astrid was done. She stepped back from the finished endoskeleton. "What do you think?" Astrid asked Nexie.

Nexie studied the endoskeleton. "It is good," she said. Then she reached into one of the big patch pockets on her dress. She pulled out the little metal scissors she'd used to show Astrid how to cut through her silk-fabric "skin."

Because of the biting incident, Remy had missed a few days of school. His mother had kept him home because he was traumatized and needed emotional support. The whole time Remy had hung out with his mom, he'd thought about Astrid. She was the one who probably needed emotional support. Astrid, in addition to being so pretty and so smart, was a very nice girl. She must have felt awful about what her doll had done.

And speaking of Astrid's doll . . .

As Remy settled himself at his desk, he looked up to see the ghoulish doll with the gross eyeball, the mushed-together face, and the alien-looking braids coming through the classroom's doorway as if riding on air. Of course, the doll wasn't floating. Even though Remy couldn't see Astrid behind the doll, he knew she was there. Who else would be carrying that thing into the classroom?

Remy wondered how a girl as great as Astrid could have ended up with a doll so totally and completely wrong. When he'd first seen the doll, Remy had wondered whether Astrid had gotten it with the intention of fixing it up. But other than repositioning its arms and legs, Astrid hadn't done anything to it. It looked the same today as it had when it had tripped Camilla and ripped its teeth into Warren's leg.

Johnny tapped Remy on the shoulder, and Remy turned to look at his friend. "Did you hear Warren had to get a rabies shot in case whatever bit him was rabid?" Johnny asked.

Remy ignored the shiver that rippled down his back. "Couldn't happen to a nicer guy," he joked.

Johnny kept his voice as low as Remy's when he joked back, "Maybe it was a zombie that bit him. But if he turns, he wouldn't be much different." Johnny chuckled.

Remy opened his mouth to respond, but a scream stopped him. As he started to turn to see what was going on, another scream joined the first one. Then another.

Remy rotated completely around. His gaze landed on Astrid's doll and then on . . .

Remy's breath caught. His heart started pounding. He turned to stone.

Sitting at Astrid's usual desk, a horrifying version of Astrid held her doll and looked toward the front of the classroom as if all was as it should have been. But it wasn't.

What had happened to Astrid?

His mouth hanging open and stomach churning up into his throat, Remy stared at the awfulness that used to be a special, pretty girl. He goggled at what looked like a patchwork version of Astrid.

It wasn't possible. It couldn't be real.

But it was.

Pieces of Astrid's skin had been crudely cut apart and elongated to fit over a body that was much taller and broader than her own body had been. It was almost translucent because it was so tautly snug on longer hands and fingers, the skin was sewn together with ragged, looping black stitches.

Astrid's face, seemingly all in one piece, had been cut away from her neck, and it was now expanded to cover a large skull. The blonde hair that had always been charmingly messy on Astrid had been smoothed over the top of the skull; it had been flattened and was stiff as if held in place with some kind of gel.

Astrid's small face on the large skull resulted in stretching that widened the eyes and set them farther apart. It flattened the cheeks and drew out the mouth. The face was like putty pulled out to its limits. All of Astrid's skin was pasty white, and dried blood crusted the seams that connected the pieces.

Ignoring the commotion around him, Remy couldn't pull his gaze from the creature that used to be the girl he'd secretly liked. He blinked, half hoping that he was hallucinating. But he wasn't. What he was seeing, although almost impossible to take in, was real.

As the collage version of Astrid sat quietly in its seat, Astrid's doll smiled contentedly. Its gaze shifted from one screaming kid to the next. It even turned and looked at Remy. He met the doll's gaze, and forced himself not to cry out or run.

Because Remy was the only one in the class who wasn't shrieking or fleeing from the room, he was the only one who saw Astrid's stretched-out mouth open. He was also the only one who heard the mumbled words that came from it.

The Astrid thing hugged her doll as she said, "Perfect now."

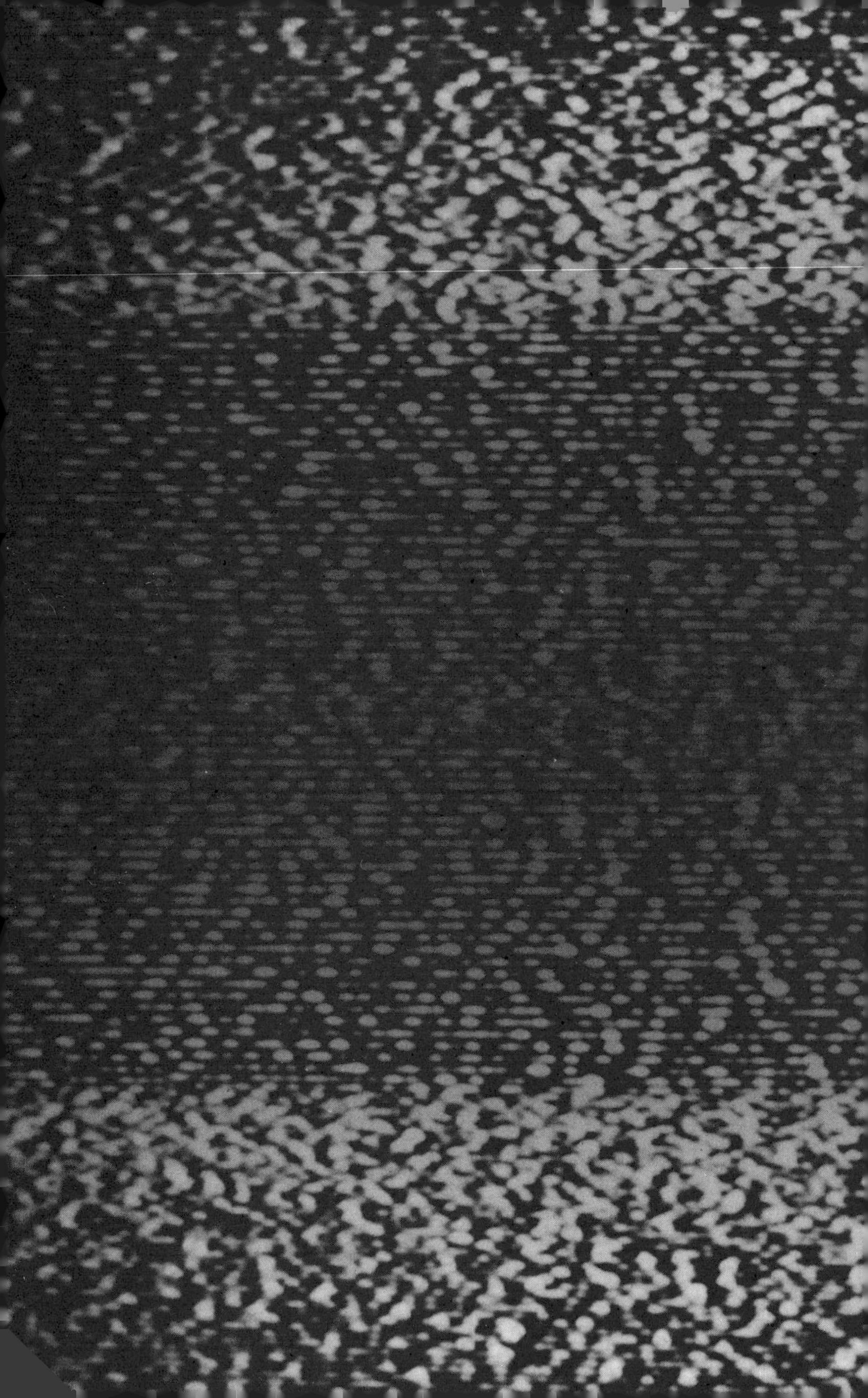

DROWNING

ARE YOU SURE THIS RESORT ATTRACTION IS WORTH THE WAIT?" KARA WALSH ASKED LOLA AND FRANCINE. KARA STRETCHED HER SOUR APPLE BUBBLEGUM OUT OF HER MOUTH AS FAR AS IT COULD GO AND THEN PLOPPED IT BACK IN. SHE WAS *SO BORED* FROM STANDING IN LINE.

Francine looked to Lola as she always did.

"Totally," Lola said, pushing her dark hair behind her ear. "My brother swears by it. He says it's one of the best VR experiences he's ever had." She pulled out a folded-up piece of paper from her faux-leather fanny pack. "Besides, it's up next on our itinerary and it's gotten a full five stars from reviewers. Can't get better than that."

"Yeah, can't get better than five stars," Francine chimed in.

Kara sighed, crossed her arms, and cocked her hip. Lola was a master planner. There was always a list. A summer plan list, a school supply list, an extracurricular activities for the school year list, things they were going to do at the Mega Pizzaplex list, and a whole boatload of others.

Blah, blah, blah.

Kara preferred to be spontaneous.

She liked to do things on a whim, to have fun in the moment instead of always planning things out. She liked action and excitement, and ultimately the feeling of being carefree.

Which usually didn't include waiting in the slowest, longest, most boring line in the history of long lines.

Yeah, they'd been waiting for over thirty minutes because the Mega Pizzaplex was so packed with kids of all ages, helicopter parents, and long-suffering employees.

It had been Lola's idea to have them each ask their parents for full-day passes as a reward for receiving good grades on their latest semester report cards, which gave them infinite gameplay and, of course, unlimited rides on the special attractions.

It turned out, though, that the special attractions only lasted a measly five minutes! It was such a scam, in Kara's opinion, since they were lucky if they got to experience each attraction even twice by the way things were moving along.

Kara shifted again and craned her neck to watch a few kids walk out of the Resort exit as they laughed, giving each other high fives.

"That was so cool!"

"I know, it's like we were really there!"

"That was the best!"

Good for them, Kara thought grudgingly. When was it going to be her turn? The line finally moved forward and she bounced in her high-top tennis shoes in anticipation, but the attendant cut the line off right in front of Francine.

Kara's shoulders sagged. "This is taking *forever*." She blew a bubble until it popped.

"We're up next," Lola told her. "It's gonna be really intense, you'll see."

Lola was not just their planner, but their resident optimist. She had long brown hair with pretty waves and light brown skin. She often dressed in red just like the frilly top she was currently wearing with her jeans, and she donned big hoop earrings that poked out from her long hair. She was also the one who had formed their friendship on the first day of middle school. They'd each been new to the school district and had been sitting alone before class started. And then suddenly there was Lola, flashing her silver braces and introducing herself with a firm handshake, with Francine already by her side, asking Kara if she wanted to be their friend. They'd been inseparable ever since, even now as sophomores. Which was *why* Kara was willing to wait in the line. Lola's ideas always turned out well.

"Yeah, it will be *so* intense," said Francine, who was the more timid one of the three even though she rocked plus-size fashion and was the tallest by two inches. Most of the time, Francine just agreed with everything Lola said and made it a point to always be nice to everyone. She had honey blonde hair that reached her shoulders, with hazel eyes that sometimes looked gray and sometimes blue. She had a habit of pulling at her clothes as if she wasn't comfortable in them even when Kara and Lola always assured her that she looked just fine.

Kara, on the other hand, often forgot to be nice. In fact, most of the time she didn't have time to remember. She liked to be on the *go, go, go*. To get the boring things done quickly so she could do fun things like ride bikes, skateboard, rock wall climb, or experience new things. Maybe it was her hair, wild strawberry blonde curls her mother always said couldn't be tamed.

But she might just die in line of boredom before they ever moved forward and got to try out the Resort.

"I'm thirsty," Francine said. "Is anyone thirsty?"

Lola said, "No," and Kara shook her head.

"I'm not really, either," Francine said, looking around, and twirling a strand of her hair around her finger.

"Next in line!" The line attendant called out and opened the braided rope to allow them into the Resort.

"Finally!" Kara gushed as they walked into the VR experience, only to find out when they had entered deeper into the attraction that there were two more groups ahead of them!

"*Ugh.*" Kara tossed her curls in frustration. "Why me?"

"Kara, relax, it's almost our turn," Lola told her. "Just look around. See how cool it is?"

Kara lifted her eyebrows. Francine's white shirt lit up like a ghost in the black light. The attendants wore pink-and-green shirts that glowed like virtual cotton candy. Neon palm trees, waves, and beach balls were the only lights along the walls. Glow-in-the-dark posters showcased the different VR experiences: Waterpark, The Beach, or Coaster City. In the pictures, the players were sliding down elaborate waterslides, others were surfing, and some were riding amusement park attractions.

Just ahead was the door to the actual VR experience. A large monitor hung from the ceiling, flashing with scenes of what the current players were experiencing. At the moment, a group of three were playing volleyball on the beach.

Kara chewed her gum absently as she eyed the posters of the Waterpark, studying the spiraled waterslides and some of the ladders that looked extremely tall.

And she felt that tingle in her gut.

It was almost fear. Almost excitement.

It told her she wanted to play the Waterpark experience *really, really* bad.

"Oooh, I know what would be fun for us," Lola said, as she pointed to the poster that said COASTER CITY: AN ACTION-PACKED THRILL RIDE! "Let's choose Coaster City!"

"Okay!" Francine agreed happily.

Kara made a face and pointed instead at the Waterpark posters. "I want to pick Waterpark. Look at those slides. They're so awesome! It would be so much fun, Lola!"

Lola tilted her head and somehow gave Kara a look her mother often gave her. "Come on, Kara, let's play Coaster City together. We don't want to choose separate experiences. We're doing this as best friends, remember?"

"Yeah, come on, Kara," Francine said.

Kara recrossed her arms, biting back a protest. It had

seemed like an especially long school year, and yeah, it was great spending time with her best friends, but a little alone time doing what she *wanted* to do sounded pretty good to her. They followed Lola's lists all year long. Sometimes it got old.

But best friends do everything together, right? So Kara did what she usually did when it came to Lola. She gave in, in order to do something fun.

Kara heaved a long sigh and nodded in agreement. "*Fine.*"

Lola clapped her hands. "It's going to be so cool, you'll see!"

"Better be," Kara muttered.

"Huh?" Lola said.

Francine looked at Kara and then at Lola.

Kara pasted on a fake smile. "Nothing, can't wait!"

Lola smiled. "Okay, great!"

When Lola turned away, Kara rolled her eyes. She was pretty sure her sarcasm was lost on Lola even when Francine seemed to see past Kara's facade. But being the nice one of the trio, Francine never mentioned anything.

A few minutes later, they finally moved up to be next in line. Kara glimpsed inside the VR room as the door slid open. There were normal lights highlighting the boxed, red room. Four large chairs were lined up together with some kind of weird helmets connected by a thick wire. She watched as the group of four before them strolled in and talked to the line attendant, then the group stood in front of the chairs as a blue laser light scanned down their bodies.

"What's that about?" Kara asked.

"Oh, it's really cool," Lola told her. "Your body is

scanned so you're uploaded into the virtual reality. When we look at one another in the VR world, we'll see *perfect* digital versions of ourselves. Awesome, right?"

Kara nodded her head, impressed.

The attendant started to walk back to the girls as the door slid closed behind him. Even under the black lights, it was obvious the attendant was a tall, cute boy with a nice smile. Lola nudged the girls with her elbow and smiled, giving a thumbs-up, telling them the boy was super cute.

Another Resort attendant, who must have been controlling the VR experience, stood off to the side behind a big console.

"Hey, ladies, you up for a virtually fun time?" the cute line attendant asked. "What's your choice at the Resort?"

"Coaster City," Lola said, excited.

He nodded his head. "Perfect. It's our most popular experience." He shifted his attention to Kara. "How 'bout you? Is that what you want to choose?"

Kara's eyebrows lifted as she chewed her gum. "Me?"

He smiled. "Yeah, you."

Lola and Francine giggled.

"Um, yeah, I mean, that's what they want. So sure."

"I'm Zachary—my friends call me Zach."

"Kara. This is Lola and Francine."

"Cool. Um, please throw out any gum or candy you may be eating. Sorry, it's the rules." Then he called out to the other attendant. "Coaster City up next, Ralph!"

Kara shrugged, stepped to a nearby garbage can, and spit out her gum. A couple minutes later, the door to the VR experience finally slid open, revealing the four chairs as the other group strolled out of the exit across from the entrance. The girls trotted in, and even though it wasn't the experience Kara wanted to do, she remained eager to try out the VR attraction.

"Stand on the big *X*, please," Zach told them. "Then hold still and look straight ahead." Seeing him under the real lights, Kara realized Zach had dark hair, tan skin, blue eyes, and dark freckles. He was definitely cute.

"Sure," she said, and glanced down to stand on a black *X* marked on the red carpet. She stayed in place and looked up as the blue light motioned down her body. An odd feeling rolled over her with the light and she slowly blinked. The room seemed to move slightly under her feet.

Must be getting hungry, she thought as the girls each chose a chair and buckled themselves in.

"Okay, ladies," Zach said to them, making sure they were each secured in the seat. "The VR chair and helmet work together to help you integrate yourself fully into the experience. They control heat sensors, movement, and visualization. You can speak to the microphone in the helmet to communicate to others and give a few simple commands. Where you turn your visual direction is where you'll be able to move toward the experience and join in a game or go for a ride."

Kara was still looking around the boxed room, taking in every detail. Signs were posted on the walls. One stated: PLEASE STAY IN YOUR SEAT UNTIL THE EXPERIENCE IS COMPLETELY FINISHED. Another stated: IN CASE OF SICKNESS, PRESS THE EMERGENCY BUTTON ON YOUR RIGHT ARMREST. Kara turned her gaze to the right armrest to see a big yellow button, then glanced up at a neon sign lit up across the wall with one word: HYPERTIME!

Zach checked on Kara last. "All set."

"Hey, Zach," Kara asked him. "What's that Hypertime thing about?"

"Oh yeah, Hypertime is pretty popular. It puts your brain into overdrive and makes you feel like you're experiencing the game longer than usual. Of course, you have to pay more." He leaned down and whispered, "It's really just an extra shot of adrenaline through the sensors for the player. But, you know, Hypertime makes it sound more exciting."

Kara smiled. "Got it."

He winked. "Okay, slip on your helmets and get ready for Coaster City!"

"This is going to be so cool!" Lola said with glee.

"So cool!" Francine added.

The girls grabbed the helmets with flat goggles from a hook on the side of the chair, and slipped them on. Kara heard the door slide shut to the VR room and the Coaster City screen flashed in front of her eyes.

Kara walked onto a beach boardwalk with tons of rides and games surrounding her. With each step, she could hear the scrape of sand beneath their feet. A seagull cried from the sky and music played from speakers attached to wooden poles.

"Wow," Lola said, looking down at herself. She smiled and then studied Kara and Francine. "Look! It's like it's *really* us. This is amazing!"

Francine giggled. "Oh, I wish I had worn a more interesting outfit."

"Francine, you look good," Lola told her.

Kara smiled. "Yeah, you're just fine the way you are."

She waved her hand in front of her face. It looked *exactly* like her hand. Down to the little freckle on her thumb. "This *is* cool."

"Look how big it is here," Lola said, gazing about. "There are more rides than I've ever seen in my life!"

It was true. The rides were packed together like a huge carnival city with bright colors and giant signs. There were a bunch of people around them, eating sweets and drinking soda. Much to Kara's dismay, there were even long lines to the rides.

"Well, it's super crowded," Kara complained, and suddenly the crowd thinned down to only a few other patrons. "Whoa, that was easy."

"Wow, this is so neat!" Lola said.

"Yeah, totally!" Francine agreed.

"Let's ride the Speedster!" Kara rushed over to a coaster that looked blisteringly fast, her friends trailing behind.

The girls tried to ride as many rides as they could. Their hair blew away from their faces and the sun shined down on their skin, warming them. When they rode a roller coaster, their bodies jerked with each rush and shift. They screamed when they dove down steep hills or when they shifted into a fast turn. The giant swings that turned in circles made them dizzy. But as soon as they finished their third ride, Coaster City faded from the VR screen.

"That's it?" Kara moaned. "What a rip. That was *so* short." She should have tried out that Hypertime.

"Wow!" Lola exclaimed. "But it was so awesome! I can't believe how cool it was. I felt like I was really there, riding the rides. I even felt the ocean air. I could even smell the popcorn and hot dogs. My brother was right. It was the best!"

They lifted off their helmets, set them on the hook, and unbuckled before climbing out of the VR seats.

"I know, it was really fun," Francine agreed. "The best."

"Yeah, it was cool," Kara said, even though it had lasted only a few minutes. "I liked the roller coaster the best. It was the only ride that gave me a real rush."

Lola threw her a look, with a twist of her lips. "*We know, Kara*. You're our fearless daredevil."

Kara grinned at that because she liked to be known for doing things that were scary. "If the line weren't so long I would have gone again and played Waterpark. Now, some of those slides look really intense."

The door on the other side of the room slid open and they strolled through the exit. Kara glanced up to view another VR monitor that hung on the wall and spotted a pool with a small waterslide. She frowned as something at the bottom of the pool caught her eye.

A movement. A shift of darkness, with long hair.

She blinked. Was someone at the bottom of the pool? "Hey, do you guys see that?"

"What?" Lola asked, looking around.

But when Kara pointed to the screen it was back to a roller-coaster ride.

"Um, nothing, I guess," Kara said, uncertain as they walked out.

"Well, it's another thirty-minute wait or longer," Lola pointed out as she looked at the long, snaking line to get back into the Resort. "I wouldn't want to wait in that line again."

Kara shook her head. "No thanks. Too bad this wasn't

virtual reality, and people could literally disappear. No more long lines for me, please."

"I know what you mean. Then let's see what's next on the itinerary," Lola said as she eagerly took out the folded paper from her fanny pack.

Kara sighed, crossing her arms. "Can't wait."

For the next two hours, the girls played laser tag, indulged in ice-cream floats, took pictures in photo booths, and giggled through a couple sessions of karaoke.

"Well, we've done everything we could on the list," Lola told them. "It's almost time for my brother to pick us up. We can go hang out in the arcade till he gets here."

"Okay," Francine agreed.

"Or we could just explore and see if we missed any-thing," Kara suggested.

Lola tilted her head. "Well, I don't want us to get stuck in a line and have my brother be waiting for us. He'll get way annoyed if I keep him waiting. It'll be better if we hang out at the arcade and just walk out to meet him when he texts."

"I guess." Kara scanned around and happened to see Zach and the other attendant closing the line to the Resort with the braided rope. Her eyes widened. "Oh, um, I gotta go to the restroom real quick. I'll meet you guys over there."

"You want us to go with you?" Lola asked.

Kara flicked out her hand. "No, it's okay. See you there in a bit *if* there isn't another long line there, too." She rolled her eyes and Lola smiled.

"Okay," she said, and then Lola and Francine took off toward the arcade.

Kara rushed past a few kids eating cotton candy and a

woman holding a crying baby before Zach could disappear on her.

"Hey, Zach!" Kara waved at him.

Zach jerked his head around and spotted her. He smiled. "Oh, hey, Kara, right? Still here, huh?"

"I'm out," the guy said.

Zach nodded at him. "See you after dinner, Ralph."

Kara expelled a breath. "It's almost time for us to go home. You closing up the Resort?"

"Yep, just for a bit. We're short-staffed today, so we have to close down the attractions for some of our meal breaks."

Kara tossed her hair nervously. "Zach, um, before you go, could you show me how the Resort works? Especially Hypertime?" She smiled at him, lacing her fingers together. This was one time she was doing her best to be nice. "I probably won't make it back for a while, and I really want to see how it works. It looks super cool."

"Um." Zach scratched his head. "I guess I could take a few minutes."

Kara bounced on her feet. "Yes! Thank you!"

Zach released the rope and looked around. "Okay, come on inside."

Kara ducked inside with excitement. She followed Zach to the control panel.

He spread his arm out in front of the panel. "So this is where the virtual magic happens."

Fascinated, Kara scanned the intricate controls and buttons that looked like some kind of scientific panel often seen in the movies. "Wow, there are so many buttons and screens. You actually know what everything does?"

"Oh yeah, we had to go through a two-week training

for all the attractions when I was hired, and then pass a big test. I usually bomb at tests, but somehow I got the call. Anyway, we try to monitor what the players are experiencing to make sure everything goes smoothly. This control here is the Hypertime. It can be set from one to ten depending on how much extended time you want to experience. It's a little confusing."

"What do you mean?"

"Well, right now it's at zero, right? But I have to punch in a number to set the *virtual extended* time frame so it knows how long to increase the experience. Otherwise, it would just keep going and going. So one is the max time at one hour, when in reality it's still a five-minute turn, the player just *experiences* it like it's longer. Pretty trippy, huh?"

"So if you set it to ten, it will only feel like an extra six minutes—and if you set it to one, it'll feel like you're experiencing a whole extra hour?"

Zach nodded. "You got it."

Kara's eyes widened at the possibility of being in an attraction for a longer time frame. "*Wow,* that sounds really cool." She looked at Zach and smiled again. "Can I ask one more favor?"

Zach lifted his eyebrows. "You want to try it out, don't you?"

"Heck yeah, please, Zach. The line was so long I could only ride once, and the experience was over way too quickly. I do have the unlimited attraction pass if that helps."

Zach stared at the controls a moment as if debating, then nodded reluctantly. "All right, I guess it wouldn't hurt to do a quick run."

Kara bounced on her feet. "Yes, you're the best!"

Zach seemed to like that he made her happy. He ducked his head and grinned. "But I have to go clock out for my break first so I can monitor you. It'll just take me a minute."

Kara thought about Lola and Francine. "Oh, but my friends are waiting for me. Can't I just start the experience first?"

He shook his head. "I can't. I'm not supposed to leave players unmonitored. It's against the rules."

Who cares about the dumb rules? Kara thought. "Come on, *please*, you said yourself the experience only takes, like, five minutes. I'll be done by the time you return. Come on, it'll be so cool."

Zach ran a hand over the back of his neck, clearly reluctant.

PRETTY PLEASE.

He blew out a big sigh. "Okay, okay. But don't let anyone know, all right? I'd like to keep my job."

Kara made a motion of zipping her mouth. "My lips are sealed."

Zach pressed a button and the door slid open to the VR chairs. "Come on and strap in."

Yes, yes, yes!

Kara practically skipped into the room. "Do I have to rescan?"

"Nope, the scans stay in the digital memory all day until they're cleared overnight."

"Cool. Can you set me up with Waterpark with Hypertime?" Kara said, hopping into the VR chair, buckling in, and placing the helmet over her head.

"Yep, I'm going to turn on Waterpark with Hypertime just for you."

"And can you set it to one, please?"

"An extra virtual hour it is. I'll see you in a few minutes."

"You mean I'll be seeing you in one virtual hour."

Zach chuckled. "Right. Have fun."

"Thanks, I sure will!" Kara said with a big smile.

Zach sighed again as he walked over to the VR controls. His mom always said he turned to mush when it came to a cute girl and found it hard to say no, even when his gut told him otherwise. He just hoped he didn't end up regretting it. He went through the player scans and reselected Kara, clicked on Waterpark, and flinched when the mini walkie clipped to his collar barked out with his boss's voice.

"Zach, have you clocked out for dinner? I need you at Gator Golf ASAP to cover a quick break."

Rattled from breaking the rules, Zach rushed to click on Hypertime for Kara and took off out the door. *She'll be done in a few minutes*, he thought. He spoke into his collar microphone. "Sure, boss, I'm on my way."

He put the rope back up and flipped the sign to TEMPORARILY CLOSED.

As he rushed over to Gator Golf, the Hypertime remained set to zero.

Kara appeared immediately inside a giant waterpark enclosed with pale blue tiled walls and a high arched ceiling. The echoing of rushing water filled her ears and seemed to echo off the numerous walls. The strong scent of chlorine hit her nostrils. In awe, she turned around to see pools surrounding her in all directions. Some of the pool areas had doors in the tiled walls that must have led to other areas. Certain water sections appeared shallow, and some looked extra deep. There were short water-slides and longer ones. There were slides that zigzagged and ones that curved into spirals. There were pool areas that appeared to have themes, like a beach, a donut shop, pirates, and outer space. There was even a slide coming out of a cool waterfall!

It was as if the Waterpark went on forever—a never-ending, giant labyrinth of water fun that continuously generated no matter where she turned.

"*This is amazing*," she whispered, turning in a circle. "They should have called this place Waterpark World. I could get lost in here forever." She almost wished Lola and Francine were with her to see the place. Almost. She'd just have to tell them all about it when she was done and met them back at the arcade. She clapped her hands together in anticipation. They were going to be so jealous that they didn't pick Waterpark the first time.

Well, she thought, *that would be Lola's fault that they'd missed out since her best friend always had to be in control.* For now, Kara would enjoy having this fun time all by herself without having to worry about them!

She looked down to see that she wore a blue wet suit with short sleeves and short pants, which was perfect for Kara. She was a water shorts with colorful tees kind of girl.

Just ahead of her, she spotted a flat waterslide that led into a shallow pool and ran toward it. She dove down and slid on her belly, arms out, and skidded straight into the little pool. Warm water splashed against her. She laughed as she rose out of the shallow water.

"So cool!" The water felt nice on her skin. She could smell a hint of chlorine, but it wasn't overwhelming. "Having the Waterpark all to myself is the best!"

With a grin, she stood and spotted a tall waterslide just ahead, about the height of a two-story building, with a skinny ladder that led to the top. She felt the nervous tingle in her hands and feet, like tiny needles biting into her skin.

Kara placed a trembling hand to her tingling stomach. "Now *that's* what I'm talking about,"

Kara determinedly jogged along the tiled floor toward the waterslide. The truth was, she had a thing about fear. She wasn't fearless, like Lola had said. She definitely *felt* fear. But dealt with the fear by trying to face it head-on, even when something made her want to run in the opposite direction. It drove her parents wild.

When Kara had been five, she'd been climbing a tree with her second-cousin Peggy, who had inched out on a tree branch that was too small, and the tree limb had cracked. When she fell out of the tree, she'd landed on her head, ended up in a coma, and suffered a traumatic brain injury.

Kara never forgave herself for not being able to help her, and as she grew older, she would have nightmares that something like that would happen to her. Her parents were always scolding her for taking too many risks.

Kara would get so angry with her mother for trying to instill fear into her that Kara just kept trying to face more and more of the things that scared her, whether it was to rebel against her parents or to try to overcome anxieties that haunted her dreams. Each time she felt that tingle in her feet, in her hands, or in her stomach, she knew it was a fear she had to break through.

Kara looked up to view the top of the slide. She shook her tingling hands, then began to climb the tall, metal ladder. With each step up, the tingling increased. Her hands grew damp with nerves. Her legs felt a little wobbly. When she reached the top, she felt herself tremble as she gazed out over the infinite selection of pools. She carefully lifted her arms up, taking in the huge park. Her heart was beating fast in her chest, but attempting to beat back a fear was a rush in itself.

She felt like she was on top of the world!

She stayed like that a little longer just to prove to herself that she could.

Carefully, she hunkered down, her breaths filtering out her mouth with excitement, then pushed off to slide down the wet tube so fast it nearly stole her breath. Adrenaline spiked through her before she splashed into a deep, dark pool, sinking to the bottom. The water surrounding her was the perfect temperature. She swam up out of the darkness and reached the surface, treading water, and suddenly jerked up.

"*Hey.*" It felt like something brushed her leg!

Unease sunk over her as she scanned the dark water around her, floating in the middle of the pool. She quickly swam to the edge and pulled herself out. She pushed her wet hair back as she gazed into the water.

"There's nothing there, silly," she told herself.

She stood and began to walk through the labyrinth. The floors and walls continued with the plain, light blue tile until she entered into different themes. The next connecting theme was a jungle. She stepped onto smooth pebbled rocks.

"Whoa." The air was humid and she felt herself begin to perspire. Palm trees surrounded a huge pool. Giant tropical flowers stuck out in various directions. There were birds chirping, and even the distant sounds of monkeys.

She spotted a parrot sitting in a tree, with pretty, colorful feathers. "Oh, hello," she said.

The bird flapped its wings at her. "Hello! Hello!" the bird squawked.

Kara giggled. "You're kinda cool." She reached out a hesitant finger and petted the parrot's soft feathers.

"Don't leave me alone," the bird told her.

Kara tilted her head as she smiled. "Well, sorry, but I have to keep exploring."

She walked to the pool and dipped her hand in the water. The water was warm and rippled on the surface. Across the body of water was a giant waterfall, with a slide attached to the cliff. It was beautiful! Kara sat down and stuck her feet in the pool as she watched the water cascade off the rocks. She glanced down as she kicked her feet.

Something moved under the surface.

A spurt of alarm shot through her as Kara snatched her feet out of the pool.

Was that a sea animal underwater? she wondered.

Then she glimpsed a flow of black hair.

Kara gasped. *Wait.* It was a girl.

Could this be like a fantasy theme and the girl in the water was some kind of mermaid?

Now, that would be cool.

Kara kneeled down and tried to scan beneath the water. Maybe she could spot a tail. But she didn't see the girl again.

"Hmm." She sat back, uncertain. "Is there a glitch in the VR program? Or was it just my imagination?" Frowning, she stood and walked out of the jungle and back onto the tiled floors. She noticed the lights dim around her and the walls darken. Her eyes widened in astonishment as she stepped into an outer space theme.

"Oh my gosh. This is the coolest!" The darkened walls had millions of tiny stars, with various planets, and even four moons. The temperature around her lowered. A comet shot across the wall and Kara ran along with it as if she could try to catch it. There were various-size pools that were highlighted with different colors of purple, blue, pink, and more. Amazed, she walked around taking the details in. She wondered if this was what astronauts experienced when they blasted into space. She passed a pale pink pool and once again she thought she saw something—*someone*—within the water.

She stepped closer and spotted pale hands, dark hair, and a flash of gray.

There's the girl again!

She wasn't imagining things.

And the girl certainly wasn't a mermaid.

What the heck was a girl doing inside the VR program with her? Kara was the only one playing the game.

Curious, she kneeled down, studying the pool. She spotted the girl floating at the bottom. "Hey, what are you doing here?"

The girl's black hair drifted around her. She wore

some kind of grayish fabric that covered her arms and legs instead of a bathing suit.

Her eyes were closed. Her body seemed unmoving as her arms drifted in the water.

She looked dead.

"Oh no," Kara whispered. She glanced around as if to figure out what to do. There was no one to ask for help. Her hands tingled and she shook them out in front of her.

Um, I have to help her. Frightened, Kara pinched her nose and dove headfirst into the pool, swimming toward the bottom. She grabbed the girl's arm that was floating in the water.

The girl's eyes popped open, her dark eyes staring directly at Kara.

Kara jerked back in shock, her mouth opening in a scream.

Water gushed down Kara's throat as she waved her arms around, trying to swim to the surface.

She needed air!

A hand gripped her lower leg and Kara's eyes widened. *No!* She kicked out, trying to get loose, but it felt like she was being pulled deeper to the bottom.

Her heart pounded against her chest.

Kara paddled her arms frantically, trying to get free.

Help! She kicked out hard, finally releasing the grip on her leg. She swam up to the surface, gasping for air. She coughed as she tried to get to the edge. It felt like snot and water dribbled out of her nose. She swam awkwardly and pulled herself up, sucking in air. On her hands and knees, she gagged out water and nearly threw up.

Her shoulders moved up and down with heavy breaths.

Her body trembled. She blinked water out of her eyes as she got her breathing under control and peered down at the small pool.

The girl was still at the bottom.

And she was looking straight at Kara with a piercing, dark glare.

I'm not alone.

That realization had thoughts juggling in Kara's mind as she walked quickly along the pools and waterslides, trying to understand what was happening. How could the girl in the water be in Kara's VR experience? Was the girl part of the Waterpark theme? She didn't understand, and the element of mystery shifted her fun experience into something uneasy.

Something scary.

Honestly, a creepy girl at the bottom of the pools was not exactly a fear she had wanted to face. It certainly wasn't a fear she'd had until a few minutes ago. Kara took a breath and tried to calm down as she walked. The tiles felt chilled under her feet. Goose bumps ran along her arms, and she rubbed her hands across her skin. It was all going to be okay. None of this was real, anyway. In reality, she was sitting back in a VR chair in Freddy Fazbear's Mega Pizzaplex Resort experience. Lola and Francine were playing arcade games, waiting for her to come back. Hypertime would run out—she was just in here for an hour. She only had to keep playing the game until it ended and avoid the girl in the water as much as possible.

"That won't be that hard," she said quietly. She would just keep away from the water.

Just to be sure, Kara came to a halt and leaned over a pool, looking down to see if the girl was still there.

Sure enough, there was the girl at the bottom of the pool, staring up at her. She reached a hand up toward Kara. Her skin was pale white. Her eyes had an eerie peacefulness to them.

Kara's gut tingled and she took off in a sprint.

She had to keep away from the girl.

Kara darted alongside the pools, through a donut shop theme. Frosted donuts floated in a pool and there were donut holes pasted on the tiled walls. She could actually smell the sugary pastries in the air. But she couldn't take the time to enjoy her surroundings as urgency thrummed through her.

Keep running.

She rushed through a beach theme. Wet sand squashed under her feet as the sound of seagulls cried in the distance. The rush of waves from a large pool filled her ears and a light spray of water touched her face. The beauty of it didn't affect her as she ran through the next theme. She stumbled upon an ice-cream shop, with giant floating ice-cream cups in the pool. Neon cones with single scoops glowed on the walls. There was an actual ice-cream counter so players could get a scoop of ice cream, with tables to sit and eat. It would have been fun if she didn't see the girl with the black hair floating in the water.

The farther she ran, Kara was sure she would lose the girl, but when Kara peeked into the closest pool, the strange girl was still there.

In every pool. In every body of water.

Kara stopped running, her breathing harsh. Her

mouth was dry and parched. She scanned wildly around her, only to see more pools, more themed waterslides. She needed out!

"Lola! Francine!" Kara yelled out in frustration. "Zach! Please, get me out of here! I don't want to play anymore. Something weird is going on here. Help me, please! I . . ."

Suddenly, she remembered the emergency button on the armrest! *Of course!* She squeezed her eyes shut. She tried to connect with her real self, sitting in the chair. She moved her arm out and pushed for the button.

Nothing.

She couldn't get a sense of herself in the VR chair. *At all.*

That couldn't be. She tried again, reaching out, but all she touched was air.

"Oh my gosh." Her eyes opened wide. She felt totally disconnected from her real body. But . . . how? What the heck was going on?

She touched her head and actually felt her tangled hair. She slid her hands over her face. She could feel her skin as if touching her *real* self. She touched her arms, her stomach, reached down to her legs.

She felt *real.*

It was as if her actual body had been completely transported into the Waterpark.

"No, no, no. This isn't reality."

But the way her body felt told her otherwise.

Her heart pounded in her chest and her breaths increased. "Oh no." She gazed at the pools around her and everything started to spin. She stepped back and hit a wall. She pressed her hands flat against the tiles so she wouldn't fall over.

She breathed through her nose calmly, just like her basketball coach had told her when she was younger and the coach wanted to calm the team down at practice.

Breath in. Breath out.

Her heartbeats began to slow and her breathing evened out.

When she finally calmed, her body felt unexpectedly heavy. She needed to rest. She wasn't sure how long she'd been running through the Waterpark. She looked around and found herself in a pizza parlor theme. She took a seat at a red pizza booth, with black-and-white checkered tables. She pulled her legs against her chest, wrapping her arms around herself. She could smell pepperoni and cheese as she stared out into the shallow pool before her.

For a brief moment from where she sat, she couldn't see the girl at the bottom of the water.

"It's not real. It's not real," she murmured, over and over, with her eyes closed, rocking herself back and forth. "None of it. This place. The girl. It's all going to end soon. I'll be back with Lola and Francine and everything will be back to normal. This is just a really, really high-tech VR experience. Everything may feel real, but it's all fake. Just make-believe."

When Kara finally opened her eyes, she was standing a couple feet away from the shallow pool. Her feet were sliding closer to the water!

"*What?*" Kara's eyes widened as she raised her arms out to balance herself. She swiveled her gaze back to the pizza booth where she had just been sitting and then to where she was standing beside the shallow pool.

Kara looked down into the water and spotted the girl

staring up at her. Kara leaped back. Her body began to tremble. "This isn't okay! I didn't get up! You can't make me do things against my will! This isn't fun anymore, okay? Zach, if you're playing a mean trick on me, I'm done now. Please, get me out of here! Anyone!"

Her voice echoed back at her through the Waterpark, empty save for the girl in the water.

"Help me!" she screamed.

Tears stung her eyes and she quickly blinked them away.

No. I'm okay. I'm not going to cry.

She blew out a breath. *Think, Kara, think.* It seemed she couldn't even sit down to rest. Well, then she would have to keep going because if she let her guard down, the creepy girl would somehow lure her into the water.

Her hands tightened into fists as she took a few more calming breaths. She had to keep moving until the game ended.

She had to.

It seemed like hours had passed as Kara continued to walk through the labyrinth of pools. *Why hadn't the experience ended?* she wondered. Zach had said the longest she could be in Hypertime was the equivalent to one VR hour. So what was taking so long? She felt like she was roaming forever through the creative themes. Her mouth was dry from exerting herself. She wished she had a piece of her favorite gum. She felt like her limbs were tiring and her mind felt foggy.

She really did need a safe place to rest.

Luckily, she found a small alcove in a rocky area that had a miniature volcano, with only one small heated pool a couple feet away. The air was extra hot, and perspiration dotted her forehead, but it seemed like a safe place to rest that was far enough from the water. Kara ducked into the small area, laid against the hard rock, and curled up into a ball. She could hear the constant rushing of water around her.

She felt very alone. There was a strange feeling in the middle of her chest that felt hollow. She rubbed a hand against the feeling to push it away.

In her daily life, she was never really alone. Her mom worked from home. She was always surrounded by kids at school. When she went out, it was usually with Lola and Francine.

She always yearned to be left alone to do her own things. To make her own choices, without having to get someone else's approval.

Now in some weird way, she got what she wanted.

And yet, she was isolated with a girl who had tried to drown her.

Not exactly what she had in mind.

Truthfully, she would give anything to be with her parents and Lola and Francine at the moment. She would have laughed at the irony if she didn't feel so sad.

"I'll be safe here for a few minutes," she whispered to herself. Her eyes grew heavy as she drifted off to sleep.

The day was warm and the neighborhood quiet for a Sunday morning. Kara was five years old and tucked up in the middle of a big oak tree in her family's neighborhood, holding as tight as she could to the tree trunk. Peggy, her second cousin, was smiling as she nudged her little body out onto a tree limb.

Peggy and her parents had come to visit Kara and her family for the weekend. They lived two towns away and usually visited about once a month. Kara liked to play with Peggy, but sometimes her cousin could be a know-it-all who never listened to Kara. Like now.

Kara's hands and feet were tingling just under her skin. "Peggy, I don't think you should climb onto that branch," Kara told her. "You're going to get in big, big trouble."

"I'm not going to get into trouble if no one tells." Peggy had black hair pulled back in pigtails. She was missing one front tooth. "Are you going to tell on me?"

"No." Kara felt envious because Peggy seemed so brave climbing the tree, and Kara felt super scared. Her palms were sweaty as she held on to the tree trunk, the bark biting into her skin. Her stomach felt like it was in a huge knot. Kara looked down to the ground. She was pretty far up. She shouldn't have climbed the tree and she wondered if she'd be able to get down. Her parents were going to be really mad if she got stuck.

"Come on, follow me, Kara," Peggy said. "It's really fun!"

Kara shook her head, and held on as tight as she could to the thick trunk. "*No.*"

"Geez, you're such a baby."

Kara frowned at her. "No, I'm not."

"Are too!" Then she stuck out her tongue in Kara's direction.

Kara gave her a mean look back.

Peggy stretched her body out on the branch. Her maroon sweatsuit reminded Kara of rotten strawberries.

"Look at me, Kara. It's like I'm a wildcat hiding in a tree!" She shoved her arms out, giggling. "Look, no hands! I'm flying! I'm really flying!"

Kara's throat tightened at the sight of her cousin as the tree limb bent lower under her weight. "Peggy, stop it! Come back right now! If you get hurt, we're both going to get in trouble."

"Stop saying—"

Something cracked. The branch shook and Peggy grabbed the branch underneath her, and she let out a scream.

Kara yelled, "Peggy! Hurry, climb back to me!"

"I—I can't. I'm stuck! Help me!" She reached a hand out to Kara as her other arm wrapped around the branch. Tears welled in her eyes.

Kara shook her head. Her body felt frozen. She was too far away. "I can't. Just climb backward. Hurry!"

"I can't move!" The branch cracked again. Peggy wrapped both arms around the branch and started crying. "Oh gosh, I'm stuck! *Please, Kara! I want my mommy! Get my mommy!*"

The girls gasped as the branch splintered really loud and Peggy began to fall.

Both girls screamed.

It was like horrible slow motion as Kara helplessly watched Peggy fall through the air until she hit the hard ground.

Thump.

Peggy's head hit against the cemented sidewalk. Blood poured out from her head.

Kara screamed for her mom.

Suddenly the ground under Peggy began to seep with water. Kara's eyes widened. The water covered Peggy; her black hair waved out of the pigtails.

"What's happening?" Kara cried out. "Mom! Dad! Help!"

The water rose higher up the tree trunk, reaching Kara's legs. Kara had suddenly grown into her teenager self. No longer a little girl.

Peggy was still at the bottom of the water, and her eyes opened as she turned and swam upward with the rising water. Her face shifted from Peggy to the girl at the bottom of the pool with dark eyes, then back to Peggy again.

Peggy/the drowned girl reached up toward Kara as the water inched closer. Kara started to climb the tree to try to get away from the water and the girl.

Her heart pounded. Her stomach tightened.

But the water kept rising, higher and higher.

A pale hand broke out of the water, latching onto Kara's ankle, digging into her skin.

Squeezing.

Kara kicked out, shouting, *"Noooo! Mom! Dad!"*

The hand yanked Kara so hard she fell from the tree and splashed into the water. The hand pulled her deeper down into the depths. Kara screamed under the water, bubbles floating up from her mouth, as the tree above appeared farther and farther away.

Kara awoke with a jolt, breathing hard. She looked around, disoriented. She was soaked with sweat. Where was she?

Was she still in VR?

Laying before her was the girl from the pool. She had crawled halfway onto the pavement.

Kara scurried back against the rock as far as she could go.

The girl no longer looked at peace or serene. In fact, it looked like she was deteriorating. Her black hair was twisted like vines on the rocky alcove. There were a few bare spots on her white scalp. Her dark eyes stared up at Kara. Her skin was discolored, with faint green veins lining her face. Her pale lips parted. Her gray garments were tattered and frayed. Her hands were pale, but the nails were smeared with black grime.

Don't leave me alone.

A voice sounded in Kara's head.

Kara felt her body slide toward the pool, toward the girl.

"No!" Kara gasped as she tried to dig her feet into the rocky floor to stop her movement. When that didn't work, she sprang up. "Leave me alone!" She leaned as far away from the girl as she could, shimmying away from her.

The girl reached out for her, with her pale hand. Kara barely avoided her.

Kara ran away as fast as she could.

She just wanted to get back home to her own reality.

She should have stayed with Lola and Francine, she realized. It didn't matter to her anymore that they always did whatever Lola wanted. They were the only true friends she'd ever really had. They put up with her impatience and her snarky attitude. She would give anything to be back with her best friends.

Francine twirled a strand of hair around her finger, watching Lola play an arcade game. Her friend had to jump across bridges and collect coins without falling to the ground or be eaten by a giant monster.

Kids were all around them, playing the Mega Pizzaplex games and talking loudly. Two little kids ran by them, with what appeared to be an older sibling chasing after them.

"Get back here, you little brats!"

"Ohhh, I'm telling Mom and Dad you called us brats!"

"Then stop acting like little brats!"

But they didn't stop running.

Francine sometimes wondered what it would be like to have siblings. She was an only child and her parents were often busy with life stuff. They joined organizations and volunteered at work and tried to get Francine to do the same at school. But Francine didn't seem to have their confidence gene. Having to talk to lots of people made her nervous. She felt awkward, and she never understood how some people could talk so much. Her parents had worried a lot about her until she'd met Lola and Kara.

Francine was just glad her best friends accepted her for who she was and didn't try to change her like her parents often did. With Lola and Kara she could just be herself. There was no pressure. It was so easy to hang out with them.

"Yes, I leveled up!" Lola said with a smile.

"So great!" Francine cheered. She didn't like to play games that much because she wasn't that good at them. Lola was pretty good. Well, Lola was good at most things. It was better to watch Lola win than to watch herself lose.

A few minutes later, Lola finally fell off a bridge with her last play.

"Shoot," Lola said.

"You got really far," Francine told her, trying to cheer her up.

Lola took out her cell phone and checked the screen. "Why isn't Kara back yet? My brother will be here soon."

"I don't know. Should we go look for her?"

Lola looked around. "Maybe, but there are three bathrooms on this floor and the place is packed." She sighed. "We should have stuck together, but Kara doesn't like to listen to me."

More like Kara and Lola both liked to have their own way, Francine thought to herself. She was used to being the neutral person between two strong personalities. It was the same with her parents.

"Let me send her a quick text while we look," Lola said. After she sent the text, she nodded her head forward. "All right. Let's go see where she is."

Francine gave her a reassuring smile. "She probably just got stuck in a line. Don't worry. We'll find her."

Don't leave me alone.

The voice kept replaying in Kara's mind. She had come across a pirate ship that was anchored onto some big rocks by a pool that resembled a lagoon. She stood on the port and gazed around her, looking across multiple pools and slides. The constant rushing of the water echoing across the walls made an ache throb in her head.

Don't leave me alone.

Not to mention the stupid voice that wouldn't shut up.

"Will you stop already?!" she yelled out.

Don't leave me alone, don't leave me alone, don't leave me alone.

Frustrated, Kara gripped her hands against her ears and screamed at the top of her lungs. She screamed and screamed until her voice was hoarse and her breaths were short and faint. She heard her screams vibrate along the Waterpark as she dropped her hands from her head. Her chest rose up and down with heavy pants.

The voice had finally stopped.

Kara was starting to get worried that there was something really wrong.

Could she be trapped inside the Waterpark forever?

That fearful thought made her nauseated and she slapped a hand to her mouth as her stomach heaved.

She let out a shaky breath. *No.* She would get back home. There had to be some kind of a way out. A doorway, maybe. A safety exit.

Yeah, that sounded right. She didn't know if that was actually possible, but it was the only plan she had at the moment.

Don't leave me alone.

Kara growled under her breath, spun around, and grabbed onto a roped ladder that looked like a giant net. She scurried up as far as she could and gazed around her.

The Waterpark was vast, but she now saw past the wonderment to how sterile and never-ending the tiled walls really appeared.

Lonely. Endless.

But it wasn't real.

Don't leave me alone.

"Just shut up already! You're not going to win!" Kara yelled out. "I'm going to get out of here and you *will* be all alone. Forever! I'm not staying here with you!"

Her hands were tight on the rope as she trembled. She swallowed hard as she gazed across the desolate park. She hoped with everything inside her that the Waterpark experience would suddenly end. But if it didn't, she would find a way out on her own. Sooner rather than later.

So there was only one thing to do: keep going. To hope that her efforts wouldn't be necessary. She climbed down the netted ropes and set out to look for an escape.

For what seemed like the next few hours, she went through every doorway she came across. She scanned the shallow pools, ignoring the girl floating in the water, hoping to see an anomaly or something that would help her leave. She looked for windows in the food theme areas, but there were no windows. Only doorways that would open to different themes. Only endless tiled walls wherever she turned.

She strode through an area with tiny floating boats, a pool with gray, blow-up pool toys floated around. There was a candy theme parlor, but instead of seeming appetizing, the candy appeared plastic and fake. Kara's stomach flipped over. She wasn't hungry and she was actually afraid of eating something from the Waterpark.

Things were not normal here, she realized.

Rules did not seem to apply.

Finally, she noticed a door in a tiled wall that looked *different*. Everything so far had been immaculate, perfect, even if it was creepy. But this door's paint was faded and chipped. The handle was rusted and discolored. Curious, Kara twisted it and pushed open the door. The hinges sighed with a long creaking sound.

She stood in the doorway of an old house.

Kara hesitated. *This* is *different.*

She felt immobilized with unease. It was like her body didn't want to enter.

"I'll be fine," she said to calm herself.

As her pulse fluttered, she entered the house.

Kara stepped into a shallow puddle of water on the floor of the house. She looked down in surprise. The water was icy on her bare feet.

Cold. When she blew a breath, puffs of air formed. A chill ran down her back.

Since she had started the experience, she was always inside the Waterpark or surrounded by an outside theme. But she was truly *inside* this house.

The house was dark, with a few candles lit on tables, lighting Kara's way. The puddled floors creaked under her feet, and as she looked closely at the walls, she noticed faint water lines running down the worn wallpaper. Patches of black mold had begun to grow on the faded surfaces.

"What is this place?" she whispered.

The front of the house speared off in three different directions. To the right was a living area with water-logged furniture. A torn couch was shifted off to the side, Chairs were thrown about with missing cushions. A rotted coffee table was covered with mold. To the left was another damp sitting room with a brick fireplace that had a crack through the center. Water trickled through the bricks and a slashed picture hung crookedly on the wall above. Lamps were broken and sunk in water. Straight ahead was a hallway with many doors and an occasional candle on the wall lighting the way.

Kara.

I need help.

Help me.

Kara froze. It was the girl's voice again in her head. *Or was it Peggy's?* she wondered. The voices were eerily starting to sound the same. She continued slowly down the hallway, her heartbeats pounding. Her hands fisted at her sides as she shivered.

She was scared. She was scared and for once, she wasn't sure what to do. Usually it was automatic to face a fear, but that was for things like riding roller coasters or diving into the ocean. Not surviving a haunted VR waterpark. She hadn't felt so scared since the day Peggy fell.

Should she run in the opposite direction, or simply face the mysterious girl and try to help her?

Wait a minute.

Kara had played plenty of video games in her life. There was always a goal for the games she played. Save the princess. Finish the maze without dying. Collect all the treasure.

Maybe this experience was the same way.

If she helped the strange girl in the water, would that be her way out of the Resort? Could it be that straightforward?

She hadn't been able to save Peggy.

Maybe this would be her chance to save someone else who needed help.

The more she thought about it, the more the plan sounded right to her. If she helped the girl, she could end the game. She could go back to her friends. Get back to her real life at home with her parents. And deep down, she could finally release the guilt she carried for Peggy getting hurt.

An inkling of hope sparked within her, and she held on to the feeling to help her move forward, trudging through the freezing water.

"I can do this," she said. "I can end this and get back to my reality."

With her stomach twisting in knots, she called out quietly, "Where are you, girl?" Then once again a little louder, "I can't help you if I can't see you."

Help me.

"I'm trying," Kara muttered. She strode down the hallway and opened the first door to the right. More cold water gushed over her ankles. She saw what appeared to be a little girl's bedroom, but everything was drenched. She heard a strange music box playing broken music from somewhere in the room.

Instead of a frilly pink bed, the cover and sheets were gray and drenched with water. Dark clothes and mildewed stuffed animals floated past it. The walls were warped. A kid's paintings hung on the walls, dripping with smeared paint. The ceiling looked to be sagging.

But there was no girl floating in the shallow water.

A fresh chill radiated down her back when the music box got stuck on the same note. Kara walked farther into the room, looking for the music box. She stepped up to a moldy dresser to see a carousel horse inside a music box, shifting up and down. Kara closed the lid and the music stopped.

She turned to walk out and the music started again.

Kara whirled around. The box was back open and the music grew louder, piercing her eardrums.

Kara rushed to the door and slammed it closed at her back. The music faded.

"Creepy." She shuddered before continuing down the hallway.

The next door she entered was on the opposite side of the hallway. Another bedroom, but for grown-ups. There was another bed soaked with water. This one was bloodred. Dead roses floated in the puddles on the floor. She wrinkled her nose. It smelled of rotting plants and something coppery. A canopy hung over the bed, with ripped material hanging from the four bedposts. A small picture frame floated in the water toward Kara and she picked it up.

The picture was faded but she could see there was a girl with black hair, sitting with two parents. However, all their features were blotted out with white as if their faces had been rubbed off. The woman had black hair and the man had brown. The picture seemed to be old, and the clothes appeared from a different time period.

Was this the girl's life before she became the girl at the bottom of the pools?

Was she somehow trapped in this virtual world of pain and heartache?

Kara could relate to being stuck in the past with the guilt she harbored for Peggy.

There were days she wondered if it would ever end.

Suddenly, water started to spill out of the photo and Kara gasped as she dropped the picture back in the water. The room creaked loudly with movement around her. The boards shifted beneath her feet.

Kara quickly stepped out of the room and shut the door.

She sucked in chilled air and moved farther down the hallway. Her feet and ankles shuffled through the water. Her teeth began to chatter. She rubbed her arms trying to warm herself but it didn't help much; it felt like she was walking through liquid ice. A decrepit staircase appeared before her. Water gushed down the stairs as if they were rocks in a creek.

Help me.

The voice seemed to come from above the staircase. Kara carefully walked up the steps, making sure to step over any that felt too unstable. The wood was weak and shifted under her feet. She gripped tightly to the railing.

But the railing broke loose and Kara had to balance herself as the railing fell down the staircase, splashing into the water.

"That was close," she whispered, trembling.

As she looked down behind her, she noticed water was rising in the house. The water had filled the hallway and was catching up to her.

A feeling of dread seeped through her.

"Oh no."

Help me, Kara.

Kara rushed up the staircase. The staircase seemed to lengthen in front of her, extending on and on.

She ran up each broken stair, her breaths huffing. Her legs began to ache. A cold sweat pearled on her brow.

Kara.

"I'm coming!" Kara yelled out. "I'm going to save you, and we'll both get out of here!"

She finally made it to the top of the staircase as the water gained momentum and spilled onto the flooring. Kara spotted a door at the end of a short hallway in front of her. There was glowing light coming out around the trim.

She ran as a wave of water chased her through the halls.

Kara ran as fast as her legs could manage. The icy waves splashed onto the backs of her legs. She looked back to see a giant swell rising higher and higher, ready to crash over her.

Kara gasped. She reached the door, grabbing the handle, but it wouldn't budge.

It wouldn't open!

Kara screamed as the wave crashed over her. She held her breath as the current rushed over her, trying to pull her away. Her body felt nearly frozen. Underwater, Kara held on to the handle for dear life. If she let go, she feared she would be washed away and never heard from again.

The knob finally twisted and Kara pulled open the door. She swam through the water, twisted around, and shut the door behind her.

The water slowly receded. Kara gasped for air as she kneeled on the floor, shivering. Her lips felt like tiny icicles. Her body was stiff. Water ran down her body and wet suit, and her hair dripped into her eyes. She shoved strands out of her face while looking around. She was in a large bathroom. The walls were tiled gray. Some of the pieces were missing and cracked. Streams of water spilled down the walls. The floor was a puddle that covered her feet and ankles. A few feet in front of her was a dirty porcelain clawfoot tub. Water spilled over the edges.

Kara, help me.

Kara swallowed hard and stiffly stepped forward through the water. She looked down in the tub and discovered the girl laying at the bottom, under the flowing water.

Her pale white eyes blinked up at her.

Don't leave me alone.

"I'm going . . . to save you . . . and we'll both . . . be free," Kara told her through chattering teeth.

She slowly reached down into the water. The girl lifted her hand to meet Kara's.

Kara gripped the cold hand and tried to pull her out.

The girl pulled back harder.

Kara's eyes widened. "*Stop*," she whispered. She dug her feet into the wet floor. Her feet slipped in the water. She gripped the edge of the tub, trying to break free from the girl's fierce grasp.

"Stop!" Kara cried out, struggling. "Let go. Of. Me!"

But the girl was too strong.

Kara lost her grip on the edge.

Her breath backed up in her lungs as she was swiftly pulled into the tub.

Underwater, Kara struggled with the girl. She wasn't in a tub anymore now but a large expanse of water. The girl's eyes squinted, her pale face scrunched up in anger. The green veins that speared off in her face were darker now, thicker. She bared her blackened teeth as she held Kara's arms in a tight grip.

Kara pulled back from her, trying to break free. She fought with all she had in her. She would survive. She had to. She kicked out with her feet, trying to shove the girl away from her.

I am free, she thought. *I am free!*

Kara broke away from the girl, shoving her away with her feet. Kara swam upward. She discovered that she was in a huge pool. The water had warmed but the surface seemed miles away. She kept swimming upward. Her lungs felt as if they would burst. She needed to open her mouth to breathe.

She struggled toward the top.

Nearly there.

But it was still so far.

So tired.

She started to slow down.

Something brushed her foot.

Kara looked down to see the girl, grabbing for her, trying to latch onto her foot.

Kara's eyes widened. Her arms felt like weights. She had to get to the surface.

Finally, she burst through, gasping for air. She swam to the edge of the pool. She hauled herself halfway over the edge, gagging. Coughing. She blinked water out of her eyes. Looking around, she was once again in the Waterpark. She pulled herself out of the large pool that had two waterslides going into it. She dragged herself as far as she could from the water. When she hit a wall, she collapsed. Her body felt like rubber. Her lungs felt raw. Her eyes drifted closed. She knew the girl was after her, but she couldn't keep her eyes open another moment.

"Mom, I want to go to the skate park. I'm tired of skateboarding in front of the house."

Kara was now ten years old, holding her skateboard against her hip. She was standing with her mom in the kitchen on a summer morning.

"Kara, I can't manage it right now," her mom said as

she poured herself a cup of coffee. "I have a meeting in ten minutes."

Kara pointed a thumb to her chest. "I can go by myself. It's just two blocks over. I'm ten!"

Her mom sighed. "Kara, I know how old you are. But I need to make sure you're making safe choices."

Kara frowned. "What do you mean?"

She sighed. "Lately, you haven't been. Your father and I don't know what's gotten into you. We hope it's just a phase you're going through. It is, right? Just a phase of making unsafe choices?"

Kara rolled her eyes. "Mom, come on. I'll be careful, I promise." She tapped the purple helmet on her head. "See, I have protection on and everything."

Her mom shook her head, her red curls bouncing. "No, Kara. Your father and I agreed. You're just going to have to skate in front of the house for now. You know I have to work during the weekdays. We'll go this weekend. I'll be able to take you then. I promise."

"This sucks!"

Her mom's eyes widened, her cheeks turning pink. "*Kara Marie.* You watch your tone, young lady."

"It's like you and Dad want to keep me a little kid forever! It's not fair!" she cried, stormed out the front door, slamming it at her back, and threw her skateboard down on the lawn. She crossed her arms and sat on the step.

Her parents' tight grip on her was driving her crazy! *Ever since Peggy . . .*

There was a pressure in her chest and Kara rubbed a hand against the funny feeling.

Other kids at school got to go places on their own, like to the skate park, or to the mini mart to get candy.

Not Kara.

Her parents were always fretting about what could happen to her if she was by herself or with other kids her age. They told her that she didn't think rationally about the dangers that could happen to a little kid. She had to think about safety and precautions.

Blah, blah, blah!

She was too young to understand, they would always say.

But Kara wasn't too young to understand. She knew her parents had changed after Peggy fell from the tree. They let their fear overtake their lives. It was like they tried to put Kara in a protective box so nothing bad could happen to her. But it wasn't fair.

Kara felt trapped!

She felt helpless.

The more her parents denied her the freedom she craved, the more Kara fought back.

Her mom and dad didn't understand that she needed to feel unrestricted. She felt happy when she was able to do new and exciting things.

Why couldn't they understand that? Why couldn't they understand *her*?

Instead, she was always forbidden to do the fun stuff. It was like she was constantly being punished for not helping Peggy. She squeezed her eyes shut against the picture of Peggy on the ground, blood pouring out of her head. Just like the dreams she had so many times. But instead it was Kara who fell from the tree, with blood spilling from her head.

She hadn't meant for it to happen! If she could do that day over again she would. She'd tell Peggy to play something else. Kara wouldn't have climbed that dumb tree so she could run and get her parents before Peggy fell.

But it had happened and she could never take it back.

Kara tightened her hands into fists. She stood and stalked over to her skateboard and swiped it up. She peered into the window and didn't see her mother.

With a tight jaw, she took off down the street to the skate park.

Mom would never even know she was gone, Kara told herself. She'd be back to the front yard before her mom's meeting ended.

When Kara arrived, kids were skating or biking over concrete ramps. Some were doing really cool tricks.

Wow, look how much air that kid got on his bike jump! And that kid spun in a circle!

Kara watched the other kids in admiration for a few minutes. Studying them. Learning. She could do everything they could. She just had to practice. When a ramp was free, she skated over to the ledge.

Looking down, she felt her hands tingle with nerves. Something inside her told her it wasn't safe, but she squashed it. She knew she wasn't that good yet on the skateboard, but she would be one day. She had to keep trying. How else was she going to learn?

She set down her board and stepped on it with one foot. She crouched and pushed off the steep ledge. She managed to get two feet on as she rolled down the ramp. Her gut twisted with excitement.

She was doing it!

Then her body leaned too far back and the board rolled out from under her. She crashed. Hard. Her elbows scraped against the concrete.

"*Ow*," she hissed as she sat up.

She saw blood on her elbow and her leg burned underneath her jeans.

A kid whizzed by her on a skateboard but didn't say anything. Kara brushed her hands off on her shirt and got back up to try again.

With her arms and leg throbbing, she returned to the top of the ramp. She set her foot on the board and pushed off again. She rolled down the ramp too fast, lost her balance again, and this time fell headfirst.

She flipped over in the air and landed hard on her right arm.

There was a click sound inside her head. Pain shot through her. A moan escaped her as she pulled her arm against her chest.

Her face flashed cold, then hot. Tears stung her eyes.

Oh no, she thought with sudden alarm.

She had broken her arm.

Her parents were going to be so mad!

She pushed to her feet, coveting her injured arm against her. She felt a strange bump under her skin and dots flashed in front of her eyes. She had to steady herself before she fell over again.

Suddenly, the sky darkened above. Kara looked around bewildered. Dirty water started rushing down the ramp.

"What's going on?" she breathed out as the water gushed around her.

The surface rose quickly. Kids ran and took off to escape the water.

Kara winced at the pain in her arm. The water had risen to her waist. She tried to walk through the rushing water but the current began to turn in a circle around her. Kara tried to walk out of the center. She slipped and was pulled into the current and then spun around in a whirlpool of water.

"Help me! Help!" she cried out.

She couldn't swim with a broken arm!

Something tugged her leg. Fear crashed over her. Kara screamed as she was jerked down into the center of the whirlpool.

Kara startled awake in the Waterpark as her body was being dragged. She looked down to see the girl pulling her toward the pool once more.

"No," Kara whispered. Her voice came out raspy. She tried to grab for anything, but the tiles were slick. Her hands slid across the flooring.

Don't leave me alone, Kara.

Kara kicked out with her legs, hitting the girl in the chest. She found herself kicking and kicking until she finally broke free.

She shoved the girl back in the pool with a foot to the shoulder.

"Stay in the water!"

Kara felt a phantom pain in her right arm from when she broke it those years ago. She ran her hand along her arm and made sure it was healed. She was okay.

Suddenly the lights in the Waterpark flickered.

Kara jerked her head up. What now?

The lights flickered again and Kara pushed herself to her feet and ran.

★　★　★

"Where do you think she is?" Francine asked Lola. They were back on the same floor in front of the arcade entrance in case Kara had come looking for them. "I'm pretty sure we searched all the restrooms on each floor. We didn't see her walking around anywhere, either."

Lola was clearly frustrated. Her arms were crossed and her jaw was tight as she gazed around. It seemed Kara was messing up her carefully thought-out plans.

"I don't know, but when I find her I'm going to tell her how inconsiderate she's being." Lola waved her phone around. "She's even ignoring my texts and calls. I mean, we all had fun today, right?"

Francine nodded. "Yeah."

"So why is Kara always against having fun with us? Why is she messing around and ignoring us now? What did we do to her to deserve this? If she didn't want to come today, all she had to do was tell us. I mean, she's not afraid to tell us anything else on her mind."

Francine ignored this, too used to Lola's and Kara's complaints about each other.

Lola's phone pinged with a message.

"Is it Kara?" Francine asked, hopeful.

Lola shook her head. "Oh shoot, it's my brother. He's waiting outside. What do I say?" Lola stared at Francine with wide eyes. She looked nervous, uncertain. "Why is Kara messing around?"

Francine blinked in surprise. Lola was asking her what to do? Lola *always* knew what to do. "Um, well, you'll have to tell him the truth. That we got separated when Kara went to the restroom and now we're looking for her."

Lola nodded slowly. "Right. Good idea."

"And I've been hearing the intercom all day, announcing lost kids. We'll have them call Kara to meet us. Then you can tell her how inconsiderate she was being."

Lola smiled as she texted her brother. "Okay, thanks, Francine. That sounds like a good plan. But I probably won't tell Kara off. I don't want to get into an argument and mess up our friendship." Then she met Francine's eyes. "Don't tell her, okay?"

Francine smiled. "Sure. Come on, let's go to the information center. Everything will be okay."

After running for some time, Kara slowed to a walk. She felt cold again and crossed her arms, trying to warm herself. The hope she had earlier about helping the girl get back to her reality had washed away in that pool when the girl had tried to drown her.

Kara had tried everything she could think of to get out of the Waterpark. She had tried to keep going until her time ran out. She had tried to look for an anomaly or a secret exit in order to end the experience. She had tried to save the girl.

Nothing had worked!

I'm never going to get out of here, Kara realized with utter shock. She was really, truly trapped this time, stuck in the never-ending Waterpark.

Her eyes stung and a tear slid down her cheek.

Maybe this was what she deserved. She'd be the first to admit she wasn't perfect, but most of the time she didn't care. She didn't care what her parents thought, even though she loved them and they loved her. She constantly fought against their restrictions. She often didn't care what Lola and Francine thought, even though they were her best friends.

She hadn't helped Peggy when her cousin needed help.

Kara mostly did whatever she wanted and didn't care about the repercussions.

And now she was paying the price by roaming this isolated place with a dead girl who was trying to keep Kara with her.

Why did it seem like, even in this VR experience, other people were always trying to make her do things against her will?

Angry, Kara quickly opened the next door in the wall.

When she opened the door, she nearly fell into nothingness, her free arm windmilling. "Ahhhhhh!"

There was absolutely nothing.

It was an empty dark space, with no floor, no ceiling or sky.

Kara gripped tightly to the door handle, trying to regain her balance. Sweat broke across her forehead. She pushed herself backward, standing upright.

Breaths gushed out her mouth as she slammed the door shut. She slid to the floor as the lights flashed around her.

The girl was ticked off now and doing her best to scare Kara.

"Is that all you got?" Kara yelled out, her face scrunched up. "Well, you're going to have to do better than that!"

The girl must have not liked what Kara said because Kara found her body slowly sliding toward a pool in front of her. She gritted her teeth and pressed her hands hard against the tiled floor, but this time she kept sliding.

"Just stop!" She shoved up to her feet and rushed to the

next doorway. She jerked open the door, glanced down to make sure there was a floor to step on, then rushed through and slammed the door at her back.

She gazed around and noticed she'd walked into a room with a mirror maze. Now there were three Karas reflected back at her.

"No way," she whispered. Kara pushed away from the door to walk closely to one of the mirrors. She almost didn't recognize herself. Her face looked so pale that her freckles stood out like strange dots. Her hair was wild. Her lips were chapped. Her eyes appeared dark and sunken in her face.

She let out a sigh. "I just want out of here before I wilt away." But she knew it no longer mattered what she wanted. The girl in the water seemed to be in charge.

Kara walked along the mirrors, mesmerized by so many Karas reflecting back at her. *Her parents would lose it if there were this many of her in the real world*, she thought. That almost made her smile.

Suddenly, she stepped into a puddle of water.

Kara looked down at her feet and froze. The water was slowly rising.

Panic shot through her and she looked back for the door she'd entered.

It was gone. She was completely surrounded by mirrors.

She started to rush through the mirror maze, trying to find a way out. The water rose, minute by minute, as it passed her ankles and then her knees.

An image flickered across the mirror in front of her and Kara paused.

Lola and Francine appeared on the mirror. They were at the arcade at the Mega Pizzaplex.

Kara stepped to the reflective glass and touched it. It was like a movie was playing on the mirror.

"It's so much more fun without Kara with us," Francine said. "Hopefully she got lost on her way to the bathroom."

Lola was playing an arcade game. She smiled. "Totally. Everything is always about her all the time, and when she doesn't get her way, she gets pouty and thinks I don't notice her attitude. Of course I notice! How could I *not* notice?"

Kara hit the glass with her palm. "Lola! Francine! I'm here! I'm trapped in this stupid VR game! I need you to come find me. Go to the Resort! Find that guy Zach! Please find me! I need your help! I'M AT THE RESORT!"

"Maybe we should just ditch her," Francine said. "You know, for good."

Lola raised an eyebrow, intrigued. "You think we should?"

"GO TO THE RESORT! I'M THERE!" Kara screamed at them. "PLEASE, I NEED YOUR HELP!"

"Then we can do whatever we want without having to ask her all the time," Francine continued on, ignoring Kara's pleas. "We don't have to argue with her about what she wants to do and what we want to do. It'll make life *so* much easier."

"No, stop. Lola and Francine aren't like this," Kara said as she shook her head in denial, her eyes watering. "They're my best friends. They care about me. You're just trying to make me feel bad. You're trying to trick me."

The glass image shifted to her parents. "Mom? Dad?" They were sitting at home on the couch, watching television. Mom had their Siamese cat, Cupcake, sitting in her lap as she petted her. Dad was practically asleep next to her.

"I don't know what to do about Kara," her mom said. "She's going to be fighting with us about more of the wild stuff she wants to do. Should we forbid her from everything?"

Her dad yawned. "What? Like ground her? She'll throw one of her tantrums and sulk around the house."

"But at least she'll be safe. She's fifteen now. It's getting harder to say no all the time."

"She'll be miserable and make us miserable. If she wants to break an arm again, let her."

Her mom's eyes widened. "Martin!"

Her dad shrugged.

"Dad! Mom! I'm sorry!" Kara yelled at them as more tears slid down her face. "I won't argue with you anymore. I'll do whatever you say. I won't take risky chances anymore. I promise! Please, I just want to come home!" She hit the mirror with her fist.

Suddenly, her parents were gone. The girl in the water stared back from the mirror. She floated under the water.

Kara stepped back.

Kara.

Don't leave me alone.

Kara turned away and tried her best to move through the rising water. Her legs were heavy and slow. She waded with her arms, trying to find a way out.

"Stop this!" she yelled as the water rose to her neck. She looked up at the ceiling and found that she was actually at the pool's surface where she might be able to escape. She simply waited for the water to rise, and she treaded the waves as they rose to the top.

Suddenly, she was submerged and she began to swim up toward the surface.

Don't leave me alone.

When Kara reached the top, she realized it was blocked by another layer of glass!

Oh no!

She hit against it with her open palms, trying to free herself.

Her breaths wanted to push through her closed mouth.

She hit the mirror with her fists, over and over.

Let. Me. Out.

The mirror cracked. Kara hit it again, shattering the glass around her. She burst out of the water, gasping for air. She pulled herself out onto a layer of reflective glass. A cracked edge scraped against her hip and she hissed. Blood dripped onto the glass.

She carefully crawled over the mirrors, hoping they wouldn't break until she reached the edge.

Relief found her sagging on the floor. She looked over to see blood dripping from her hip.

The wound actually hurt. She could really get hurt here, she realized, as she swiped at the wound and stared at the blood on her fingers.

It was supposed to be virtual reality. She shouldn't feel real pain.

But everything had felt too real since she entered the Waterpark.

The girl in the water peeked her head out of the hole in the shattered mirror and stared at her.

Kara gave her a dirty look and got up to walk away, nursing her hip.

Kara walked along the tiled floor aimlessly. The themes she would come across were fewer and farther in between. Now she only spotted the dark doors that would lead to more tiled rooms and sporadic plain pools with slides. Nothing was colorful or unique. It all looked bleak and isolated. She felt lethargic. Defeated. She was like a sponge that had been twisted and squeezed out, and there was nothing left inside her to give.

It seemed like so much time had passed. Long, continuous hours. Maybe even days. She couldn't tell. Maybe time stood still in the virtual world. Maybe years would pass and suddenly her experience would just end and when she came out, everybody would be old and Kara would still be the same age.

Kara blinked, trying to focus.

She was about to pass another door. She nearly didn't open it since walking into strange doorways hadn't been going well. However, when she got near it, she felt warmth radiating from the wood.

She touched the handle and noticed it wasn't cold. She hesitantly twisted the knob and pushed open the door.

A bright light shined down on her from the ceiling, making her squint her eyes. She smelled chlorine and the quiet flow of water. Kara stepped through the doorway.

Various tall waterslides were dotted throughout the area with clear pools at the bottom, surrounded by tiles. But the pools weren't too close together. There was a safe distance around them.

I could stay here, she thought.

For a while, at least.

She could be far enough from the water to avoid the girl.

She walked along the structures, gazing at the tall waterslides. Most of them were pretty average. A straight open slide into the pool.

Soon she came across one intricate waterslide that stood out from the rest. The long-tubed slide came down from the ceiling, twisting like a coiled snake and ultimately ended at the crystal clear, blue pool at the bottom.

She angled her head to see the very top.

"Where do you go?" Kara wondered as she realized the slide actually came out of the top of the ceiling. "Wait. Could this be a way out?"

Could she even dare to hope?

But as she gazed up at the massive slide that twisted high up, she realized there were no stairs. She was going to have to climb the structure to find out where it began. She licked her dry lips and walked around, studying the intricate waterslide. The slide was an enclosed tube with rushing water traveling down the long, twisting coil. There was no way she could climb up that way. She'd slip and fall into the water where the girl could grab her.

Her only way up was to climb the outside of the slide.

Her hands and feet started to tingle with nerves, and her stomach fluttered. There was not much to hold on to, and nothing to support her climb.

She swallowed past the lump in her dry throat. She crossed her arms and paced back and forth. The truth was that she was desperate enough to attempt it.

She could do it, she told herself. She had to see where it led.

Don't leave me alone, Kara.

Kara jerked her head toward the pool attached to the waterslide. She stepped closer, looking down into the clear water.

Of course, the girl was there at the bottom, but suddenly her gray skin was pale again, like porcelain. There were no more green veins on her skin or black teeth in her mouth. Her black hair looked thick and healthy under the water as it floated around her.

She was actually pretty, Kara realized.

She reminded her of Peggy.

"This isn't my place," she told her. "I'm sorry you're here, but it's time for me to be back in my own reality. I miss my best friends. I miss my parents. I miss my life." Kara turned away and looked at the tall structure. "I have to go."

Don't leave me!

Don't. Leave. Me!

The hairs on the back of Kara's neck lifted at the anger in the girl's voice. Kara ignored the voice and gripped the top of the tube, hiked up her right foot, and hefted herself up. She balanced herself on top of the hard material, and then reached up for the next row of the coiled slide. She could hear the water stream down inside the tube as she reached up higher for the next twisting row.

She was done with this virtual reality.

She was going home.

The girl at the information desk called for Kara to meet Lola and Francine.

"Kara Walsh, please come to the information desk on the first floor! Kara Walsh, you are needed at the information desk immediately!"

Lola paced back and forth, her arms crossed. Francine looked around, twirling her hair. The Mega Pizzaplex was still packed. Everyone seemed to be going about their business, playing games, eating pizza, and having a grand time.

No one knew Lola and Francine were worried about their best friend.

Minutes passed. Lola kept pacing. Francine kept twirling. Kara didn't show up.

"This is getting ridiculous!" Lola called Kara's phone, seething. It went straight to voicemail. "Where is she?" Lola asked with a little whine.

Francine tugged at the hem of her shirt. "Um, I don't know. I'm sure we'll find her, though."

"She wouldn't have left without telling us." Lola pushed her hair behind her ears and shook her head. "Something's off. I know it."

Francine was beginning to feel the same way, but someone had to stay calm and reasonable. Her responsible, organized, take-charge best friend was pretty much fraying around the edges. "Let's look around some more. Maybe her phone died and she didn't hear the announcement. It is pretty loud in here. There could be any number of reasons she's not answering."

Lola tapped her cell phone to her chin, staring out into the crowd. "I guess her phone could have died . . . .I'm just getting worried. My brother is waiting. He keeps texting me." She turned her attention to Francine. "Should I tell him to leave and come back later?"

"Tell him we're looking for her and to please hold on."

Lola texted him and Francine scanned the floor around her. With so many people, it was as if Kara had been swallowed up by the Mega Pizzaplex. Then she spotted that cute boy from the Resort, walking among the crowd. "Hey, there's the kid from the Resort VR attraction. Let's ask for his help."

Lola's head shot up. "Where?"

"Over there. Come on." Francine led her through a crowd of people until they finally cut him off.

"Hey, remember us?" Francine asked him. "Do you remember our friend, Kara, with the reddish-blonde curls?"

Zach nodded, with his cute smile. "Oh yeah, hey."

"Have you seen Kara?" Lola asked him, urgently. "We can't find her anywhere."

Zach's eyebrows tugged toward each other as he looked at his wristwatch. "Yeah, I left her at the Resort about twenty minutes ago. Had to cover a quick break. Her game should have ended already, though." He glanced at Francine and Lola, scanned their faces. "She didn't meet up with you guys?"

"No, she won't answer her phone, either. And we're really worried." Lola frowned at him. "What do you mean you left her at the Resort?"

Zach rubbed the back of his neck, with a nervous smile. "Oh, well . . ."

Kara climbed up the tall, tubed structure slowly and carefully. It was a long and arduous climb since she had to maneuver herself from each twisting part of the coiled tube, pulling herself up to the next row. It took a bit of time to find a foothold or to secure a good grip on the structure. She glanced down at how far she'd come and the height made her gasp. The ground began to spin. She closed her eyes as a wave of nausea washed over her, perspiration pearling her brow.

"No, don't get sick," she whispered to herself. "You can do this, Kara. Just keep going."

She reached up to the next hard tube and pulled herself on top of the hard material, climbing higher. The lights above were harsh and her hands and feet began to sweat. She wiped her right hand down her wet suit to keep it dry while a bead of sweat ran from her head to her nose.

As she hugged the tube above, she suddenly lost her footing on the hard top below. Her arms gripped tightly to the upper tube as she hung for a second.

She squealed in surprise.

"*Please, please, please.*" She carefully got her feet back on the hard tube and stayed there for a minute, catching her breath. "Okay, that was close."

She looked back up. The light was so bright, she squinted. But she could still catch glimpses of the tubed structure twisting into the tiled ceiling.

Halfway there.

Keep going.

It seemed like she'd climbed for a long time, but the goal was just within her sights. She allowed herself a small smile. She could be back to her own reality soon.

She would never take things for granted again.

She'd always believed she was trapped by circumstances as if she had no freedom with her strict parents, even with her best friends. But now, being confined in the virtual Waterpark gave her a new perspective, where she truly understood the meaning of being helpless.

When she was back in her reality, she would listen to her parents. She would agree with Lola and Francine on everything. If Lola wanted to make lists, Kara would make them with her. If Francine was uncertain of her outfits, Kara would encourage her more often with her wardrobe. They would be so surprised that soon Kara would be known as the nice girl in the group. If her parents wanted her to stay home, she would happily do so and maybe help around the house more often. She'd tell them she loved them. She couldn't remember when she told them last. She'd tell them as soon as she got home. She smiled at that thought.

She couldn't wait to be back with them all.

Kara glanced down once again and this time she looked into the pool.

The water was clear. She could see the girl way at the bottom as if waiting for her.

Come to me, Kara.

The voice sounded sinister, and Kara's gut clenched. Gone was the young girl's voice—it was now heavy, deep, and terrifying, echoing in her mind. It rattled Kara's nerves, made her hands and feet tingle even more. Anxiety shuddered through her.

In a rush, Kara reached up while looking down at the girl. She grabbed air instead.

Kara sucked in a breath as she glanced up.

She'd missed the next part of the tube, she thought in horror.

Her arm wavered, throwing her off-balance. As she

tried to gain her traction on the bottom tube, her damp foot slipped off the surface beneath her.

Kara grabbed for air.

Her body fell backward.

Falling.

Falling.

Kara's arms flailed around her. Her mouth opened to scream but nothing came out as she flipped over and over.

She slammed hard on the tiled floor around the pool. The wind knocked out of her in a whoosh. She heard a harsh cracking echo in her ears. Pain ripped through her legs and hips. Her back and arms slapped hard against the floor, pain radiating through her body.

"*Ahhhhh . . .*" Kara moaned at the wretched throbbing from her legs and hips. Tears overflowed and streamed down her face as she looked down at her twisted, contorted limbs.

Her legs . . . were broken.

No . . .

She blinked rapidly in stunned shock and agony. She couldn't walk. She couldn't climb the structure. She didn't think she could even move.

Kara.

Kara shook her head in denial. The girl from the pool reached out of the water, pulling herself up onto the edge.

The pretty version had disappeared. The creepy girl with the twisted black hair, green veins lining her face, and piercing dark eyes came to get her.

"No!" Kara screamed at her. "Please, don't take me!

I don't belong here. Please, I just want to go home. I'm begging you to let me go!"

The girl kept coming, crawling toward her.

Kara grabbed at the slippery tiles around her, trying to pull herself away. But she slid against the smooth surface as if an invisible force pulled her against her will.

"Nooooo!"

The girl grabbed onto Kara's ankle and then the other. Excruciating pain shot through Kara's legs as she screamed out.

The girl dragged Kara toward the pool.

"Stop! Stop! Let go of meeeeee!" Kara screamed. "You're hurting me!"

The girl jerked Kara into the pool and deep into the watery depths.

Kara grabbed at the water around her as the light above her disappeared.

Francine rushed behind Zach and Lola as they made their way to the Resort. Zach pulled down the rope to the entrance as they all ran toward the control panel. He looked up at the VR screen but it was blank. Nothing was showing but static.

"That's weird," he muttered. Then he seemed to look at something on the controls and his eyes widened. "Ah, man."

"What?" Lola asked him urgently. "What's the matter? Is Kara here?"

"Um, it's nothing. Something wasn't set right. Looks like the game was left on, so she's still here." He flicked off a switch called HYPERTIME and then another one labeled WATERPARK and pushed the button to slide open the door.

Francine rushed behind Lola over to the VR seats. Kara was there seated in the first chair, thank goodness!

"She's here!" Francine yelled out in relief. "Kara, we couldn't find you! You gave us a terrible scare!"

"Kara!" Lola snapped. "We've been looking for you everywhere! My brother is waiting for us! We were so worried. We have to go now!"

Zach rushed to Kara and lifted the helmet off. "Kara?" he asked, frowning.

"Kara!" Lola's eyes widened. She grabbed Kara's arm and shook her. "What's the matter with you? *Kara.*" Lola shook her harder. "Stop playing around. This isn't funny!"

Francine looked at Kara and then stepped back in shock. Kara had the strangest look on her face. Her eyes were wide with dark circles under them as if staring at nothing. Her skin was pale. Her lips were dry and parted.

Francine slapped a hand to her mouth to keep from screaming.

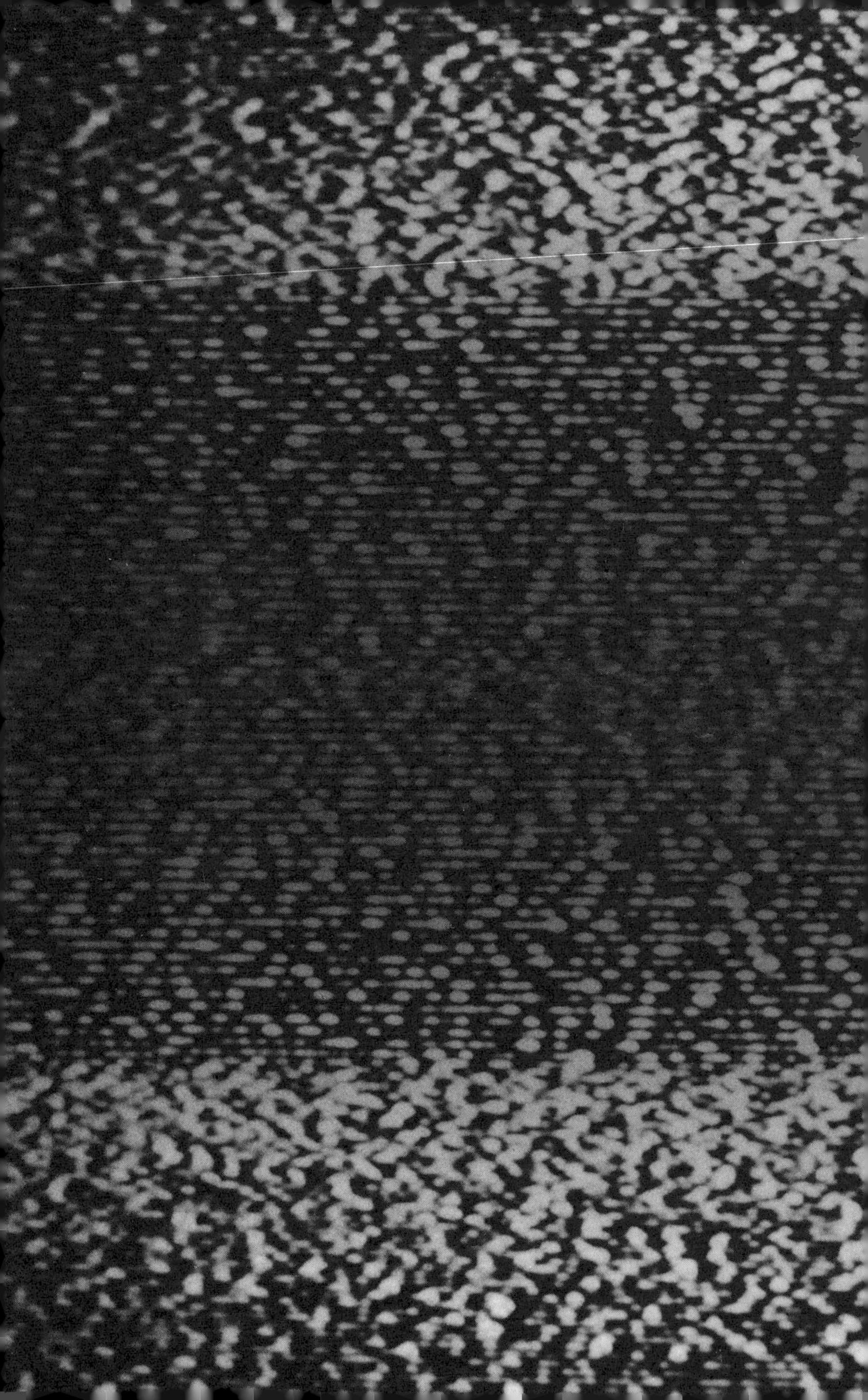

THE MIMIC

DADDY, I'M A GHOST!"

Edwin Murray, his brow in its usual deep furrow, swore when his son's small but insistent hand tugged at Edwin's flannel shirtsleeve. The motion forced Edwin to give up on the intricate wiring job he was attempting.

"Stop that, David!" Edwin snapped.

Edwin looked down, expecting to see the badly cut thatch of David's fine brown hair. Instead, Edwin found himself looking at yellowing lace. The lace was draped over the brown hair, and the rest of David as well. The fragile mesh fabric was undulating and moaning—or rather, the four-year-old under the fabric was moaning, in a pretty decent approximation of a scary ghost.

At the end of the undulating lamentation, however, the lace (actually, the boy) sneezed. Then it coughed. The lace churned as if about to erupt.

"That's what you get for playing with dusty old lace," Edwin said, his annoyance ebbing a bit. He had to admit that he enjoyed David's creativity, and watching the lace thrash was amusing. Edwin just hoped the boy wasn't picking up some noxious disease from the ancient fabric.

It was early March, and spring rain was seeping in through a few of the cracks in the factory's old brick walls and dripping down from a couple leaks in the tin roof. The water from those leaks collected on the third floor, but the moisture pervaded the entire building. And although the factory had dozens of tall, skinny paned windows, several were boarded up and the thick glass panes of most of the rest had been painted gray. When he'd bought the building, Edwin had painstakingly scraped the paint off the second-floor windows so the living space would have light, but he'd left the lower windows painted over. He liked the privacy, even though the lack of light made the expansive space damp and musty. Edwin was already concerned that David was going to catch a bad cold as he had the past two springs. He didn't relish the idea of adding the potential bugs and bacteria lingering on lace to the mix.

When Edwin had bought the abandoned factory to house his new business, he'd found yards and yards of knotted, crumbling lace throughout the building. The lace was piled against the factory's brick walls, strewn across its rough cement floors, mounded beneath the Leavers Machine in the main production room, and even wrapped around its dozens of concrete support pillars. That lace was sprinkled with the pillars' pale green peeling paint. Edwin wasn't sure why the factory's owners had left such intricate work behind. However, Edwin rather liked the lace. Although some of it had mildewed, he thought much of it might be salvageable, and he was sure his creative mind could come up with some use for it. So, he had left it where it was.

His wife, Fiona, had liked it, too. Five years before, when Edwin had acquired the building, he and Fiona had also just purchased the old Queen Anne mansion they'd planned to restore to its original grandeur. Fiona had been delighted by all the lace in the old factory because she'd envisioned using it to make *"yards and yards and yards of luscious window coverings." "And a canopy for our bed, my love,"* she'd added, winking at Edwin. Edwin had blushed. Back then—and it now seemed so long ago— Edwin had been a deliriously happy man.

After Fiona had died giving birth to David, Edwin had been tempted to get rid of all the lace. He hadn't wanted to trigger memories of a time that was forever lost to him. However, throwing it out felt like just another loss. He couldn't bear to do it. And so the lace remained. And so did the memories.

The lacy ghost sneezed again. Edwin reached down and pulled the dusty fabric off his son. His impish, freckled face revealed, David grinned, sneezed once more, and wiped his nose so hard it was a miracle that the uptilted snoot remained on the boy's face at all.

"I thought you were going to play with your toys while I worked," Edwin said, doing his best to sound stern. "We had an agreement. Remember? You play quietly for an hour, Daddy gets work done, and then we go for ice cream."

"Ice cream!" David shouted. "Chocolate chip ice cream!" David, who was clutching a plush white tiger in his left hand, grabbed the lace again with his right. He threw the lace over his shoulders like a cape and began dancing around. "Chocolate chip! Chocolate chip! Chocolate chip!" He turned the words into part chant, part song.

Edwin crossed his arms and studied his son. As he often did, Edwin looked for some evidence of his own looks in the little boy. He never found any, beyond a similar slope to their eyes.

Edwin was happy that David looked more like Fiona than Edwin. Fiona had been far lovelier than he was, as he often told her. Edwin had never understood what Fiona had seen in him. Whenever he'd asked her, she'd tweak the full sandy-brown mustache that Edwin had worn since his senior year in high school. "I fell for your mustache," Fiona would tease. Then she'd giggle and give him a big kiss, and he would forget to care about why she loved him. He was just so happy that she did.

David's song grew louder, and it picked up some percussion. He'd taken up a wooden slat from the old Leavers Machine and used the stick to pound on the cement floor in time to his chant.

Edwin shook his head. Ice cream was the last thing

David needed. The boy was already worked up. In fact, he was nearly always worked up.

Edwin remembered how excited he'd been when he'd learned he was going to be a father. He already had a job he loved, a gorgeous wife he adored, who, inexplicably, adored him back, and enough money to buy what he and his wife wanted. Now, he'd have a child, too. He'd have a legacy, someone to pass his life's work on to.

For nearly all Edwin's twenty-four years of life, he'd loved building things. When he'd been about David's age, he'd begun taking apart his mother's small appliances so he could see how they worked, though they rarely still worked when he put them back together. His mother was amazingly tolerant of the need to frequently replace things. By the time Edwin was eight, he knew that he wanted to build useful machines that would change people's lives. He believed in automating life's most mundane tasks, and he was sure he could create robots to replace most household chores people didn't enjoy.

His got his first patent on a robotic vacuum cleaner when he was still a college student. Despite the bugs and high price point, it had sold well enough to allow Edwin to start his business right out of school. The vacuum also funded a good life for Edwin and Fiona, who had met at school and married as soon as they graduated. The vacuum was wildly popular—at first. Unfortunately, the machines didn't have the longevity that customers expected, and complaints began rolling in. Eventually, sales fell off.

Edwin watched his son cavort around in front of the metal garment rack that held a circus-like array of animal and other character costumes and imagined, for at least the thousandth time, how different things would have been if Fiona had lived. If she'd survived giving birth to David, Edwin wouldn't have been derailed by grief, and he wouldn't have had to try to figure out how to invent his machines and take care of his infant son at the same time.

David Sean Murray, now attempting to do a somersault while still wrapped in lace, had come into the world just before dawn on a stormy fall morning, and he'd arrived in full screaming fury. Given that Fiona had been bleeding to death as David caterwauled, Edwin assumed that David's protest against being taken from his mother's womb had been amplified by his probable understanding, on some unfathomable mother-son-bonded level, that he was about to lose his mother for good. Or maybe Edwin was being fanciful. Maybe David was just a noisy baby.

Whatever the reason, David's vocal protestations didn't end on the day of his birth. They continued on and on and on. Edwin had spent the next several weeks trying to function on an hour or two of sleep (if he was lucky) per night. Instead of being able to throw himself into his work and either fix the vacuum or come up with something even better, Edwin had to spend the better part of his days feeding David, burping David, rocking David, changing David's diapers, and listening to David cry and cry and cry and cry.

Edwin loved his son. He really did. But without Fiona, Edwin was a man hanging on to a cliff's edge by the tips of his fingernails. He wasn't sure he could do what he needed to do. Four years had passed, and he still wasn't sure.

David's chocolate chip chant was getting louder and louder. The boy was spinning faster and faster.

"David!" Edwin shouted.

David stopped spinning, but the momentum sent him

staggering across the cement floor. He careened into Edwin's worktable, knocking over the animatronic head that Edwin had been wiring. The head, that of a bright yellow chick, rolled across the table and fell to the cement floor. A spark shot out of the chick's eye.

"David!" Edwin yelled even louder. "That's enough!"

David lost his balance entirely and landed on his rump. The boy's dark brown eyes blinked twice, then David's severely arched brows bunched. He buried his face in his tiger and started to cry.

Edwin sighed and picked his son up. "Come on," Edwin said. "I think you need a nap."

David, remarkably big for his age, in spite of having two short parents, wasn't an easy carry. He weighed close to fifty pounds, and he was three-and-a-half-feet tall. Pretty soon, Edwin, only five-foot-five himself, wasn't going to be able to cart his son around. Perhaps he could build a robot to do the job for him.

Edwin's steps faltered. "That's not a bad idea," he said to himself.

David stopped his crying in mid-gulp and looked up. "What's a bad idea, Daddy?"

"No, not a *bad idea*," Edwin attempted to clarify. "Just *not a bad idea*. Which means a good idea."

David twisted his nose and pursed his full, small lips. Edwin didn't blame the boy for his confusion.

"Never mind," Edwin said. "How about I read you a story and you take a short nap, and then we'll get that ice cream?"

David stuck a stubby index finger in his mouth and sucked on it while he pondered the proposal. Finally, he nodded.

"Good boy," Edwin said.

He'd reached the top of the steep cement stairs that led to the second floor of the building. He put David on his feet, took the boy's hand, and led him down a wide hall to what used to be part of the factory's office and storage space.

After Fiona passed away, Edwin had known he couldn't manage a house and his business property at the same time. And since the factory was where Edwin did his work, the choice of which to keep was an easy one. Thankfully, Edwin was an engineer-slash-architect, so he converted part of the factory's offices to a small apartment with a compact sitting area, a tiny galley kitchen, one bedroom, and one bathroom with an old clawfoot tub. All the little rooms except the kitchen, which was floored with blue linoleum, now had wall-to-wall brown carpet (chosen to hide the dirt). All the apartment's exterior brick walls and interior white-painted walls were decorated with an eclectic mix of David's "artwork," aka scribbled drawings, and old photographs (in the factory's offices, Edwin had found dozens of black-and-white photos of the factory in its heyday). As David grew older, Edwin would have to create a second bedroom, but for now, keeping an eye on David was easier when they slept in the same room. Not that they slept there very often. Much of the time, Edwin worked on the factory's main level at night, and David slept on a cot nearby.

Edwin knew that this wasn't the ideal setting for raising a child. There were hundreds of ways a child could get injured in the five-thousand-square-foot building. David, though, in spite of his penchant for noisy tantrums, was a good kid. He hadn't defied Edwin's orders to stay away from the machines—yet. Edwin had noticed that David was getting a little bolder in his adventures. That might become a problem as he got older.

And that was what made the idea Edwin had just had such a brilliant one. But would he have time to implement it?

"Daddy?"

Edwin was peripherally aware that David was climbing onto his small mattress, which was nestled inside a wooden white tiger's head. The head, which Edwin had carved to mimic the look of David's favorite toy, arched up and over the top of the mattress. David loved the tiger bed, almost as much as his plush tiger, named, appropriately, "Tiger."

"Daddy!"

Edwin, who had been contemplating the notion of mimicking, blinked and frowned at his son, who was now standing on the mattress, holding up said plush tiger. "What is it, David?" Edwin sighed and pointed at the mattress. "Lie down."

David obliged, but he kept holding up his plush friend. "Tiger wants to know if he can have ice cream, too. Chocolate chip."

"Of course. What other flavor is there?"

David giggled. "So, he can have some?"

Edwin stroked his mustache. "I suppose we could ask Lucy to get some of the special, invisible tiger ice cream made just for tigers out of the back for him when we get to the ice cream parlor."

"Lucy's nice," David said.

"Yes, she is." David liked the grandmotherly woman who owned the ice-cream parlor so much that Edwin had a feeling David's love of ice cream was more related to a desire to see Lucy than it was about eating the ice cream itself. "But you won't see Lucy unless you and Tiger take a nap."

"Grrr," David said. "That's what Tiger says about naps."

"Very wise," Edwin said.

David leaned over and rooted around in a mess of books that were scattered over the floor by his bed. Edwin looked at his watch. His shoulders tightened.

"Uh, David?"

David's head popped up. His eyes were bright and eager. Edwin felt like a jerk for what he was about to say, but . . .

"How about we skip the story?" Edwin asked.

The bright eyes dimmed. A quiver appeared around the dimple in David's chin.

"Just for now," Edwin said. "I'll read two stories before you go to bed tonight. But if Daddy is going to be able to take you for ice cream, he has to get work done."

David pushed out his lower lip. Then, remarkably, he shrugged. "Okay, Daddy."

David flopped onto his stomach and tucked Tiger up against his chest. He closed his eyes, and within seconds, his breathing slowed.

David might have been a noisy—almost hyperactive— child, but he had some wonderful qualities. Not only did he listen pretty well, but he could also fall asleep nearly instantly. If only Edwin could learn that skill.

Edwin lightly smoothed David's silky-soft hair. David stirred, then his breathing slowed even more.

Edwin headed back down to the main floor of the factory. He had so much work to do, and he might get just a half hour of uninterrupted concentration.

One of the old exposed pipes that crisscrossed the ceiling on the factory's first level clunked. Edwin could hear David's voice in his head: "*It's the pipe fairy, Daddy.*"

David had names for all the sounds the factory made. He'd named its distinctive features as well. Although the factory was dark, filled with old debris, and dirtier than it should have been, David wasn't scared by it. To David, the factory was home. He'd made friends with it.

More than one visitor to Edwin's business had expressed concern about David's safety in the large, old building that sat at the edge of the four-lane highway that ran through the industrial part of town. The land that the old factory sat on wasn't much bigger than the factory itself, so David had no yard to play in, and their only lawn was a vacant gravel lot. Sometimes they'd play catch there, or they'd sit in folding chairs and play Name That Car. Edwin was teaching David the makes and models of the cars they spotted on the highway. David had an amazing memory and was learning quickly.

Recently, Fitz, the deliveryman who brought Edwin all his current projects and the supplies he ordered, had asked, "*Don't you worry about the kid falling down stairs or getting hurt in the machines or locked into a room or something?*"

Edwin looked up from the clipboard he was signing. "What?" He noted that Fitz was looking past his shoulder toward the Leavers Machine that dominated the east wall of the main factory floor. Edwin turned to look at the mammoth lacemaking machine. It was dark and silent; none of its thousands of moving parts could so much as twitch now. As far as Edwin knew, it had been frozen in place for over thirty years. The machine had been turned off mid-job, and a now moth-hole-riddled expanse of lace hung loosely over the machine's beam roller. Limp, yellowed threads stretched like spiderwebs from spools stacked on a nearby bobbin-winding unit.

"*Oh, he knows better than to go near that,*" Edwin said. He felt a need to reassure Fitz, so he continued, "*All of the extra rooms are closed up, and I usually help him with the stairs. I built him a slide for coming down.*"

"*You built your kid an indoor slide?*" Fitz raised his bushy black eyebrows as he took back the clipboard.

"*Yep,*" Edwin said.

It had been fun. Edwin had found a secondhand slide that had once been in an amusement park, and he'd bolted it to one wall of the secondary stairs between the first and second floor. He'd placed a couple mattresses at the bottom of the slide. David loved the thing. Sometimes, he loved it too much. He frequently demanded that Edwin carry him up the sharply canted stairs over and over so he could slide down repeatedly.

Edwin returned to his worktable and frowned at the yellow chick head lying near one of the table's legs. He sighed. He really had no interest in continuing the project. But he had to.

Edwin bent over and picked up the chick head. He sighed again.

It occurred to him that he sighed a lot. But why shouldn't he?

Edwin was trapped in a life he didn't want to live, and he was doing projects he never in a million years thought he'd be working on. He was turning weird creature costumes into entertaining robots, for heaven's sake. What was useful about that?

Edwin set the metal chick head on the table in front of

him. This was the eighteenth animatronic character he'd been asked to create. He'd spent the last year and a half abandoning his own work to bow to another company's agenda.

Edwin thought back to the day that he'd signed away his own enterprise. *"You're doing the right thing,"* Grant Starling, the portly Fazbear Entertainment exec who'd negotiated the buyout, said as he watched Edwin scrawl his signature on the bottom of the twelve-page contract.

Am I? Edwin had wondered.

When Edwin had started his company, he'd thought his timing was perfect. It was the early '70s. People wanted more time to play, and their minds were opening as well. Edwin had assumed these things would translate into a huge market for his machines. Unfortunately, he'd been wrong. Either that, or his personal tragedies had undermined his ability to create machines that were good enough to attract a big market share. The machines he designed were intricate and required thousands of hours of focused work—not to mention very expensive parts and tools. Raising a son on his own had pulled the rug out from under Edwin. He just hadn't had enough in him to do everything he'd needed to do. When his finances ran dry, he'd had no choice but to sell his company to Fazbear Enterprises.

"You have a real talent," Grant had said. *"We're happy to welcome you to the Fazbear family."*

Edwin turned over the chick head. He pressed his lips together in disgust. The fall to the floor had dented the chick's beak and snapped off one of the metal "feathers" atop its skull. "Great," Edwin muttered.

He was behind schedule and totally overwhelmed. He didn't have time to take David to get the promised ice cream today, or any other day for that matter. But he'd have to do it. David would throw a tantrum to end all tantrums if Edwin didn't keep his promise.

Edwin contemplated the chick's head. He really had to get to work on it. But a new idea was leaping around in his mind. It was demanding attention. And rightfully so. If Edwin could pull off what he had in mind, it would open up an enormous amount of time for him. David would be entertained, and Edwin would be free to concentrate on his work.

Edwin pushed aside the chick's head. He grabbed his drafting pad and a pencil.

It put him three weeks behind in his projects for Fazbear Entertainment, but Edwin, working feverishly and essentially giving up sleep entirely for many bleary-eyed days, was able to take his idea from spark to completion in an amazingly short amount of time. Edwin attributed this speed to the passion he held for the project.

Edwin had been so caught up with Fazbear that he'd forgotten what it was like to pour himself into his own creations. He felt like he'd been gasping for air for months and now he could finally breathe again.

"Whatcha building, Daddy?" David had asked the first day that Edwin had begun implementing the plan he'd sketched out.

"I'm building you a new toy," Edwin had said.

"What kind of toy?"

"One that will keep you company while I work," Edwin had said.

David had twisted his lips into his *I don't understand* expression.

"I'm building you a friend," Edwin had clarified.

"Tiger is my friend." David held up the white tiger. The tiger wasn't all that white today. David had taken the tiger on an "aventure" behind the stacks of spools. The area had decades of accumulated dirt, and much of it now smudged Tiger's muzzle.

"Well, once I finish what I'm building, you and Tiger will have another friend," Edwin said. "Now, why don't we take Tiger upstairs and clean him up. Then we can have dinner."

"Mac and cheese!" David screamed.

As Edwin had helped David climb the sharp flight of stairs, Edwin's chest had tightened at the thought of his son having just a plush tiger . . . and soon, a robotic torso . . . for a friend. Next year, that would change. Edwin would be able to put David in kindergarten. Even though he'd relish the time to himself, Edwin didn't have the money to pay for a preschool program at the moment, and the free class was across town. Besides, the one time he'd tried to enroll David in a community program, too many busybodies had started sticking their noses into his business. David apparently told some hair-raising stories about sleeping in an abandoned factory that groaned and clanked at night. No, for now, David was better off with Edwin. And if Edwin's idea worked, Edwin could keep his son close *and* have enough time to work.

Edwin didn't have a lot of money for supplies to build what he wanted to build, so he'd come up with a design that would allow him to cannibalize machinery in the factory. By pulling wiring from rooms that he never used, taking pistons from a defunct industrial washing machine, and borrowing steel and spools and gears and springs from the Leavers Machine, Edwin had fashioned the torso, arms, and head of a primitive-looking endoskeleton. This physical housing was the easy part.

Once Edwin had constructed the legless robot, he had to build the computer for it. This he did by stealing hardware from some of his abandoned projects.

Now came the challenging part. Edwin wanted to create a thinking mind that would learn by mimicking what it observed. It had been Edwin's observation of how the bed he'd built for David mimicked David's favorite toy that had given him the idea. Thinking about the concept of mimicking so soon after casually contemplating having a robot to entertain his child had brought the whole idea together.

Perhaps because the idea was inspired, or perhaps because Edwin was so desperate to find a way to take care of David without actually having to take care of David, Edwin was able to write the code for the program at nearly the speed of light. It was like the program wanted to be written, so it helped him create it.

He'd used a combination of Pascal and C to write his code. What he did was unusual, and some might have called it slapdash as he hurried to get the robot finished. He took several shortcuts that any other programmer would have frowned upon, but he was happy with the result.

David was happy, too.

After twenty-two days of feverish work, Edwin was about to boot up his creation for the first time when David and Tiger zipped down the back staircase slide and trotted over to Edwin. David charged up to Edwin and leaned against his dad's leg.

David wrinkled his nose. "Daddy, you stink," he announced.

"Thank you for pointing that out," Edwin said.

His son was right. Between taking care of David and building his brainchild, Edwin had let a few things fall by the wayside. Personal hygiene was one of those things. His breath, he suddenly realized, was stale, and his armpits might have been lethal.

But none of that mattered. It was done.

"Check this out," Edwin said to David.

Lifting the endoskeleton off the table, Edwin set it on the floor in front of David. Then Edwin sat down cross-legged next to it.

David plopped down next to his dad. "What's its name, Daddy?" David asked, studying the endoskeleton's face.

Edwin also looked at his creation's face, wondering how a four-year-old boy would see it. He glanced at David as he realized that the endoskeleton's features might have been scary for a little kid.

Given what Edwin had been able to work with, he thought the endoskeleton's head had turned out pretty well. Edwin's first attempt to form the skull had started with simply placing two large white doll's eyes within the boxy confines of a piece of metal housing he'd scrounged from a broken-down compressor. Because the square top looked nothing like a real head, though, Edwin had tried again. He'd found a rounded bit of metal in the guts of the Leavers Machine, and he'd used it to form a narrow protuberance that jutted up from between the big white eyes. Under the eye housing, Edwin had welded in place a hinged "jaw" that he formed out of parts of the Leavers Machine's guide bars. Using a set of novelty chattering teeth he'd found in a box full of old bits and bobs on the third floor, Edwin had given his creation a big, white-toothed mouth.

Getting all this hardware connected to its programming required welding a large processor to the back of the skull and running a tangle of wires all around the skull. Wires stretched toward the back of the skull, dove in and out of both eye sockets, snaked through the mouth, and extended down the articulated neck that in turn connected with a metallic spine, which connected with a makeshift rib cage that was not as curved as Edwin had wanted it to be (but it worked), and the rib cage was linked to two robotic arms that ended in pincerlike hands.

Okay, so maybe the thing wasn't pretty. In fact, its appearance was a tad disturbing.

David, however, didn't look scared. His eyes were sparkling, and his head was cocked in what looked more like curiosity than any sort of trepidation.

"I haven't given it a name," Edwin said. He thought about the program he'd written. He'd called the program Mimic1. Well, that would work. "How about Mimic?" he suggested.

David made a face. "That's a weird name, Daddy."

Edwin had no response to that comment.

"But I like it," David continued. "Mimic." He nodded. "Yeah, that's okay."

"I'm glad you approve," Edwin said.

David shifted position and frowned. "What does it do, Daddy?" David asked.

"Well, let's find out," Edwin said.

Taking a deep breath, Edwin reached behind Mimic's neck and activated it. Mimic's eyes lit up. They fluttered. Its mouth opened and closed.

David leaned forward, rapt.

In slow motion, Mimic leaned forward.

Startled, David whipped his head back and hugged Tiger. But he giggled.

Mimic, still moving slowly, pulled its head back and pantomimed hugging a tiger-size invisible object. David giggled again.

"He's copying me, Daddy!" David said, clearly delighted.

Edwin smiled. It—he—sure was. Mimic was working!

David put out a finger and touched Mimic's chest. Mimic put out a pincer and touched David's chest.

David set down Tiger. "Wanna play patty-cake?" David asked his new friend.

Edwin blinked in surprise. He'd played the clapping game with David when David was much younger, but they hadn't played in a couple years. David, however, clearly remembered the game.

On some level, apparently understanding that he had to show Mimic what to do, David clapped his hands slowly and then put his hands out, fingers up, palms toward Mimic. Mimic matched the movements as best he could. He spread his pincer fingers to approximate David's hand position. David clapped again. Mimic brought his pincers together with a metallic clink.

Edwin closed his eyes and rolled his shoulders. He'd done it. Now, he could get back to work on his paying jobs.

But first, he had to clean himself up. Edwin opened his eyes and looked at David, who was still teaching a complex version of patty-cake to his new friend.

"David," Edwin said, "How about we take Mimic upstairs? You two can play while I take a shower."

David stopped playing. He dropped his hands. Mimic did the same.

"That's good, Daddy," David said. "You need soap." He pointed at Edwin, then put his fingers over his nose.

Edwin laughed as Mimic moved his pincers to the space that separated his eyes.

"Mimic agrees," David said.

Edwin laughed harder and stood. He leaned over and picked up Mimic as David jumped to his feet.

David took Edwin's free hand. "I like Mimic," David said.

Mimic reached out and wrapped his pincers around Edwin's wrist. The feel of the cold metal against Edwin's skin made Edwin stiffen for a moment. Some primitive part of his brain felt a surge of fear. Would Mimic clamp down and hurt Edwin?

No. Mimic's touch was gentle, even hesitant. Edwin relaxed and took his son and his son's new friend up the stairs.

The next two weeks were the best Edwin could remember having since Fiona had died. After catching up on some sleep the first night Mimic was completed, Edwin woke up energized and ready to go back to creating the characters Fazbear Entertainment wanted. And because David was occupied with his new friend, Edwin had long stretches of uninterrupted work time. It was fantastic. It was amazing how much he could get done when he wasn't interrupted every other minute.

When Edwin had programmed Mimic, he hadn't had the parts he needed to give Mimic the ability to speak.

He'd been concerned that this would be a problem for David, but he shouldn't have worried. David had no issue with Mimic's muteness. He started developing a sort of sign language to communicate with his robotic friend.

David's sign language involved often hilarious imitations of the things he was trying to communicate. *Ice cream*, for example, was conveyed with a gesture that involved turning one hand into a bowl-like shape and using the other hand to approximate the shape of a spoon. David would dip the spoon hand into the bowl hand and put the spoon hand to his lips. Then, in what Edwin thought was adorably brilliant, David would rub the front of his chin as if ice cream was dripping there.

Mimic copied every move David made. This encouraged David to teach Mimic more and more things.

At first, what Mimic could do was somewhat limited. He could slowly copy David's simpler movements. It was impressive for a robot held together with the engineering equivalent of two pieces of tape, but it wasn't a replacement for a friend.

So Edwin tinkered with Mimic, to make sure that David wouldn't get bored. Edwin wanted Mimic to be able to move as smoothly as possible. He still wasn't sure how Mimic was learning so quickly, but he was very pleased by this development. Edwin was even starting to kick around ideas for how he could use the evolving program to get his company back. The Mimic1 program, if it matured as Edwin hoped it would, could be applied to many tasks.

The first time Edwin realized he hadn't checked on David for hours, he was shocked. It felt irresponsible, almost. For all he'd known, David could have left the building. But he hadn't.

When Edwin looked up from finally finishing the giant chick robot that he'd been working on, he found David and Mimic on the floor, coloring. Mimic was actually using crayons.

Mimic's use of the crayons was clumsy, and he definitely didn't color inside the lines. But David didn't, either. David had always been prone to coloring the entire page. Mimic did that, too.

Later that same day, Edwin's concentration was broken by a rhythmic thwacking sound. At first, the sound was just enough to make him frown, but as it got louder and was joined by David's giggles, Edwin grumbled and looked around.

A few feet from his worktable, Edwin spotted David and Mimic tossing a red rubber ball back and forth. Because David wasn't all that good at throwing or catching a ball, the ball frequently missed its target and bounced across the floor. Undaunted, David scampered after it, retrieved it, and tried again. Mimic's throws, because they were a copy of David's, were just as inconsistent, but David was clearly delighted by the clumsy game of catch.

Edwin smiled. Although the noise was distracting, at least David was content. Edwin returned to his work, satisfied that Mimic was doing what Edwin had designed the robot to do.

Mimic went everywhere that David went. He sat at the table when David ate. He perched at the edge of the sink when David brushed his teeth. And all the while, he copied all David's motions.

One evening, as they ate, David pushed his bowl of mac and cheese across the table so it was in front of Mimic. Mimic immediately took the spoon and scooped up some of the noodles. Edwin had to scramble to stop Mimic from dropping the mac and cheese through his open mouth. It wasn't as if the food would hurt Mimic. It would have gone through the novelty teeth and out the opening behind them, tumbling down the back of Mimic's neck. But Edwin didn't want to scrub cheese off Mimic's parts.

"Whoa there," Edwin said to Mimic. "I'm afraid you're not designed to digest food."

David thought this was hilariously funny. He was taking a sip of milk, and he laughed so hard that milk came out of his nose. Mimic opened his mouth and approximated the head-shaking, open-mouthed action of a laugh. David laughed even harder. Then he jumped up and said to Mimic, "Let's play trains."

Edwin put his hand out in a STOP gesture and shook his head. "What do you do first?"

David looked up and to the right and twisted his lips, then he giggled. "Sorry, Daddy." He turned to pick up the carton of milk sitting next to his plastic cup. "Always put things away in the fridge," he said.

Using two hands, David carefully carried the quart carton to the fridge and stowed it away. Mimic watched his every move.

Because David always carried Tiger, Mimic usually had one of his arms curved in a way that suggested an invisible tiger. One day, David decided Mimic needed his own tiger.

"Can we buy Mimic a tiger?" David asked Edwin just before bedtime.

Edwin looked at Mimic's inwardly curved arm. The gesture tugged at his heartstrings, but he shook his head. "Sorry, sport," he said, "but money's a little tight right now."

David had heard this often enough that he knew what it meant. He shrugged. "Okay."

Later that day, when Edwin was finishing up the programming on a pirate fox character, he looked around and spotted David and Mimic by a pile of lace near the Leavers Machine. Both were bent over the lace, folding and refolding it.

Edwin got up and walked over to his son. "What are you doing?" he asked.

David looked up and grinned. Then he looked back at Mimic. "Is it ready?" he asked Mimic.

Mimic nodded.

Edwin's brows rose. This wasn't mimicking. It was responding. When had *that* happened?

David leaned back and pointed at Mimic. Mimic opened his mouth in his version of a smile.

Edwin blinked in amazement.

Cradled in the curve of Mimic's left arm was an approximation of a tiger. It was made of lace and held together with string. David . . . and Mimic . . . had used the old material to form a head, a body, two arms, and two legs. They'd even managed to create little nubbins atop the head that looked like tiger ears.

"Now Mimic has a tiger, too!" David said triumphantly.

Edwin reached down and ruffled David's hair. "Yes, he does. Very well done. Very clever."

David beamed. Mimic's eyes lit up brighter than usual.

Now even more confident that he could leave David in Mimic's care, Edwin threw himself into his work. He put in long hours, stopping only to feed David or answer David's occasional questions.

The questions, however, weren't as occasional as Edwin would have preferred. Although Mimic could entertain David in many ways, the robot couldn't talk to the boy.

"Why do we have to brush our teeth, Daddy?" David asked one day when Edwin was trying to rush David through his morning routine.

"Because if we don't, we get cavities," Edwin said.

"What are 'cavties'?" David asked.

"*Cav-i-ties*," Edwin enunciated.

David repeated the word, correctly this time. "What are they, Daddy?"

"Holes in the teeth."

David looked alarmed. "I can get holes in my teeth?" He pointed at Mimic. "He doesn't brush. Won't he get holes in his teeth?"

David had stopped brushing, and he waved his toothbrush. Toothpaste and water flew everywhere, including onto the clean shirt Edwin had just managed to get on his son.

Keeping himself and David in clean clothes was a challenge. Edwin had no washer or dryer in the factory. That was on his list of improvements to add once he got more money, but for now, he had to go to a laundromat. And he hated going to the laundromat.

"Stop that!" Edwin said. He shook a finger at his son. "Don't be careless."

David's face screwed up. His lower lip quivered.

"Don't you dare start crying," Edwin snapped.

Of course, the command had the exact opposite effect of what Edwin wanted. David started crying. Turning away from Edwin, David hunched over. Mimic, perched by the sink, hunched over as well.

Edwin grabbed David by the shoulders and shook him. David's cries turned to screams of rage.

"Oh, for heaven's sake!" Edwin said.

He forced himself to take a deep breath. He knew better than to do what he'd just done. It was just that he had so much work to do, and he only wanted David to brush his teeth and go sit and play with Mimic. Was that too much to ask?

Edwin crouched down in front of his son. "David, I'm sorry," he said. "I'm sorry I yelled."

David wasn't in a forgiving mood. He turned away from Edwin and reached for Mimic. Mimic wrapped his pincer hands around David's fingers.

Edwin spent the next several minutes trying to calm David down. The whole time, he promised himself he'd do better by his son.

But he didn't. His resolve fled him a mere ten minutes after the incident.

By then, David was wearing a fresh T-shirt with his brown corduroy pants, and he was bouncing up and down in anticipation of playing with his cars. Edwin looked at David's rumpled bed and the zebra pajamas that lay crumpled on the floor next to it. As David started to skip past Edwin, who grabbed Edwin's shoulder. He pointed at the pajamas. "What have I told you?" Edwin asked.

David looked up and to the right in his classic *oops* expression. "Sorry, Daddy." He bent over and picked up the pajamas. "Always put things in the closet," he said.

David opened the door leading to the next room and stowed his pajamas on the shelf next to a hanging rod of Edwin's clothing. Mimic watched David the whole time.

For the next couple hours, Edwin was able to focus on work. But then his focus was abruptly interrupted.

"Look at me, Daddy!" David screamed.

Edwin lifted his gaze from his task. His eyes widened.

"What do you think you're doing?" he shouted.

David, clad in one of the costumes sent by Fazbear Entertainment, was no longer a little boy. He was a yellow dog frolicking around on all fours. Because the costume was too big for David, the dog's limbs flopped all over the concrete. They were getting filthy.

And it got worse. Next to David, Mimic was stuffed inside the top part of a green alligator costume. It too was now dirty. Edwin was going to have to clean up both costumes . . . like he didn't already have enough to do!

"Those costumes aren't for play!" Edwin yelled. He shot up out of his chair and charged over to his son. Yanking David off the floor, he shook his index finger. "Get out of that costume right now!" He turned toward Mimic. "You too!"

David, predictably, started to cry. Edwin ignored the tantrum and worked on extricating his son out of the faux fur.

Once he had both child and robot costume free,

Edwin placed Mimic next to one of the pillars. He pointed at David. "Now, go over there and play quietly."

David sniveled. "Okay, Daddy."

Setting aside the costumes to deal with later, Edwin returned to his work. But he only got in another half hour or so before he was interrupted again.

"Daddy, I'm hungry," David announced when Edwin was right in the middle of doing a tricky soldering job.

David poked Edwin in the forearm. Edwin's hand slipped. The solder blotched in the wrong place.

Edwin swore. "David! Watch what you're doing!" Edwin crossed his arms and glared at his son. "You just made me mess something up. Now I have to redo it."

David looked at his feet.

Edwin noticed Mimic gazing down at the bottom of his own legless torso.

"Sorry, Daddy," David said.

Edwin took a deep breath and looked up at the ceiling's exposed old oak beams. He watched a spider toiling in the middle of its web, which was monstrous, over three feet wide, anchored against one of the green pillars and stretching out to the top of one of the factory's tall boarded-over windows. Edwin noted that the spider was alone. Unhampered by spiderlings, the huge black insect was managing far more productivity than Edwin was.

Edwin pulled his gaze from the spider and rolled his shoulders. He ruffled David's hair. "It's okay, David. But could you please play quietly with Mimic for a little bit longer while I finish what I'm doing here?"

"Okay, Daddy," David said. He turned toward Mimic. "We'll draw."

A few days before, Edwin, while looking for a part on

the third floor, had come across a box of construction paper in a variety of colors. He'd carried the reams of paper down to the first floor and shown it to David.

"You can use this to draw whatever you want," Edwin had said.

"Neato, Daddy!" David had said.

Since then, David and Mimic had been doing all manner of odd little drawings that were surrounded by markings that looked vaguely like hieroglyphics. When Edwin had asked David what they were, David had shrugged. "It's made up, Daddy."

It might have been made up, but it riveted David and Mimic. So now, David pulled out more paper, and he and Mimic began scribbling more drawings and symbols. Edwin, both amused and baffled by his son's creative efforts, turned back to his work.

As Edwin finished the soldering job, he resolved to make time to tinker with Mimic after David was asleep later. This was something he'd been doing regularly since he'd created Mimic. He kept tweaking Mimic's functionality so Mimic could do a better job of entertaining David. Clearly, however, it needed more work. As the rainy spring days continued, David was getting more and more restless.

Perhaps if Mimic was a bit more mobile, Edwin thought.

That night, after tucking David into his cot near Edwin's worktable and watching Mimic copy David's big yawn and the little eye rub that always preceded settling in with Tiger for sleep, Edwin picked up Mimic and carried him over to the long worktable. There, he worked at updating Mimic's program so Mimic could use his arms and lower torso more fluidly. This new agility would give Mimic an expanded ability to play with David. Mimic would be able to scoot along the ground, in approximation of the way David often butt-scooted across the floor when he was playing. He also would be able to get himself up and down stairs. And he'd be able to throw the ball farther and retrieve it as well. Edwin also adjusted Mimic's processors so that Mimic could continue to execute more and more complex tasks.

There, Edwin thought when he was done. That should give him more time to focus on his work.

And Edwin could do more while David slept, too. Rubbing away his exhaustion, Edwin returned to the latest project he was doing for Fazbear Entertainment. He worked until just before dawn and then carried David, still sleeping, up to the apartment. There, Edwin dropped into bed himself and fell into a restless sleep.

Two hours later, Edwin awoke abruptly when his excited son landed on his stomach and screamed, "Sunshine, Daddy! Let's play catch!"

Trying to get back the breath that had been stolen from him when David's full weight had hit his solar plexus, Edwin blinked at the vivid yellow ray of sun that was streaking in through the closest window, beneath a shade that Edwin hadn't bothered to lower the night before.

David began bouncing up and down on Edwin's stomach.

"David!" Edwin shouted. "Cut that out!"

David slid off his dad. Edwin took a deep breath to refill his lungs.

"I'll go out and wait for you to come and play with me, Daddy," David said.

Edwin nodded vaguely, only half processing what David had said. Edwin sat up. As he put his feet on the floor, he heard David slide down to the factory's first floor.

Good, Edwin thought. Mimic was down in the workshop. He'd keep David occupied while Edwin grabbed a quick shower and make breakfast.

Edwin stood and headed toward the shower. He started thinking about how he was going to tackle the next part of his current project.

Edwin was still thinking about his plans as he set out bowls and spoons, a box of cornflakes, and a carton of milk. He continued to strategize in his head as he trotted down the stairs to get his son.

"David!" Edwin called out as he got to the first floor. "Breakfast!"

Edwin expected an immediate squeal of joy because David loved to eat. But Edwin didn't hear anything.

He did, however, *feel* something.

The factory, as cool and dank as it was, didn't get a lot of air movement. Edwin never felt drafts. But he did now. He felt a strong current of warm air.

Edwin's muscles tensed. In spite of the warmth that wafted across his bare arms, Edwin felt a chill skitter down his spine. Frowning, Edwin looked around.

Edwin's workshop looked as it should have. Mimic was sitting on Edwin's worktable. Nothing was out of place.

So why was Edwin on the alert?

"David?" he tried again. This time, his son's name came out louder, with just the slightest edge of fear.

Edwin took a step forward. And that's when he saw that the factory's main double doors were standing wide open.

"David!" Edwin yelled.

Edwin took off toward the open doorway. Looking right and left past the pillars as he went, scanning the massive factory floor for his son, Edwin's stomach lurched up into his chest.

As Edwin dashed through the factory's open doors, he shouted for David again. Under the shout, he could hear his mind repeating over and over, "Please, no. Please, no."

He wasn't sure who or what his mind was talking to. But it didn't matter. The appeal wasn't heeded.

The next ten seconds of Edwin's life played out as any normal ten seconds would. They unfolded one second at a time. For Edwin, however, the ten seconds compacted into an expanded infinite experience of horror that at once happened instantaneously and also went on forever.

Edwin rushed out into the brilliant morning sun and breathed in a mouthful of humid air just as David's ball bounced out into the nearest lane of traffic. Oblivious of the oncoming white van, David, a wide grin on his eager face, his legs churning, dashed out onto the highway. His gaze was locked on the bright red ball.

Time compressed even more. Edwin could no longer process what he was seeing as a string of events. His mind shut down. All he had were his senses.

The roar of an engine. The smell of exhaust. A blur of white skidding past Edwin's gaze. A screech of rubber on asphalt. The stench of burning rubber. The blur of white vibrating to a stop. A sickening *thud*. A scream. More screeching rubber. Shouts.

Edwin, as he streaked toward his son, tried to convince

himself that what he'd just watched hadn't happened. He tried to tell himself David was fine. But he knew he was lying to himself. As he flew toward his son, Edwin knew he was running both toward something he'd never reach and away from something he'd never escape.

"Call 911!" someone screamed.

Edwin reached David's side. He bent over and tried to gather David into his arms. But another set of stronger arms pulled him back. "Don't move him," a man's voice said.

Edwin lashed out, fighting to free himself. Everything lost focus; Edwin could only see flashes of color—crimson red spreading across an expanse of black, bright blue pressing down from overhead, snatches of white and orange and darker blue and yellow.

Edwin opened his mouth, and he heard a high-pitched keen. The sound, he realized, was coming from him. The arms that gripped him held on even tighter. Edwin's senses failed him. The sounds faded into a distant roar. The colors blurred together. The sun was blotted out by a darkness that Edwin intuitively knew was coming from someplace within his soul.

Out under the bright morning light, in the road near his son's broken body, Edwin had lost his ability to process reality. But after that, he lost two weeks of his life entirely. He disappeared into a fugue he didn't even know was a fugue until he came out of it and realized that time had marched on after David had passed. Edwin had no memory of anything since then except the seemingly endless loop of David's death, which replayed in Edwin's mind's eye over and over and over again.

Edwin came out of the lost time one morning on

another sunny day. Opening his eyes, Edwin found himself in his own bed, alone.

Edwin blinked and rubbed his face. He struggled to get his mental bearings. And when he got them, he wished he hadn't.

Although he couldn't remember any of the discrete details, Edwin had an intellectual understanding that he'd lived through burying his only son. He grasped that he was alone in the factory, and that life was supposed to be going on.

Not sure he had the strength to stand, Edwin tried putting his feet on the floor and pushing himself off the bed. Amazingly, his legs held him up. They also took him to the bathroom and got him through a normal morning routine.

As if anything could be normal. As if anything would ever be normal again.

When Edwin faced his mirror, he wasn't surprised to be looking into the eyes of a stranger. He didn't feel like Edwin anymore. He felt like a husk. He looked like one, too. Apparently, he hadn't eaten much, if anything, during his lost two weeks. The gaunt face of a broken man looked back at Edwin from the bathroom mirror. A scraggly beard was filling in around his full, and now drooping, mustache.

Turning away from himself, Edwin left the bathroom. He headed toward the stairs and shuffled to his worktable. There, his gaze landed on Mimic.

I should deactivate him, Edwin thought. But Edwin didn't have the energy to do it. He barely had the energy to get to his worktable.

Dropping into his rolling chair, Edwin surveyed his current project. He'd been working on it, he realized, during the two weeks he couldn't remember living through. It was further along than it had been the day that David had died. Edwin had no memory of doing the work.

And he had no desire to continue it now. But what choice did he have? His son was dead, but Edwin had obligations. Sighing, he bent over the worktable and told himself to concentrate.

Edwin picked up a pair of needle-nose pliers. He looked at a tangle of wires and then gazed at the endoskeleton he was supposed to be merging with Fazbear Entertainment's latest costume, a blue bunny. Edwin frowned at the pliers. For the life of him, Edwin couldn't remember how to grip them. Did he use a fisted grip or a fingertips grip? He tried both. Neither felt right.

A long scrape preceded a metallic clunk. Edwin shifted his gaze from the pliers to Mimic, who had just climbed up onto the table. Mimic clutched his makeshift tiger. Edwin stared at it, frowning.

Slowly, a memory clawed its way through the murk that was his mind. In the recollection, Edwin was snatching David's Tiger from Mimic's grasp. Mimic had tried to start carrying around Tiger, Edwin realized. He'd blocked it out. Now, he could remember squeezing Tiger, crying so hard that his tears soaked Tiger's fur.

Edwin shook his head, willing the memory to go back where it had come from. Blankness was better than the jagged shards of scenes like that.

Edwin glanced at Mimic. "Don't you have something better to do than stare at me?" Edwin grumbled.

Mimic set aside his tiger and lifted both sets of pincers. Forming one set into a bowl shape, he used the other pincers to create a makeshift spoon. Mimic mimed lifting the spoon to his mouth. Then Mimic used his pincers to approximate the gesture of wiping ice cream from his chin.

It was David's code for wanting ice cream. Seeing Mimic use David's sign language was too much for Edwin to process. He roared in fury and self-recrimination.

Reaching out blindly, not knowing why he needed it, Edwin sought something to wield. He had a sudden, out-of-control imperative to hit something . . . no, to *destroy* something.

Edwin's hand closed over a length of metal. Sharp-edged and cold, the metal was heavy. The weight of it felt good in Edwin's hand. So did lifting it. So did bringing it down on the animatronic's head.

Howling like a wild animal, Edwin battered Mimic over and over and over with the metal rod. Metal sparked against metal. The reverberation of each blow bounced up Edwin's arm, sending jabs of pain into his shoulder. But Edwin didn't care. He only cared about destroying Mimic, pulverizing the only real thing that Edwin could attack in an effort to annihilate his pain.

Edwin pummeled Mimic again and again and again. He battered the animatronic's head, thrashed at his chest, and lashed at his arms.

Edwin's swings were big and wide and wild. His muscles burned with the effort of pulling back the rod and arcing it toward Mimic in one strike after another. Edwin was panting, his chest heaving. The spittle that had shot from his mouth when he'd screamed at Mimic was now a froth that jetted from Edwin in great gushes.

When his sputum landed on one of Mimic's eyes, Edwin realized that the eye was dangling out of its socket, hanging against Mimic's cracked fake teeth. Edwin, who had been so lost in his rage that he'd been nearly blinded by it, blinked to clear his vision. That's when he saw how much damage he'd done.

Mimic's eye wasn't the only thing that was out of place. The metal Edwin had used to form Mimic's forehead and jaw was crimped together, compressing Mimic's face. The broken teeth were shoved back into Mimic's head, caught up in torn and tangled wires. The remainder of Mimic's wiring had been raggedly wrested away from Mimic's metallic spine, and the spine itself was bent backward. Mimic's rib cage was crushed in multiple places, and Mimic's arms hung askew. Mimic's pincers were mutilated.

Edwin was destroying his creation.

But he didn't care.

For two weeks, Edwin had been lost in a void of despair, and now his despair had turned to rage. He had to get it out somehow or it would consume him. Because Edwin knew, even as he continued to scream and foam at the mouth, that the real object of his anger was himself. And that infuriated him even more. He wanted to destroy himself, but he couldn't. So, he sublimated his wrath onto Mimic with an intensity he hadn't known he had in him. He lost control of his humanity. He was devolving into the primitive version of himself, into something ferocious and savage. He could almost feel his murderous thoughts pouring through his muscles and transfusing through the metal into Mimic's systems.

Edwin wasn't sure how long he whaled on Mimic before he finally ran out of strength. And he ran out of anger.

Edwin's legs went out from under him. He collapsed to the ground and stared at the remains of his creation, the remains of his son's friend.

Mimic, though not completely destroyed, was now a pathetic picture of total defeat. At some point during Edwin's assault, Mimic had toppled over, and he now lay, arms bent, in one last tragic copy of Edwin's little boy.

Edwin dropped his head into his hands. His anger dissolved into regret. And the regret brought tears that he thought just might flow forever.

Dominic put his hands against the peeling paint of the square brick building's double doors. He pushed. The doors creaked.

Beyond the doors, the feeble light of a sun attempting to squeeze a few rays past wispy gray clouds reached into darkness so heavy and complete that Dominic felt like he was looking not at the interior of a building but rather at a solid black wall. Dominic hefted his heavy-duty tactical flashlight. Behind him, Harry's breath fell hot and moist against Dominic's shoulder blades.

"What do you see?" Harry asked.

Dominic flipped the switch on his flashlight. He aimed the radiant beam through the open doors.

Glen, who pressed against Dominic's left shoulder, sucked in a breath. "What *is* that thing?" he asked.

Dominic, who'd felt his neck muscles tense when the flashlight beam had landed on what looked like a huge, toothy behemoth, forced himself to get a grip. "It's just some kind of loom, I think," he said. "From what I heard, this place was a lace factory before that Murray dude bought it. That thing is probably a lace-making machine."

"It's creepy," Glen said.

Harry sidled out from behind Dominic. He chewed his

lower lip and sniffed as he gazed in the direction of the flashlight's glow. "The whole place is creepy," he said.

A little guy—maybe five foot four if he stood up real straight, which he rarely did—Harry had the courage of his stature . . . meaning, not much at all. The only reason he was here was that he'd been ordered to be here. And even then, Harry had told Dominic he'd debated whether to quit the job rather than take the assignment.

"What are you afraid of?" Dominic had asked, resisting the urge to laugh at his friend.

"I've heard stories," Harry had said.

"What stories?"

Harry had shaken his head. "My mom always says that talking about something gives it more power."

Dominic had snorted at this superstitious idea. Now, however, he wondered what Harry had heard. What was so bad that Harry didn't want to give it more power?

"Are we going to just stand here like three scaredy-cats?" Glen asked. "Or are we going in?"

Glen flicked on his own flashlight. He gave Harry a pointed look, and Harry pulled a stubby flashlight from the pocket of his baggy khakis. He turned it on and squared his shoulders.

"All righty then," Glen said. "Let's get this done so we can go back to my place and barbecue those ribs."

Harry turned and frowned at Glen. "Ribs? I thought we were doing hot dogs. I hate ribs. They're so gory. They make me think of dead things."

Glen rolled his eyes. "So are hot dogs."

Dominic decided someone had to take charge. "Okay," he said. "Come on." He stepped through the doors.

Glen and Harry followed Dominic. Together, all three walked into the darkness.

Because Dominic and his friends were wary, they shined their flashlights this way and that. The beams cut through the gloom like searchlights. The swooping beacons scythed over a dozen or so thick pillars that lined up precisely in three rows equally spaced between the building's outer walls. The pillars' pale green paint was peeling; under the paint, they were dingy gray and cracked.

"Is this place sound?" Harry asked.

"They wouldn't have sent us in here if it wasn't," Dominic said.

"Are you sure?" Harry asked.

A sudden whoosh of air rushed into the building. Dominic's long hair whipped around his face and got in his mouth. He was swiping it free when a deafening slam whirled him around. Dominic's flashlight beam landed on the now-closed double doors.

Harry, who also had rotated to face the closed doors, stared at them with wide eyes. His face, above the pale yellow of his flashlight's glow, looked ghostly white.

"Boo!" Glen yelled.

Dominic flinched, but Harry nearly jumped out of his skin.

"That's not funny!" Harry protested.

Glen laughed. Dominic couldn't help it; he snickered. But he patted Harry on his bony shoulder. "Come on," he said. "Let's scope the place out and see what we're up against."

Harry swallowed hard and nodded. Dominic put his back to the closed door and took a tentative step forward.

Dominic hadn't been sure what to expect before they'd gotten here. The instructions they'd been given were vague, to say the least.

"Just get in there and clean up the mess. Make repairs. Get it handled," Dominic's supervisor, Ron, had instructed when Dominic and his buddies got the assignment.

"Get what handled?" Dominic had asked.

Ron, a balding man with a beer belly, had waved a vague hand and said, "Edwin Murray left that place in *quite* a state when he disappeared a few months ago. The property reverted to Fazbear Entertainment due to breach of contract."

Dominic didn't think that answered his question, but Ron hadn't added anything else. Dominic and his friends, therefore, now each carried a satchel. They'd brought an array of tools. They were prepared, they hoped, for whatever the task might require. The only thing they'd known they'd need for sure was the flashlights.

"Take flashlights," Ron had told them. "The power's out in the building."

"How come?" Harry had asked, fidgeting.

"Paperwork mix-up with the power company," Ron had said.

Harry's pale brows had bunched into a deep frown that still contorted his face. In fact, now the frown was even deeper.

Dominic couldn't blame Harry for his expression. Even Dominic, who wasn't easily spooked, was a little intimidated by the building.

Dominic dropped his satchel on the floor. It landed with a thud and several clanks as the tools inside jostled together. Glen and Harry set down their bags as Dominic slowly arced his light through the room, squinting into the narrow beam to try to see everything he could. Not that he was happy with what he was seeing.

Besides the massive loom on the far wall of the big open space, this first floor of the three-story building was pretty wide open. The floor looked to be flanked by two staircases. One was wide and steep. The other, hidden in the murk, appeared to be a secondary staircase. Partially hidden behind a wall, it was probably one assigned to the people who had worked here, Dominic thought.

Throughout the open area, piles of lace lay in limp, dirty tangles at the base of several support pillars and against the exposed-brick walls. To Dominic's left, a long worktable was piled with wires and scrap metal and what looked like robotic parts. A rolling stool sat near the table. Behind the table, a metal garment rack held a bunch of Fazbear character costumes. Dominic's flashlight glow picked out a brown Freddy Fazbear costume, a yellow Chica costume, a Foxy costume, a Bonnie costume, and a couple bright pink and yellow-green court jester costumes. A visible layer of dust lay like gray fuzz on all the costumes.

Just past the row of costumes, a cot was set up. Its graying canvas sagged in the middle as if someone heavy had used it regularly. Dominic took a step forward and directed his flashlight's beam at the concave depression in the center of the cot. Something was nestled there. What was it? It looked like a small, dingy, white animal. Dominic squinted. No, not an animal. It was just a bundle of lace. He laughed at himself for thinking he'd been looking at a tiger cub.

Dominic turned and shined his light on the other side of the room. There, he saw a bunch of gears and metal rods scattered over the floor. Near them, countless spools of old grungy thread were stacked on a warped wooden stand.

"What's that over there?" Harry asked. His voice, never particularly deep, was a little higher and breathier than usual.

Dominic shifted the direction of his flashlight so its illumination joined that of Harry's. The light reflected off something silvery and slanted.

"Cool," Glen said, redirecting his flashlight to aim it in the same direction as the other two. "That looks like a slide."

"A slide?" Harry squeaked.

Dominic, intrigued, walked forward past two of the pillars. He found himself at the base of the secondary stairs. They were, as he'd suspected they would be, plain and functional. They had, however, a feature he hadn't expected. Someone had attached a long metal slide to one wall of the staircase, so the stair treads were now only eighteen or so inches wide. The slide covered the rest of the stairs' width. It ran from a landing above, one now obscured by the darkness, to the first level's concrete floor. A couple old, lumpy mattresses covered the concrete at the base, as if to give a user of the slide a cushy place to land.

But Dominic wouldn't want to land there now. In the beam of his light, he could see one of the mattresses move. Something was inside it. Probably a rat.

Dominic turned away and aimed his flashlight someplace else. The light landed in a shallow pool of water and reflected off a ripple along the puddle's surface. What had made the water ripple? Just an air current? Or something else?

"What exactly is it we're supposed to do here?" Glen asked.

"I was hoping it would be obvious when we got here," Dominic said. "But so far"—he shrugged—"your guess is as good as mine."

Harry, with uncharacteristic courage, walked over to the long worktable. "Maybe we're supposed to finish Murray's projects. Get them functional and get them out of here."

"Could be," Dominic said. "But we should probably scope out the whole building before we jump to any conclusions."

"We should split up and explore," Glen said.

"Split up?" Harry gasped.

"It would speed things up," Glen said.

Harry shook his head so emphatically that his blond curls bounced around it. He blinked pale blue eyes several times.

Not for the first time, Dominic was struck by how young Harry looked. Dominic knew Harry was actually three years older than Dominic's twenty-four years, but he didn't look it. His narrow chin covered with little more than peach fuzz, Harry's stature wasn't the only thing that was stunted. Harry's features, dominated by large round eyes and a small nose that was perpetually stuffed up, were boyish. So was his nature. His brain, however, was advanced. Harry was an electronics and robotics whiz. That was why Fazbear Entertainment had hired him, and that was why he was on this team.

Dominic had an engineering background, but he wasn't any kind of wunderkind. Neither was Glen. His expertise was also in engineering, and his hobby was woodworking, so he was pretty handy to have around.

Dominic and Glen had something else in common. They both looked older than their years. This was so for Dominic because of the premature gray in his thick, wavy dark hair and also because of his stark features. In addition, his was the kind of facial hair that needed shaving again four hours later. Dominic was also big. So was Glen although Glen's size was more in his musculature than in his height. Dominic was six-foot-four. Glen was only six feet tall.

"I am not wandering around this place by myself," Harry said. "Who knows what's even in here?"

As if to punctuate the sentiment, a click and a faint scratching sound came from the opposite end of the first level. Dominic and his friends whipped their flashlight beams in that direction, just in time to watch a rat scurry out from behind the big loom-like machine.

"No way," Harry said. "I won't go anywhere alone in here."

"You're a—" Glen began.

Dominic spoke over the top of him. "That's fine," he said. "I think we've seen what there is to see down here. That just leaves two more floors. Glen, why don't you and Harry go on up to the third floor and check that out? I'll take the second floor. Then we'll meet back down here and take stock of what we're facing." Dominic looked at Harry. "That work for you?"

Harry swallowed hard, but he nodded.

Dominic looked at Glen, who shrugged. "Whatever," he said.

"Okay," Dominic said. "Let's go."

Without waiting for his friends to respond, Dominic turned away from the secondary flight of stairs and started walking toward the main stairs. Although they were steep, they were wider. They also had what appeared to be a reasonably sound, black wrought iron handrail climbing up the wall with them.

Dominic's athletic shoes made scuffling sounds as he padded past the worktable and circled around a pillar to get to the stairs. Behind him, Glen's and Harry's footfalls echoed his own.

Dominic paused at the base of the stairs and aimed his light up the steep flight. The light revealed that the wooden stairs had once been painted the same color as the pillars. The paint had mostly worn off, leaving dirty gray depressions between what little fading green paint remained at the stairs' edges. Not sure about the state of the wooden treads, Dominic hung on to the black stair rail as he tested the first step.

The step had some give to it, and it groaned in protest of Dominic's weight, but it held. Dominic tentatively tried the second step. It was the same. He continued on up the stairs. Glen and Harry followed.

On the second-floor landing, all three men shined their flashlights down a narrow hallway. A series of closed doors and one open doorway were visible in the flashlights' beams.

As one, the men turned and shined their lights up the next flight of stairs. Not as wide but just as steep, the remainder of the stairs extended up toward the arched opening of an inky maw.

Harry groaned. "Oh man, that's not good."

Glen gave Harry a gentle punch. "Come on. It'll be an adventure."

"I don't like adventures," Harry said, sounding like a whiny child protesting his mother's attempt to get him to try something new.

Glen laughed. "Tough. Come on."

Glen pulled him up the stairs as Harry looked forlornly over his shoulder at Dominic, who gave Harry a thumbs-up and then turned toward his own adventure.

He wouldn't have admitted it, but Dominic wasn't too excited about his task, either.

Don't be a wuss, Dominic thought. He took a step down the narrow hallway.

The first two doors were locked. He thought that was weird, but he decided not to worry about it at the moment. Better to explore what he could reach easily before he took on battering down a locked door.

The third door led to a storeroom filled with boxes. Dominic opened one of the boxes and found robotic parts—circuitry and wiring, some gears, nuts, and bolts. In the second box, Dominic found a robotic vacuum in its original packaging. The other boxes contained more of the same.

The next room was also filled with boxes. These were all sealed but labeled. The boxes were stacked to the ceiling, but Dominic read the labels he could see.

"Fiona's hats," Dominic read out loud. "Fiona's shoes. Bakeware. Photo albums. First-floor books. Games. Puzzles. Souvenirs. Edwin's photography equipment."

Dominic stopped checking labels. These were apparently Murray's belongings. Dominic didn't know much about Edwin Murray, but he did know that his wife and kid had died. Poor guy. Fiona must have been his wife.

The boxes were dingy and dusty and musty. Moisture had gotten to them. They were sagging. Probably much of their contents were damaged. All the packed-up evidence of a guy's previously happy life was quite depressing. Dominic backed out of the room.

So far he hadn't found anything helpful. Certainly nothing that Fazbear would want.

Dominic continued on down the hall. In the next room, he found more boxes of Murray's belongings. Still nothing interesting.

In the room after that, however, things changed.

Given the glass half wall at the edge of the next room Dominic entered, he concluded he was in one of the factory's old offices. This office, however, had been redone into a living space. It held an old-fashioned high-back sofa, like the kind of thing you'd find in an old mansion, and two wing-backed chairs. They'd probably been pale yellow at some point, but now they were a dirty tan. Heavy dust was layered on what looked like antique end tables and an antique coffee table.

Dominic moved past the old furniture toward an opening on the far side of the room. Stepping through the opening, Dominic found himself in a small galley kitchen, which was lined with yellow Formica-covered counters, held a narrow fridge, a small four-burner range, and one deep, off-white farm-style sink. At the end of the kitchen, a two-person table was flush against the wall under a boarded-up window.

Dominic looked at the window. For the first time, he thought about all the boarded-up windows. He knew the building had been empty for months, but why were all the windows covered with nailed-into-place plywood, both inside and out? It wasn't like this was a dangerous part of town. It seemed a little weird.

Dominic's nose twitched as he realized he was smelling rotting food. Or, something he hoped was rotting food. He aimed his flashlight around the tiny kitchen. The counters and the table were empty, but when Dominic's light whipped across the lower part of the refrigerator, he froze. He peered at a large reddish-brown stain on the dirty light blue linoleum floor near the fridge's vent. A stiff wire, partly silver and partly rust-colored, lay in the middle of the stain.

Domonic took a step toward the fridge. At the same instant, a rat crept out from the narrow crack between the fridge and the end of the counter.

"Later," Dominic muttered to himself.

Dominic retraced his steps through the little living room and returned to the hallway. He poked his head through another door and shined his light around a tiny gray-tiled bathroom with a clawfoot tub. He continued on.

The next room Dominic came to was a large bedroom that held a dresser, a couple nightstands, a double bed, and a single bed that had been styled into a pretty impressive-looking white tiger. Dominic smiled, but then his smile faded. This bed must have belonged to Murray's kid. That was just plain sad. Dominic looked past the bed to a closed door. He took a step toward the door, but then his flashlight beam flitted past a set of narrow shelves. Piles of toys and a row of children's picture books filled the shelves. Both toys and books were shrouded in dust, and the books were limp, their spines blackened by mold. The building's moisture had taken its toll.

Dominic started to step past the bookshelf. Then he spotted something on the shelves that didn't belong.

Dominic walked around the end of the tiger bed and aimed his light next to a row of plastic cars. The light landed on a satchel not unlike the ones Dominic, Glen, and Harry had left on the first floor of the building. In fact, this satchel was identical to those. Given that Dominic's satchel and those of his friends were Fazbear Enterprises–issued satchels, Dominic had to conclude that this one was, too.

Had there been another team assigned to "handle things"? Why hadn't that team finished the job? And why was the satchel still here?

Dominic stepped forward and picked up the satchel. He sat down on the edge of the tiger bed and opened the leather case.

Amid the expected tools, Dominic was taken aback when his flashlight beam landed on a small, battery-powered tape recorder. Curious, he picked it up and looked in through the recorder's little window. The cassette tape in the recorder was stopped in the middle.

Dominic pressed rewind to see if the recorder's battery was still good. It was. The tape began spinning, returning to its start with a purring whir. When the tape was rewound, the recorder clicked off. The click felt unnaturally loud in the little room.

Dominic shook off a shiver and shined his light around the room to be sure he was still alone, which made him feel like a first-class fool. He shook off the heebie-jeebies that had suddenly set in for reasons he couldn't explain. He returned his attention to the recorder and pressed PLAY.

A shushing sound filled the room, followed by a crackle. Then a man's voice.

"I can't believe they sent us in here the week before Christmas," the man said. He sounded young, probably about Dominic's age. "Joan wants to kill me, and I don't blame her. We were supposed to decorate the tree with her nieces tonight. Instead, I'm trapped in here. And what the hell is up with that?"

Dominic stared at the recorder. Trapped? What did the guy mean by trapped?

". . . think we should pry the board off one of the windows," the voice on the recorder continued, "but Terrence says if we do that, we'll get fired. We're supposed to clean up a mess in here, not make another one, he says. But seriously? We can't get out and go home to our families tonight? I don't get why the door locked behind us to begin with. Why would it lock from the outside?"

Dominic, his finger trembling ever so slightly, pressed the STOP button on the recorder. He thought about the doors that had slammed shut behind him and his friends when they'd entered the building. He hadn't gone back to check the door. He'd just assumed they'd be able to get back out when they were ready. What if they couldn't?

A faint whir and a tapping sound came from the hall-way. Dominic stiffened and shined his light toward the doorway. It was empty. So was the hallway behind it. He didn't hear anything else.

Dominic shifted positions so he was facing the door. He pressed PLAY on the recorder.

A long sigh came from the recorder. "Okay, so I might as well document what we've done so far. For the record. I'm not about to get fired over this project. It's weird, and it sucks, but we're doing our best." The sound of rattling papers came from the recorder. Then a cleared throat.

"Terrence is the one who suggested we do what we've done," the voice on the recorder said. "Because we weren't given real clear instructions on what to do, we were pretty much at a loss at first. I mean, we're in an eerie building filled with old stuff and even older stuff and what are we supposed to do with it? Sort it? Catalog it? Terrence says that because he's a tech guy and I'm an engineer, we're probably not expected to go through boxes. He figured we're here to finish the projects we found on the first level. So that's what we've been doing. We started a few hours ago, and we worked until just past midnight. It's a good thing we have watches. With the windows all boarded up, you can't tell if it's night or day outside. I'm just glad we found that generator. Without it, we'd have had to rely on our flashlights, and who knows how long they'd have lasted."

Dominic stopped the recorder again. Generator?

Dominic stood. Taking the tape recorder with him, he left the small bedroom. He'd check behind the door near the beds later. If there was a generator in this building, he wanted to find it, and he doubted it was in what he suspected was a closet.

Dominic returned to the hall.

The unmistakable sound of an engine powering up sent a rumble through the building. The bare light bulb over Dominic's head came on.

He looked up and grinned, enjoying the ongoing

thrum of the motor. Glen and Harry must have found the generator.

"Way to go, guys," Dominic said.

He turned off his flashlight. Even though the overhead bulb wasn't doing much to push back the shadows in the hallway, Dominic could see well enough, and he had a feeling he should conserve his batteries.

Dominic looked up and down the hall. He figured he should continue to search this floor. Now that they had power, Glen and Harry probably would do the same with the third floor.

Dominic moved on down the hall, toward the next closed door. As he neared it, the same rotting smell he'd noticed in the kitchen returned. This time, though, the smell was more pronounced, and Dominic could tell what it was. He was smelling decayed flesh. Something nearby was definitely dead.

A rat? Probably.

Dominic looked at the closed door. Did he really want to go in there?

He exhaled and shrugged. He opened the door.

A bit of the hallway light bulb's weak light slipped in through the open doorway. Dominic pushed the door open wider, realizing that his shoulders were bunched up in anticipation of finding whatever was causing the foul odor.

But all he saw when he looked into the room were two rows of hanging clothing and a shelf of folded clothing. He also saw another door. That door, he realized, led back to the bedroom he was just in. Clever. Murray had turned one of the factory's small storage rooms into a closet.

Dominic wrinkled his nose. The smell was definitely stronger in here. It was probably just a dead animal, maybe behind one of the walls. Dominic backed away from the door and continued down the hall.

For the next several minutes, Dominic explored the remainder of the factory's second floor. He found nothing but more storage rooms, most of which were empty, and two more office spaces. These hadn't been converted to living space. They were stacked with old desks and chairs and also some pretty cool vintage office equipment. He found a 1920s Underwood typewriter that he planned to take with him when the job was done. He was pretty sure he could restore it, and he could envision it sitting on the shelf in his living room.

The farther Dominic got from the little apartment area, the less he smelled the decay. The rooms on the far end of the hall smelled mildewy, but he didn't get a whiff of anything rotting. That was nice.

Because power was running through the building again, he was able to turn on at least a bit of feeble lighting in each room. When he flipped the switches in some of the rooms, nothing happened, and then he'd pull out his flashlight for a quick inspection of each space.

The increased illumination, however, had relaxed Dominic enough that he was comfortable turning the tape recorder back on while he explored. The man's voice . . . Dominic wished he knew the guy's name . . . kept Dominic company while he poked around.

"The first thing we did," the man on the recorder said, "was make a few repairs to the building. The roof had some pretty bad leaks, and we took care of the worst ones . . . at least for the short term. The old tin roof obviously needs to be completely redone, but we plugged things up the best we could. We also shored up a few steps and tackled some of the building's old wiring. We realized we had to do that when we got the generator going and still didn't have much light. There was a short in the system that was causing a cascade failure. We rerouted a few things and got the lights working in most of the rooms. The bulbs are old, though, and we couldn't find any replacements, so that's a short-term fix as well."

Dominic reached the last room on the second floor. It was an old restroom. He tried the tap at one of the sinks. No water came out. Three stall doors were closed. Beneath the old wood panel doors, darkness puddled. Dominic didn't see the point in looking into the stalls, and he wasn't keen on doing it anyway . . . especially after he thought he saw movement in the blackness under one of the doors. *More rats*, he figured. No need to deal with that.

Dominic swiftly left the restroom and headed back down the hall. The man on the recorder continued to talk. ". . . assessed the condition of the endoskeletons we found on and near the worktable. Some were in early stages and needed a lot of work, but some just needed some adjustments. So, we went ahead and did that. Also, after we take a break and share Terrence's protein bar, we're going to go ahead and complete one pretty cool endoskeleton. From the waist up, it looks like it should be functional, but it's not moving." The man snorted. "And no wonder. The thing doesn't have legs. So, we're going to take some legs off one of the clearly nonfunctional animatronics and add them to the more advanced one."

The tape recorder clicked off just as Dominic made it back to the main staircase. From the floor above, he heard a heavy thud. Then he heard a murmur of voices and clomping footsteps coming down the stairs.

While he waited for Glen and Harry to join him, Dominic took the tape out of the recorder, flipped it over, reinserted it, and hit the PLAY button. He listened to the whisper purr of the tape looping around, but no other sound came out of the machine. Dominic fast-forwarded the tape and hit PLAY again. Still nothing. That was too bad. He wanted to know more about the other team.

Dominic stared at the recorder. Why had the recorder's owner left it behind? Dominic felt the skin on the back of his neck prickle as an unwelcome thought crept up from his subconscious.

"I wasn't seeing things," Harry said as Glen and Harry reached the second level.

"Sure, you were," Glen said. "You're spooked, and it's messing with your head."

"It is not," Harry insisted.

"Is, too," Glen said.

Dominic cocked his head and studied his buddies. "Are we back in kindergarten?" he asked. "What's going on?"

Glen rolled his eyes. "Nothing's going on. Harry thought he saw something move up on the third floor."

"I did!" Harry said.

"What's up there?" Dominic asked.

"Bunch of junk," Glen said. "Boxes of thread and machine parts. Old furniture. Some lumber. A mess of half-finished inventions. Not sure what most of them are supposed to be. Weird machines. The whole floor is one open space stuffed with old crap."

"And a generator," Dominic said, pointing at the faint yellow light coming from the bulb over their heads.

"Yeah, and a generator," Glen said. He clapped Harry on the back. "I thought it was a lost cause when we found it, but genius here got it going."

Harry shrugged and chewed on his thumbnail. "It's not going to run for very long," he said. "There's not much gas left in it."

"How long?" Dominic asked.

"A couple hours, maybe," Harry said.

"I think we should call it quits for the day," Glen said. "We can get some cans of gas and some light bulbs . . . most of the bulbs up there are on their last legs, like that one." He pointed over his head. "We can come back tomorrow."

"I hope we can," Dominic said.

"What's that mean?" Glen asked. "What did you find?" Glen looked down the hall. He put the back of his large-knuckled hand to his nose. "And what is that smell? I got a whiff of it as we passed this level, and I didn't think much of it. But now that I'm standing here . . . ." He contorted his puffy features. The bags under his eyes pleated, and his round cheeks expanded as he blew out air. "That's rank!"

Harry sniffed. "I don't smell anything."

"You never do," Glen said. He turned toward Dominic. "Seriously, did you find a dead animal or something?" Glen's eyes were suddenly jittery, and the ruddy skin around his nose was tight.

Dominic shook his head. "It must be behind a wall or something." He moved toward the stairs. "Come on. Let's head back downstairs, and I'll tell you what I found."

Glen looked down the hall and frowned. Then he shrugged. "Yeah, okay."

As Dominic led Glen and Harry down the sagging old steps, Dominic relayed what he'd found. He also explained what he'd heard on the tape.

"Trapped?" Harry yelped as they reached the main level.

"Another team?" Glen said. "Why didn't Ron tell us about them?"

"I plan to ask him," Dominic said.

Together, the three men strode past the main level's support pillars. Although still filled with darkened corners and relentless half-light, the factory floor was at least now illuminated by the flickering bulbs in several dust-coated, black-metal warehouse pendant lights. The lights, rather than lowering the freak factor of the factory, added to it. The intermittent gleam accentuated the cavernous feel of the place. Dominic couldn't wait to leave.

He and the others headed toward the closed double doors. There, however, they discovered that, like the other team, they, too, were stuck inside the building. The doors wouldn't open.

"There has to be another way out," Harry said breathily after they'd done everything they could think of to get the doors open.

"Why didn't we bring an axe . . . or a chainsaw?" Glen asked only half sarcastically.

"There has to be another way out," Harry repeated.

But there wasn't.

When they'd explored the main level before, Dominic and the others hadn't been looking for doors leading outside. Now they did look for those doors. And they found none.

"What kind of factory has just one set of doors?" Glen asked when they finished examining the perimeter of the first level.

That is a good question, Dominic thought. But this one didn't. He thought he could make out where two other doors used to be. Two door-size sections of brick looked newer; they were redder instead of the more faded pink of the rest of the factory's walls.

Dominic, Glen, and Harry gathered next to the long worktable. "What now?" Dominic asked. "I don't suppose there was a balcony or a fire escape on the third floor?"

Glen shook his head. "Nah. Nothing but boarded-up windows, just like down here."

Harry let out a gasp.

"What?" Glen asked, obviously exasperated.

Harry lifted a shaky finger and pointed at the garment rack behind the worktable. "Weren't there *two* court jester costumes when we first got here?"

Glen frowned and looked toward the row of costumes. "Who knows? It's not like we could see much with just our flashlights."

Dominic studied the costumes. Instead of hiding in shadows as they had been when Dominic had looked at them before, the costumes were illuminated by one of the hanging pendant lights. Dominic frowned. Had there been a second jester costume? He thought there had been. But there wasn't now, and since he and Glen and Harry were the only ones in here, Dominic must have remembered wrong.

"There were two," Harry whispered. "I notice stuff like that."

Glen and Dominic exchanged a look. Dominic noticed that a vein near Glen's temple was pulsing visibly.

Glen cleared his throat. "I hate to say this, but I think we need to go back up to the second floor and figure out what's causing that smell."

Dominic's chest tightened. "Why?" he asked. Although he knew the answer.

Glen shook his head. "I've smelled something like that one other time, and . . . well, let's just say I'm not so sure it's a dead animal up there."

"What do you mean?" Harry squeaked.

Glen ignored Harry. He looked at Dominic.

Dominic thought about the stain in front of the refrigerator. "I think you're right," he said to Glen.

Dominic pulled up the top of his T-shirt and breathed through it as he and Glen stared at what they'd found inside the refrigerator. He tried to block out the disgusting sound of Harry vomiting on the linoleum behind him. The sour stench of Harry's stomach contents merged with the sickly sweet smell of decaying flesh.

Glen lifted a foot and used it to push the refrigerator door closed. He turned away and strode out of the kitchen. Harry, wiping his mouth, stumbled after Glen. Dominic, his legs unsteady, followed the others.

Why hadn't he opened the refrigerator door earlier? He'd seen the stain. And he'd known what it was. Even in the mottled light of his flashlight's beam, he could recognize a bloodstain when he saw one. But he'd used the rat as an excuse not to listen to the little voice that had been nagging at him ever since he'd gotten his first whiff of the stench that permeated much of the factory's second floor.

Had he, on some strange level, known what was inside the refrigerator? No. How *could* he have known?

Dominic's mind replayed, in vivid detail, what he'd just seen. As it did, his stomach heaved. He didn't begrudge Harry for throwing up.

Dominic wondered if the man who'd been broken down and compressed like a compacted doll before being crammed into the fridge was the man who'd made the tape recording. Or was it Terrence? Or maybe it was someone else. Whoever it was had been garroted so violently that he was nearly decapitated. Then his limbs had been snapped and crimped so that his entire body could fit inside the fridge.

Glen stopped in the hallway and looked farther down the hall. He inhaled and closed his eyes. When he opened them again, he caught Dominic's gaze. "You're thinking what I'm thinking, right?"

Dominic thought about how strong the smell was in the makeshift closet. He also thought about how many parts of that closet lay in darkness and how he hadn't bothered to check to see what it might hold. He nodded. "Yeah."

"What?" Harry asked. He clutched at his stomach. His face was white and taut. His legs wobbled, and he started to sway.

Glen gave Harry an uncharacteristically gentle pat and helped Harry sit down on the top step of the staircase. "You wait here."

Harry didn't answer. Now seated, he leaned over and put his head between his knees.

Glen looked at Dominic. Dominic nodded. "Follow me," he said.

It took only seconds to reach the door that opened into the room Murray and his son had used as a closet. And it took just another second to flip the light switch by the door. Why hadn't Domonic turned on the light when he'd looked into the room earlier?

Probably because of that, he thought, when he saw the body hanging among the clothing that was stored on the rod running along the back wall of the room.

"Oh man," Glen breathed. "That's just . . ." He shook his head, but he didn't turn away from what they'd found.

Dominic couldn't look away, either.

In the gloom that had filled this room when he'd looked into it earlier, the man stowed tidily among a row of men's suits could have passed, at a glance, for more clothing. In even the unsteady light of the room's fading bulb, though, it was clear that the clothing was on a corpse, and the corpse was caught up on a hanger. A metal rod had been speared through the corpse's chest, running left to right, and the rod had been wired to a wooden suit hanger. The man hung upright from the hanger, like a side of beef dangling on a meat hook.

"Oh jeez," Glenn said. "He's been eviscerated."

Dominic dropped his gaze to the corpse's midsection. He put a hand over his mouth. What he'd first thought were just wrinkles in the man's jeans were actually entrails slopping over his belt.

"Do you think that's—" Glen began.

His question was cut off by the sound of Harry's shrill scream.

As one, Dominic and Glen whirled around and looked down the hall.

At first, Dominic wasn't sure what he was seeing when he gazed toward the top of the steps. Maybe his brain, not accustomed to witnessing such things, refused to process it. Maybe he was in shock. Maybe he was in denial.

Whatever caused his initial confusion abated quickly as Dominic faced the fact of what he was witnessing. He also faced the fact that there was nothing he could do to stop it. Before Dominic could even think about moving, Harry was dead.

And the court jester . . . not a real jester, obviously, but a bright pink and yellow-green court jester costume with a wide, leering grin—something *in* a grinning jester costume—was pulling Harry's brain out of the top of Harry's open skull.

Harry was dead—he had to be—but he was still sitting upright as whatever was in the jester costume scooped the grayish-beige pulpy lump out of Harry's head as if the jester wasn't a jester at all but rather was a bear pulling honey from a beehive. Harry's lifeless torso collapsed, and his body tumbled forward onto the stairs with a whump.

The jester, brain in the costumed jester's hand, turned and aimed his creepy, huge smile directly at Dominic. Dominic couldn't move.

Glen grabbed Dominic's arm. "Come on!" Glen shouted.

Dominic let Glen drag him backward along the hall. Dominic's legs were jelly, and he was having trouble breathing, but he was able to stay with Glen as Glen rushed them down the hall toward the secondary flight of stairs.

Dominic's head, which he realized was filled with a roaring sound as if his shock was a waterfall thundering through his consciousness and wiping out any semblance of reason or functionality, managed to grasp onto a coherent thought. *The slide*, he remembered.

They reached the slide just seconds after Harry's body landed on the main staircase treads. Glen manhandled Dominic into a sitting position on the top of the slide. He planted a hand between Dominic's shoulder blades and gave Dominic a shove.

"I'm right behind you," Glen said as Dominic started down the slide.

Indeed, Dominic could feel Glen's oversized work boots against his back as he skimmed down the slide. And when he landed on the lumpy, filthy, moist mattresses on the first floor, Glen landed almost simultaneously with him.

Glen was on his feet in half a second. He reached down and took Dominic's hand, pulling him up.

Glen looked right and left. "We need a place to hide," he whispered. His gaze snapped back and forth between the top of the slide and the bottom of the main staircase.

Dominic, now starting to think more clearly again, nodded. Unfortunately, the main floor didn't have a lot of hiding places. He pointed toward the big loom machine. "Maybe under the lace over there behind the machine?" he suggested.

Glen nodded sharply, once. "Good a place as any."

Dominic took the lead this time. Moving as quietly as he could, he ducked behind the nearest pillar and then hurried across the twenty feet or so that lay between the pillar and the machine. Checking over his shoulder to be sure they weren't being observed or followed, Dominic dove under a rotting pile of lace. Glen, again, was right behind him. Together, they huddled under the limp material. The lace was fetid. Dominic began breathing through his mouth. From the noisy inhales and exhales in Dominic's ear, it was clear Glen was doing the same.

For probably a full minute, Dominic and Glen breathed in silence. Dominic didn't want to talk. He was trying to hear through their panting respiration; he was listening for footfalls.

Eventually, the sounds of labored breathing turned into quieter quick puffs. They were calming, marginally. Still, Dominic couldn't hear anything else.

Dominic, who couldn't see anything through the filmy lace anyway, closed his eyes. He needed to think.

Harry had been right, Dominic realized. There had been a missing jester costume. But who, or what, was inside it?

Dominic badly wanted to get Glen's take on what was going on, but he knew better than to make a sound. Since they couldn't get out, they had to stay hidden. And quiet.

Dominic wouldn't have believed it was possible, but he fell asleep. Under the skin-crawlingly disgusting lace, he had closed his eyes and lost consciousness. He was only aware of this fact, though, when Glen elbowed Dominic and then clawed his way free of the lace.

Dominic blinked several times, remembered where he was, and hissed, "What are you doing?"

Glen extricated himself from the frilly material. He wiped cobwebs from his eyes. "Don't worry," Glen said.

"Whatever it is isn't down here. I've been listening for a while. I haven't heard a thing."

Dominic frowned, not convinced. He looked around. Everything looked the same as it had when they'd headed toward the doors, expecting to leave.

"We need a weapon," Glen said.

Dominic nodded. He wanted to ask what kind of weapon could stop something that could lop off the top of a man's head, but he didn't say anything.

"All I have in my toolbox that could work is a wire cutter and a wrench, and it's not a big one," Glen said. "Anything in your box that could work?"

Dominic shook his head. His tools were designed for intricate work, not for fighting off a serial killer.

"Maybe on the worktable," Glen said.

Dominic nodded again.

It wasn't normal for Glen to take charge, but Dominic was okay with it. He was out of his depth.

Their heads swiveling constantly, alert for any sign of danger, Dominic and Glen crossed the factory floor to the worktable. They began searching the area for something they could use as a weapon.

"You realize what's going on, don't you?" Glen asked.

Dominic frowned. Did he? Probably. But he kept silent. He waited for Glen to put in his two cents.

"Fazbear Entertainment is trying to clean up a mess," Glen said. "Then sent in a team to do that. Team A, let's call them. They failed."

"Understatement," Dominic muttered.

In spite of the situation, Glen forced a chuckle. "Yeah. So, we're Team B. And we're either going to stop whatever killed those other guys and killed—" Glen's voice caught. He cleared his throat. "Poor Harry," he said. He cleared his throat even louder. "Anyway, either we stop whatever's in that costume, or we're going to be sealed up in here just like those other guys."

"That's what I was thinking," Dominic said, but his mind wasn't on the conversation.

Dominic had just spotted something lying under the worktable, something that shot ice water through his veins. He froze as he gazed at the discarded, bloodied court jester costume that lay under the worktable.

Dominic sucked in his breath sharply.

"What?" Glen asked.

Dominic straightened. "I think—"

That was as far as he got because as he spoke, Glen walked around to the far side of the worktable. When Glen brushed past the costumes hanging on the garment rack, he didn't notice the movement of a fuchsia-and-white mushroom costume with gaping, round dark eyes and an O-shaped cavernous mouth.

"Glen!" Dominic shouted. "Look out!"

Glen didn't bother to turn around and find out what Dominic had seen. Wisely, he just started to run.

But it didn't make any difference. The mushroom man, or whatever was wearing the mushroom costume, had faster reflexes than Glen did. Before Glen could even take a step, the mushroom man's hand caught Glen by the back of his shirt collar. Glen flailed, but his efforts weren't enough.

The mushroom man's other hand grasped the back of Glen's brown leather belt. Then, in a motion so fast Dominic could barely follow it, the mushroom man lifted Glen off the ground and held him, belly down, back up, for an instant before taking one long stride and ramming Glen headfirst into the brick wall behind the garment rack.

Whatever wore the mushroom man costume had superhuman strength. Glen's head cracked against the brick and was instantly pulverized like a smashed melon. The crushed head, still attached to Glen's spine, was driven into his neck. And then Glen's shoulders accordioned into the wall. Glen was shredded tissue and mangled bone from the rib cage up when the mushroom let go of Glen's belt and dropped the corpse on the concrete.

That was when Dominic's brain finally got a message to his feet. He turned and ran.

Dominic burst onto the top level of the factory. He looked around wildly.

The factory's third floor was like his grandmother's attic on steroids. Over 1,500 square feet or so of brick-walled, cement-floored open space was crammed full of everything from basic cardboard boxes to wooden crates to old furniture to bolts of lace to stacks of character costumes similar to the ones on the first floor to mounds of unidentifiable machinery. Dominic felt like he'd walked into a musty, filthy flea market. Everything that stretched out before him was covered in dust and wilting from the moisture in the air.

On the far side of the expanse, the generator grumbled and chugged. Even over that racket, though, Dominic could hear something nearby. Probably another leak in the roof. Hopefully.

Dominic couldn't see the generator from where he

stood. He'd have to check it out, but for now, it sounded steady enough. And he had more immediate issues.

When Dominic had fled the murderous mushroom, he hadn't even thought about pausing on the second floor of the building. He knew by coming to the top level, he was boxing himself in, but he also thought the level, given what Glen had said, would have the best hiding spots.

Dominic had no way to get out of the building, at least not that he could think of at the moment. He thought the only way he could survive was to hide long enough for someone from Fazbear Entertainment to come in and look into the status of his team . . . although if he was being honest with himself, he wasn't sure anyone would actually check. And if they did, it wouldn't be soon. Terrence and the unnamed man on the tape recorder had been here a month before, and clearly no one had come in here since then. Dominic had a candy bar in his satchel, but that was it. And if the other faucets were as dry as the one he'd checked, he had no water unless he counted whatever was dripping through the roof.

Dominic wasn't going to last a month.

But would he even survive long enough to have the chance to last?

Dominic scanned the shadows on the stairway behind him. He was alone. But for how long?

"You could fight," Dominic muttered.

Yeah, he thought. He could fight. And he had to fight. Trying to wait out whatever wore the costumes wasn't an option.

Dominic, of course, understood that whatever he was up against wasn't something easily defeated like a man in an animal suit. Whatever he was facing was much more than a mere man. It was a monster, probably a robotic monster, but not necessarily. No matter what it was, however, there had to be a way to stop it.

Dominic looked at the jumble of machines. Maybe there was something he could use.

For the next several minutes, Dominic sorted through the machinery available to him, frequently pausing to check that the stairway was still empty. And he discovered that he might have a chance to survive.

The conglomeration of inventions stashed on this level of the factory was extensive, and because it was extensive, it contained nearly every motor part an engineer could hope to have on hand to build a monster-killing machine. Now, if only he had tools.

Dominic looked down the staircase for the hundredth time. It was still clear.

No way was he going down to the first floor, but he might get away with a quick jaunt to the second floor. That's where the other guy's satchel had been.

Dominic looked at the boxes and crates beyond the machinery. Maybe what he needed was already up here.

Yeah, but how long would it take to find it? No, he had to get the satchel on the second floor.

Dominic steeled himself. He began to tiptoe down the stairs.

His heart pounding the whole way, every nerve ending in his body on full alert, Dominic got to the second floor and began sidling down the hall. Every couple steps, he stopped and listened. Other than his own breathing and the continued drone of the generator, he heard nothing. The factory didn't even have the usual creaks and groans associated with old buildings. Other than the sound of the generator's motor, everything was preternaturally silent.

Rotating constantly to be sure nothing snuck up on him, Dominic darted down the hall. He was about to dash into the apartment when his footsteps faltered. He stopped and turned to goggle at the top of the staircase.

When Dominic had fled the first floor and ran to the third floor, he'd passed Harry's body on the second-floor landing. Now, however, Harry's body was gone. In its place, the pink-and-white mushroom costume lay in a crumpled pile.

The thing that was wearing the costumes had been up here.

Dominic's whole body went cold. What should he do? What *could* he do?

He looked up and down the hall. Finally, he made a decision.

Dominic dashed into the apartment's bedroom. Because he'd lost his flashlight long before Glen was killed, Dominic had to flick on the bedroom light to spot the satchel. As soon as he did, he hurtled around the tiger bed, grabbed the satchel, and retreated from the room even faster than he'd entered it.

No longer caring about being quiet, fully unglued and wanting to be back on the third level where his potential monster-killing machine waited for him, Dominic tore back out into the hallway and galloped up the stairs to the third floor. At the top of the steps, Dominic stopped and bent over to catch his breath. He clutched the satchel's handle like it was a lifeline.

Now that he had tools, he was confident he could build something to stop the costume-wearing killing machine. All he needed was a little time.

But time wasn't something he was going to get.

Before Dominic could take even one step toward the machinery that he'd hoped to transform into what he needed, the top costume in the pile of costumes near one of the wooden crates sat up. The costume, its faux fur matted and rotting, was a grayish-purple lion with a bedraggled mane and broken whiskers. The costume's decrepit appearance, however, did nothing to diminish the horror as it rose up from the pile and took a step toward Dominic.

Dominic whirled and lunged toward the stairs.

He didn't make it to the first tread.

The thing in the lion costume caught Dominic by the ankle just as he was about to descend the stairs. Dominic's feet went out from under him. He fell face-first, and his chin hit one of the hardwood treads.

Dominic cried out, but the impact of his chin was just the beginning of his discomfort. Yanked backward roughly, thudding up the stairs, Dominic was spun onto his back and slammed to the floor.

The impact vibrated through his entire skeletal system, and the pain was intense. But again, that pain was nothing.

A fireball of agony tore up through his midsection. Starting at his solar plexus, between his ribs, the torture seared up through his chest and grabbed him by the throat from the inside. It felt like a band of molten metal was choking him from within.

Dominic looked down, and he immediately opened his mouth to scream, however, it couldn't come out. This was because the thing in the lion suit had reached up through Dominic's solar plexus and grabbed his trachea from the inside. The lion was now yanking his trachea back down through his chest.

Dominic's heart, hammering impossibly fast, exploded in his chest. He fought for breath but couldn't find it. He reached for a coherent thought, but he couldn't grab that, either. Instead, Dominic could do nothing but give in to the darkness that, mercifully, smothered the fiery torment ripping him open from the inside out.

ABOUT THE AUTHORS

Scott Cawthon is the author of the bestselling video game series *Five Nights at Freddy's,* and while he is a game designer by trade, he is first and foremost a storyteller at heart. He is a graduate of the Art Institute of Houston and lives in Texas with his family.

Kelly Parra is the author of YA novels *Graffiti Girl, Invisible Touch,* and other supernatural short stories. In addition to her independent works, Kelly works with Kevin Anderson & Associates on a variety of projects. She resides in Central Coast, California, with her husband and two children.

Andrea Rains Waggener is an author, novelist, ghost-writer, essayist, short story writer, screenwriter, copywriter, editor, poet, and a proud member of Kevin Anderson & Associates' team of writers. In a past she prefers not to remember much, she was a claims adjuster, JCPenney's catalog order-taker (before computers!), appellate court clerk, legal writing instructor, and lawyer. Writing in genres that vary from her chick-lit novel, *Alternate Beauty*, to her dog how-to book, *Dog Parenting*, to her self-help book, *Healthy, Wealthy, & Wise*, to ghostwritten memoirs to ghostwritten YA, horror, mystery, and mainstream fiction projects, Andrea still manages to find time to watch the rain and obsess over her dog and her knitting, art, and music projects. She lives with her husband and said dog on the Washington Coast, and if she isn't at home creating something, she can be found walking on the beach.

Help!"

The voice on the radio came through loud and clear. It filled the small office space so forcefully that Kelly exhaled sharply. Her breath created an air current that rippled the memos and children's drawings pinned to a bulletin board on the wall above the radio.

Kelly had just finished installing a new electrolytic capacitor into the radio's workings, and when she heard the crystal clear voice, she whipped her hand back and stared at the radio in awe. She'd fixed it!

"Help!" the voice repeated.

Or had she? Kelly frowned. That voice . . . it was clear now, not lost in static like it had been when she and the others had first heard it. But it was the same voice.

Lucia, who had been sitting cross-legged on the floor flipping through a small crumpled notebook, got up. She crossed the room and leaned over Kelly's shoulder.

"Help me. I'm trapped in the old pizzeria," the voice said.

Kelly looked up at Lucia.

"It's the Mimic," Lucia said unnecessarily.

Yeah, Kelly thought, *tell me something I don't know.* She shook her head. "I thought I'd be able to fix it when you found those parts, but all I was able to do was clear up the local signal. I'm still not getting outside the building." She sighed. "I can't believe the Mimic thinks we're going to fall for that trick again."

A couple hours before, when they'd first heard the garbled version of the voice, Kelly, Lucia, Adrian, and Jayce had thought they'd found others trapped in the old pizzeria with them. It was heartening to think they weren't on their own. Even though Kelly tended to be a loner, she knew that in dire situations, strength in numbers was a real thing. Unfortunately, there weren't any others. There was just the Mimic, which had used the radio to lure them to a room off the area behind the stage.

Kelly shivered when she thought about what would have happened if she or anyone else had just barged all the way into the room when they'd gotten the hidden door open. The fact that they'd managed to run before the Mimic got one of them was a miracle. Not that Kelly believed in miracles. With a hypochondriac mother who spent most of her time in bed nursing this or that only-in-her-head illness and a father who was a workaholic police detective, Kelly's life hadn't given her any evidence of miracles. All she'd learned from her experiences was two things: One, it was best to know how to entertain yourself; and two, really bad things happened. Her dad, on the rare occasions he was home, told horrific stories of pain and loss. He made it clear that Kelly would be a fool to think life was anything but suffering.

Lucia waved the notebook she held. "I think I might have a little insight into how the Mimic's programming works." She opened the notebook and pointed at a page of penciled handwriting.

Kelly squinted at the smudged hen scratch. "You can read that?"

"A little." Lucia pointed at a battered shoebox sitting on the floor next to the desk. "This was in that box I found at the back of the bottom desk drawer, the one the radio parts were in. Apparently, this notebook belonged to one of the engineers on the original Fazbear Entertainment animatronic creation team, the ones who built all the characters that provided entertainment in the Freddy Fazbear pizzerias." She flipped through the notebook and tapped one of its pages. "I can't make it all out, but from what I can tell, when the team created the Mimic line, they didn't want to have to program in every show routine, step-by-step. That was a lot of coding, so they just programmed the Mimic to basically watch and learn. Not only could a Mimic fit into any costume, it was designed to observe the other routines and then mimic them."

Kelly raised an eyebrow. "That sounds like tricky programming."

"Yeah, too tricky." Lucia flipped a page of the notebook. She screwed up her face as she pointed at the few unsmudged words on the page. "I wish I could read all of this, but it seems like the original Mimic began mimicking not just the other animatronics but also people.

And it did it in ways that weren't intended. I'm not sure what it did. I can just make out the words *misconstrue, scared, potential disaster,* and *deactivate remaining Mimic endos.*"

Kelly rubbed her arms. "Okay," she said, "but what does that have to do with the Mimic's attempt to trick us?"

Lucia closed the notebook. "I think the Mimic might seem like a malevolent creature to us, but it's really just a robot that was designed to copy what it observes. At some point, it must have seen maybe something like a hide-and-seek game, or whatever. It probably can't reason that the trick would only work once."

"Help!" the voice said again.

Kelly looked at the radio. "Maybe we can use this to our advantage. If it wants to lure us to it, it will be where it says it is, right?"

Lucia nodded. Her wild curls bounced. "Brilliant." She reached out and picked up the mike. "Where are you?" she asked.

"I'm trapped in the janitor's supply room," the voice said.

"Well, now it's just being stupid," Kelly said. "We searched that room. There's no way anyone is trapped in there."

"Clearly, its internal logic doesn't extend to reasoning out what we might or might not have done yet," Lucia said. "Maybe . . ." She stopped when a metallic thud sounded inside the duct leading away from the vent opening under the table that held the radio.

Kelly jumped up. Both she and Lucia retreated to the other side of the room.

"Maybe it's smarter than we think," Kelly whispered. She stared at the vent opening.

After Adrian and Jayce had crawled into that opening, Kelly and Lucia had simply leaned the vent cover over the opening; it wasn't attached. Whatever was coming toward the office through the duct would easily be able to get out into the room.

"Maybe it's not the Mimic," Lucia whispered back. "It could be Adrian and Jayce."

Kelly listened hard. She heard a faint clunk followed by a *skirr* that sounded like fabric slipping over dusty metal. She leaned toward Lucia and whispered even more quietly into Lucia's ear. "The sound is too uniform to be coming from two. Whoever, or whatever, is in there is alone."

Lucia frowned and listened. She turned and glanced at the makeshift barricade blocking the office door. She looked back at Kelly, who nodded.

Without exchanging another word, Kelly and Lucia each took an end of the filing cabinet that was lying on top of the desk shoved in front of the door. Kelly knew she and Lucia were thinking the same thing. If the Mimic could fool them once, maybe it was doing it again. It made them think it was someplace else and was now trying to sneak up on them through the ductwork. They had to get out of the office.

Kelly and Lucia set the filing cabinet on the floor, and they started to move the desk. But they weren't fast enough. The vent cover fell onto the floor with a clatter.

Lucia ran over and picked up the desk chair Kelly had been using moments before. She raised it above her head and stood by the table.

Kelly continued shoving at the desk on her own, but she kept an eye on the vent opening. When she saw a thick thatch of disheveled black hair and a pale face with equally thick and black framed glasses, she called out, "Wait! It's Jayce."

Lucia exhaled loudly and set down the chair. She bent over and held out a hand to help their friend out of the duct.

"Where's Adrian?" Lucia asked as she hauled the small, skinny guy up onto his feet.

One look at Jayce's expression told Kelly all she needed to know about Adrian. The dust covering Jayce's face was bisected by light trails running down from his eyes. They were the tracks left by tears, Kelly realized immediately. Jayce's red eyes and dull gaze confirmed her conclusion.

Lucia, maybe because she didn't want to understand, took longer to realize the obvious. "Jayce? Where's Adrian?"

Jayce started to shake. He shook so hard that Kelly rushed over and helped him sit. Once he was in the chair, she kept her hand on his shoulder to try to steady him. She leaned down and said, "He's gone, isn't he?"

Jayce leaned forward and put his face in his hands. He started sobbing and babbling. His words were mostly incoherent, but one sentence was clear: "I couldn't do anything."

Lucia took a step backward and stared at Jayce. Her face had lost all its color. Her eyes were glassy.

Kelly knelt down and put an arm around Jayce. She had no idea what to say, but the guy clearly needed comfort. Whatever had happened—Kelly couldn't make sense of what he was saying—had been bad.

Lucia suddenly rushed forward. She grabbed Jayce's wrists and snatched his hands from his face. "Get it together. Tell us what happened!"

Kelly blinked at Lucia's harsh tone. Then she got it. Lucia was coping with her grief by going right to anger. Kelly tried to calm her. "Lucia," she said, "Jayce is in shock."

"I don't care!" Lucia yelled.

Lucia's outburst snapped Jayce out of his stupor. He freed himself of Kelly's embrace and shot to his feet.

"There was nothing I could do!" he shouted back. "Adrian was trying to get out through the fan, and he must have fallen. The Mimic had him before I could even move! If I'd come out of my hiding place, I'd be dead, too! Is that what you wanted?"

"Yes!" Lucia screamed.

Jayce blanched and blinked. Then he said softly, "Well, you probably won't have to wait long. We're the only three left. Maybe I'll be next."

Lucia didn't say anything. She just balled up her fists and glared at Jayce.

Kelly sighed. "Wade and Joel . . . you found them?" she asked Jayce.

Jayce looked her way and nodded. "I think they'd been trying to get out through the fan, too. We found their . . . We found what was left of them when we went to the systems room."

Lucia turned and crossed to the other side of the office. She faced a yellowed, curling Fazbear Pizzeria poster and dropped her head. Kelly watched as Lucia's shoulders hunched and started shaking.

The fact that Lucia had a crush on Adrian had been

obvious to Kelly for a long time. Kelly never said much at school, but she observed. She was well aware of the dynamic between those around her. Hope had been pretty straightforward; she'd loved Adrian. Adrian had been equally transparent; he'd loved Hope back. Wade had loved Hope, too, but he'd tried to hide it. Jayce was crazy about Lucia, but Lucia only had eyes for Adrian. Joel had never seemed to care much about anyone but Joel. Kelly, if she'd been honest with herself, had liked Nick, but Nick had never shown any interest in her.

Maybe because she'd always been on the fringes of social life at school or maybe because she'd been hardened by the stories her dad had told about his work, Kelly had been shocked by the others' deaths, but she wasn't devastated. Not like Lucia was right now anyway.

"Help!" the voice on the radio said again.

Jayce sucked in a breath and stared at the radio. His eyes got huge. "Is that—?"

"The Mimic," Kelly said. "It's trying to lure us out again."

Jayce wiped his face. He frowned at the radio. "But that means—"

"That we know where it is right now," Kelly finished for him again. "Yeah."

Jayce swallowed and adjusted his glasses. He rubbed his jaw, clearly thinking. Glancing once at Lucia, who still stood with her back to the room, he cleared his throat.

"I had to crawl through a lot of the ductwork to get back here," Jayce said. "I took a couple wrong turns and learned more than I wanted to about how the ducts are laid out. The ducts are old, and some of the seams are rusting out, maybe on the verge of collapse, but they're mostly passable. While I was in them, I got an idea." He glanced at Lucia's back. "I was thinking we could lure the Mimic into one of the rooms. I thought I could go into the room and wait until the thing came after me, then I could escape into a duct while you two block the door."

Lucia whirled around and glowered at Jayce. "That's stupid. Why wouldn't the Mimic just go after you in the ducts? It can expand and contract, remember?"

Jayce flinched away from Lucia's anger. "I know, but it's the weight of it. I don't think the duct could hold it. As long as I could get ahead of the Mimic, if it tried to follow me, I think the duct seams would fail, and the Mimic would fall through the duct."

Lucia frowned and thought about that. She looked at Kelly.

Kelly shrugged. "You're the one who read the user's manual, but it makes sense to me. And if we could convince the Mimic we're coming to the janitor's supply room, we won't have to worry about it jumping out at us while we're setting up the trap."

Lucia nodded slowly. Then, ignoring Jayce, she walked over and picked up the radio's mike.

"Hello," Lucia said into the mike. "Are you still there?"

The voice replied immediately. "Yes. Help. I'm trapped in the janitor's supply room."

"Okay," Lucia said. "Stay where you are. We're coming to find you." She looked at Kelly, then she keyed the mike again. "It might take us a while because one of us is hurt, but we're coming."

"Thank you," the voice said.

"How nice," Lucia said in a voice heavy with sarcasm, "it's a *polite* murderous robot creature."

One corner of Jayce's mouth lifted up in a half smile. Kelly felt sorry for him. He so wanted Lucia to like him as much as he liked her.

Kelly put her back to Jayce and caught Lucia's gaze. Kelly used her head to indicate Jayce. She raised her eyebrows and gave Lucia a pointed look. *Apologize to the guy,* Kelly tried to say with her expression.

Lucia was quick to catch on. That was why Kelly liked her. Lucia scowled, but then she stepped over to Jayce. She took his hand. "I'm sorry I yelled at you," she said.

Kelly didn't think Lucia sounded all that sorry, but the words were a start. "We're all in shock," Kelly said, trying to help along the apology. "We're not acting like ourselves."

Lucia quirked her lips, but she nodded.

"It's okay," Jayce said. "I understand."

Lucia was lying when she'd said she was sorry. She wasn't sorry. She was still furious with Jayce for letting Adrian die. But she didn't have time to indulge her feelings right now. Jayce might have been a coward, but he had a good idea. And they needed to act on it while the Mimic was waiting for them to come to the janitor's supply room.

"We need a plan," Lucia said. "And I think I have one."

Lucia started telling Kelly and Jayce about the key she'd found. Kelly listened intently. Jayce looked past Lucia's shoulder. His child-size fingers kept fiddling with the drawing pens in his pocket protector; she knew he was itching to pull one out and retreat to a corner so he could draw his way into oblivion. If only he could draw Adrian back to life.

Every time Lucia let herself take in the reality of Adrian's death, she couldn't breathe; it felt like an invisible hand was reaching into her chest and crushing her heart. Adrian was gone. Adrian, who had been the shining light in her world since her family had moved to this miserable town, was gone.

"Lucia?" Kelly said.

Lucia summoned her willpower, and she managed to take in a breath. What had she been saying?

"You were telling us about the key that you think goes to the deadbolt on the door to that storage room at the end of the back hall," Kelly said. "Then you stopped talking. You might have stopped breathing, too."

Lucia forcefully pulled in another lungful of air. "Sorry. I—" She shook her head. "Yeah, so since we can lock that room, I thought that would be the best place for our trap. But we need to know whether there's ductwork to that room."

The radio spit static. Then the voice asked, "Are you coming to help? I'm scared."

Lucia snorted. "Scared. Ha!"

Kelly reached for the radio. "Hang on! We're coming. It won't be much longer!"

She looked at Lucia.

Kelly's expression was tight. Her eyes were slightly narrowed, and a furrow bunched between her brows. Lucia interpreted the look as judgment for what Lucia had said to Jayce—she'd basically told Jayce she'd rather that he'd died instead of Adrian. But that was true. No matter what she said now, Jayce wasn't going to feel any better. And besides, they didn't have time to deal with Jayce's feelings.

Jayce continued to fidget with his drawing pens, and he continued to avoid Lucia's gaze. But he spoke. "If I was oriented correctly, I'm pretty sure I crawled past the vent in that room," he said. "It's actually exactly what we want. It's behind some boxes; I could see them through the vent grate. If we could get in there and take the vent cover off but leave it propped over the opening, the Mimic wouldn't even see it behind the boxes. And it's a smaller vent opening than most of the others, too; the Mimic might not even be able to get into it. Once the Mimic comes for me, I can run behind the boxes and escape into the vent while you two deadbolt the door."

"That could work," Lucia said. She pursed her lips. "Like I said before, we don't know exactly how compact the Mimic can get, but hopefully you're right about its weight."

Jayce nodded without looking up.

"Why does it have to be you, Jayce?" Kelly asked. "Being the bait is going to be dangerous. Maybe we should put our names in a box or something and draw for it."

Jayce lifted his head. He blinked at Kelly and gave her a small smile. "That's nice, but no. It has to be me. I've been in the ducts. I know how to move through them. And . . . I need . . . I need to do this." He flicked a glance at Lucia.

Kelly sighed. "Okay." She looked at Lucia. "But what if the Mimic is strong enough to break through a deadbolt?"

Lucia thought about the question. It was a good one. The Mimic was a powerful machine. It ripped apart human bodies as if they were made of gauze; it could very well snap a deadbolt.

"You have a point," Lucia said.

"We need to barricade the door, too," Kelly said.

"How do you barricade a door that opens inward?" Jayce asked.

Lucia frowned. She chewed on her lower lip for a few seconds while she ran through possible options. "Okay," she said finally, "I have an idea. Come on, Kelly. Help me move the desk." Lucia stepped toward the desk.

"Where are we going?" Jayce asked in a pitifully small voice.

Lucia blew out air and turned toward Jayce. She didn't want to take the time to explain her plan. She just wanted to do it. But she knew Jayce was scared, and he had every right to be. She forced herself to be patient.

"We need a couple tables," Lucia said. "We need a long one, bigger than the storage room doorway. We'll break the legs off it so it's basically a slab we'll use to cover the door opening. Then we'll need a smaller table, one about the width of the hallway. We'll use that to wedge the longer tabletop in place; we'll shove the smaller table between the longer table on one side and the hallway wall on the other side. That way, even if the Mimic breaks through the deadbolt, the doorway will be blocked. I think we can find both tables in the employee's lounge."

Kelly slowly nodded. "That should work. So, we'll need to get the tables ready, right? Like leave them in the hallway or something? Then Jayce," she looked at him, "you'll lure the Mimic into the storage room and go for the vent to escape. While you're doing that, we'll close and deadbolt the door and position the tables. Because we hope the vent will be too small or heavy for the Mimic to make it through, it will be trapped." She shifted her gaze to Lucia. "Right?"

"That's it in a nutshell," Lucia said.

Kelly and Jayce were silent. No one moved.

Lucia's patience ran out. She positioned herself at one end of the desk. "If we're doing this, the first thing we need to do is move this desk. Kelly?"

"Hang on a second," Kelly said. She picked up the radio's mike. "Hello? Are you there?"

The radio was silent.

Lucia felt the muscles in her neck and shoulders clench. Her stomach constricted.

"Hello?" Kelly repeated. "I'm sorry we were delayed. But we're coming now." She leaned over the radio as if telepathically commanding the voice to come through its speakers.

Nothing.

Kelly turned and looked from Lucia to Jayce. The skin around Jayce's eyes pulled inward. His breath started coming in quick little bursts.

Kelly tried one more time. "Are you there?" she said into the mike.

Lucia counted to five. Then she said, "I think the Mimic has caught on."

Jayce hugged himself. Kelly set down the radio's mike. Her hand was trembling.

"But it doesn't matter," Lucia said. "The only chance

we have is to trap it." She looked toward the office door. "We have to go out there."

When Lucia had agreed to Adrian's suggestion of a double date, Jayce had been over the moon. He had fallen for Lucia the first moment he'd met her, on a rainy afternoon at Adrian's house.

"This is my new neighbor," Adrian had said when he'd introduced Lucia to Jayce.

And Jayce was a goner. He wasn't sure what had gotten him. Was it the wild hair? The funky clothes? The sensual mouth? Maybe it was the way one of Lucia's eyes was larger than the other; it gave her a quizzical look Jayce thought was beyond charming. Maybe it was none of those things. Maybe it was her mind. She was the smartest girl Jayce had ever met. She thought in ways no one else did. He was in awe of her. He'd been so excited about the double date; he'd thought it was going to be the start of their future together.

Jayce understood now that he and Lucia had no future. Not even if they survived. And he didn't think the odds were that great that they were going to make it. Not him anyway. The real reason he'd insisted on being the bait for their trap was because he didn't think the bait would live for long.

For the moment, though, he let himself enjoy watching Lucia. He loved the way she moved. She always walked with purpose, her head and shoulders tilted slightly forward as if she couldn't wait to get where she was going.

Now, she led Kelly and Jayce down the red-walled hall toward the door to the employee's lounge. Her head swiveled right and left as they passed a torn poster of Freddy Fazbear. From the tilt of her head, Jayce could tell Lucia was listening hard. So was Jayce.

It took just a couple seconds to reach the doorway to the employee's lounge. Lucia led the others through the shadowed opening.

Lucia was stepping carefully, but hiking boots weren't the stealthiest of shoes. Her rubber soles scuffed the dirty tiles, making a rough sliding sound. Jayce and Kelly were quieter; they tiptoed around the crumpled papers and flattened paper cups that were scattered over the floor.

A few feet into the room, Lucia stopped and looked around. Her gaze landed on a long table leaning against a few of the black metal lockers. She motioned for Kelly and Jayce to follow her, and she headed that way.

A faint clink froze Lucia mid-step. Jayce and Kelly stopped, too. Jayce's breath caught at the back of his throat. His legs quivered, and he clutched Kelly's arm. Kelly didn't protest; she didn't move at all.

No one spoke.

What direction had the sound come from? Jayce thought the noise had originated from someplace close. Could something in the ductwork have made the sound? Air did move in there. Metal expanded and contracted. Could that have been the source of the sound?

Lucia looked up at the recessed ceiling lights. Though dim, they were steady. Jayce knew what she was thinking—lights always flickered when the Mimic was close.

How close could it get before they flickered, though? Jayce had never paid enough attention to answer that question.

Jayce rotated silently and peered into every shrouded

part of the room. He squinted at a couple coats hanging in a corner opposite the lockers. *Were* they coats? Jayce had already seen that the Mimic could get into and out of costumes. What if the seemingly limp, empty sleeves in the corner weren't empty at all?

Lucia had apparently decided it was safe to continue. She took another step. And another.

Kelly and Jayce began moving forward again, too.

Lucia was now passing a locker door that was slightly ajar. Jayce's gaze zeroed in on the two-inch gap that revealed absolute blackness within the locker. Had that locker been open when they'd been in here before?

The last time Jayce had been in this room, he'd been scared out of his mind. He had a vague memory of standing with his back to the lockers. Had they all been closed then? He couldn't remember. But something about that locker . . .

The locker door twitched.

"Lucia!" Jayce shouted.

Lucia whirled, her eyes wide, her face flushed. Jayce couldn't tell if she was scared or angry. Probably both.

"Wha—?" Lucia began.

The lights flickered.

The locker door shot all the way open. Metal slammed against metal.

The room went dark.

Kelly immediately jerked Jayce around. He stumbled but stayed upright as she hauled him back the way they'd come.

Jayce wanted to call out Lucia's name, but he couldn't get his voice to work. His throat had closed up; his mouth was dry.

Another bang. A scrape. The familiar *tap-hiss-rasp*. Pounding footsteps. A loud crash and a grunt.

Kelly whisked Jayce out into the front hall. There, the lights were still on. Jayce tried to turn back to see if any of that light could pierce through the inkiness in the lounge so he could see Lucia.

Kelly didn't give Jayce enough time to look. She immediately hauled him down the hall toward the office. She didn't enter the office, though. She just pulled the door closed. Then she turned around and raced, with Jayce in tow, down the main hall toward the lobby. As she went, she closed every open door.

Jayce strained to hear the sounds coming from the lounge. He heard the crunch of wood. A slap. A slithering sound.

Jayce tried to free himself from Kelly. He had to go back and help Lucia. He knew she was still alive because he hadn't heard her scream. Maybe she was hiding. He needed to get to her.

Kelly, however, wouldn't let Jayce go. When he wriggled his arm, she clutched him tighter.

They'd reached the lobby when the resounding whack of a door slamming preceded thundering footsteps. Jayce wanted to cheer. He knew that sound. Lucia was tearing down the hall after them.

Even as Kelly dragged him toward the dining room, Jayce watched Lucia coming toward them. He winced. Lucia's face, rigid and white, was streaked with blood that ran down over her forehead from her hairline. Jayce whimpered when he realized that Lucia's scalp was torn. She was missing a chunk of her wonderful curly black hair.

Lucia caught up with Kelly and Jayce when they were just a few feet into the dining room. "We have to hide," she hissed. "The closed door won't slow it down." She wiped blood from her eyes as she dashed toward a pile of rubble outside the door of one of the party rooms. "Back there," she said.

Kelly apparently agreed with Lucia's course of action because she immediately tugged on Jayce's arm and led him around a stack of concrete blocks so they could hunker in next to Lucia, who was already tucking herself behind a tangle of endoskeleton parts and broken lumber.

Lucia curled herself into the smallest space possible to make room for Kelly and Jayce. They squeezed in next to her. They all attempted to slow their breakneck pace and much-too-loud breathing.

The *tap-hiss-rasp* they all knew too well sounded from beyond the lobby. Kelly gripped Jayce's hand.

The dining room lights flickered . . . and went out.

Lucia wasn't sure how long they crouched in the blackness. One minute? Ten? An hour?

Time stopped having significance when you were hiding in the dark. Every muscle in Lucia's body was bunched in readiness to flee. Adrenaline made her so jittery she could barely stand being in her own skin.

Warm wetness continued to flow down Lucia's face. She made no move to staunch it.

Even though she was trying to be silent, Lucia couldn't hold her breath. Her lungs were desperate for air. She tried to take tiny breaths, but she could hear herself inhaling and exhaling. She could hear Kelly and Jayce, too. Could the Mimic hear them?

Lucia closed her eyes and thought about the user's manual she'd read. Unfortunately, the manual had been miserably lacking in details about the Mimic. She understood its ability to change its size and configuration to fit different costumes. She understood its strength. But she knew little about its sensory processors. How well did it see and hear?

Lucia's eyes flew open when a hand closed around her wrist. She flinched but immediately realized it was only Kelly. She also realized that the dining room lights were back on.

Lucia tilted her head and listened. She could hear the barest hint of the tap–hiss–rasp in the distance, the sound was heading down the front hallway. The Mimic was retracing its steps and going toward the office. Maybe it thought they were hiding in one of those rooms. Maybe it intended to get a different costume from the Parts and Service Room.

Lucia had only seen a brief glimpse of the Mimic when it had erupted from the locker in the employee's lounge. That glimpse had revealed what had looked like an upright gray mouse . . . maybe. Lucia had been more concerned about jumping out of the Mimic's reach than trying to label its costume. The Mimic almost had her. It had grabbed her by the hair and twisted. If it had gotten a grip on her head, as it had obviously intended to do, she wouldn't have her head any longer. Thankfully, her thick, curly hair had misled the Mimic. It had painfully relieved her of a good hunk of that hair, but at least her head was still connected to her neck. She'd been able to scramble out of the Mimic's reach and thrash her way out of the lounge before it caught up to her.

Lucia continued to listen. Now, she couldn't hear anything except her breathing and that of Kelly and Jayce.

Lucia lifted a hand and held it flat in front of Kelly, a signal for them to wait a little longer. They needed the Mimic to get as far from the dining room as possible.

Lucia counted to sixty—three times. Then she nodded to Kelly, who nudged Jayce, and the trio carefully crawled out of their hiding place.

When they were all on their feet, Lucia immediately took off, moving as fast and quietly as possible. Skirting around one of the piles of body parts, she headed toward a heap of broken furniture.

Lucia picked up a one-legged chair, carefully set it aside, and pointed at a long table. "This is what we need," she whispered.

Lucia looked toward the archway to the lobby. The lobby lights were on steady. No sound came from the hallway. With any luck, the Mimic was at the far end of the hall. Would it hear the noise they were about to make?

Lucia looked at Kelly and Jayce. Jayce was shivering; he was barely holding it together. Kelly was stoic.

"We need to get the legs off that long table," Lucia explained. "We'll carry it down the hall and lean it against the wall by the door to the storage room. We also need that smaller table." Lucia gestured at a two-seater table lying on its side against a pile of endoskeleton parts. The little table still had all four of its legs.

"Kelly, do you think you could lift that?" Lucia asked. "Or drag it? I think it's just the right size."

Kelly nodded. "That looks pretty light," she said. "I can handle it."

"Okay, good," Lucia said. "We're going to need to do this fast because we're going to make some noise." She looked at Jayce. "If I kick off one of these table legs, can you manage the other one?"

Jayce wiped his nose and looked at the table leg. He nodded.

"Good. Once the legs are off, we'll each take an end. I'll go backward. You'll go forward. Move as fast as you can. I'll keep up."

Jayce nodded. His Adam's apple bobbed up and down twice.

"Ready?" Lucia asked Kelly. "You can go ahead and start carrying your table to the back storage room."

Kelly shook her head. "Wait." She leaned over and grabbed the hem of Lucia's long skirt.

Before Lucia could protest, Kelly ripped the bottom of the skirt. She tore off a strip of fabric.

"If we don't stop that bleeding," Kelly said, pointing at Lucia's head, "you're going to start feeling pretty faint."

Lucia frowned and started to shake her head. She was immediately dizzy. Okay. Maybe Kelly had a point.

Lucia let Kelly wrap a strip of the skirt around Lucia's head. The fabric scraped at the raw wound; it stung, and Lucia's eyes moistened. She blinked the tears away.

"Okay," Kelly said. "That should do it." She stepped back and studied Lucia. "And now you look badass. Doesn't she, Jayce?"

Jayce flicked a shy glance at Lucia. "Like a warrior goddess," he said.

Lucia snorted.

"Now, Kelly," Lucia said. "You need to go."

Kelly nodded. She picked up the table and began carrying it, legs away from her, through the dining room.

"Okay," Lucia said to Jayce, "let's do this."

Lucia positioned herself next to one of the long table's legs. She waited for Jayce to move over to the other leg.

"On three," Lucia said to Jayce.

Jayce readied himself.

"One, two, three." Lucia swung her foot back and kicked the table leg. Jayce did the same.

The wood legs cracked. Lucia and Jayce kicked again, and the legs broke away from the table. As soon they did, Lucia bent over and lifted one end of the table. Jayce quickly hefted the other end.

Lucia started walking backward as fast as she could. Jayce trotted forward. They carried the table past the other broken furniture and past the piles of metal and flesh-and-blood body parts.

Jayce helped Lucia prop the tabletop against the wall next to the storeroom door. Kelly pushed her little table into the open doorway of the systems room. Jayce tried not to think about what was beyond that door. Three people he'd known were in pieces inside that room; if he let himself think about it, he wouldn't be able to function.

"Okay," Lucia said. She looked at the tables. "I don't think the Mimic will think anything about these tables. I doubt its ability to reason is that advanced."

"I hope you're right," Jayce said. His voice cracked on the word *hope*. He was ashamed of how terrified he sounded.

Lucia, however, surprised him by touching the back of his hand. The ferocious expression she'd worn since she'd come barreling out of the employee's lounge softened for an instant. "Are you sure you want to do this? I can be the bait instead."

Jayce nodded. He was so scared, he was afraid he was going to pee his pants. But he wasn't going to wuss out now.

"Okay," Lucia said. "We should do this before the Mimic finds us all here." She turned toward Kelly. "I think you and I should go to the arcade. There are plenty of places to hide there, and we'll be able to see down the hall. We'll know when the Mimic is heading toward the storage room, and it will only take a few seconds to run down the hall, lock the door, and position the tables to block it."

Kelly nodded.

Lucia rotated back to Jayce. "It's all you now. Get the Mimic into the storage room and then get into that duct. Make sure you're fast, really fast. Yeah?"

Jayce nodded. His bowels felt like they were shriveling up inside his belly.

"Like I said before, after the Mimic follows you into the room, Jayce," Lucia said, "Kelly and I will deadbolt the door and use the tables to barricade it."

Jayce nodded again. A sharp nod. He wanted Lucia to go now. If he thought anymore about what he was going to do, he wouldn't be able to do it.

Lucia seemed to understand that. She reached out and patted his shoulder awkwardly. "Okay. Let's do this."

Kelly gave Jayce a long look. Her eyes were soft, as if she fully understood all the complexity of his feelings right now—his longing for Lucia's caring and approval, his regret, his dread.

"Go," Jayce said.

Kelly looked like she wanted to hug Jayce, but she didn't. Neither did Lucia. They both just turned away.

"Wait!" Jayce blurted.

Lucia and Kelly rotated back toward him.

Before he could talk himself out of his whim, Jayce reached out and grasped Lucia by the shoulders. Quickly pulling her close, he kissed her.

Jayce had never kissed a girl before, so he wasn't sure what he was doing. But he knew right away that his kiss wasn't the tentative kiss of a shy boy initiating his first kiss. His kiss was firm and long and passionate . . . it was a hero's kiss. It was a kiss that let Lucia know how he felt, in case he didn't make it and was never able to tell her.

For several long seconds, Jayce put all his focus on Lucia's soft lips. He savored the warmth of being so close to her. He lost himself in the moment, willing it to last forever.

But of course, it couldn't.

Jayce ended the kiss and let Lucia go. She stumbled back a step and gaped at him. He half expected her to slap him. When she didn't, Jayce said quietly, "Now. Go."

Lucia blinked at him. Her eyes were moist. Then she turned and gestured to Kelly. Together, Kelly and Lucia trotted down the hall.

Jayce watched Lucia's skirt swish as she ran. He watched until Lucia and Kelly crossed through the dining room and disappeared behind an arcade machine near the small stage.

For several seconds, Jayce just stood in the silence. He concentrated on breathing in and out. *I can do this*, he told himself.

Seven excruciatingly long minutes later, Jayce was rethinking their whole plan. Why had he volunteered to be the staked goat? What was he thinking? He wasn't a hero. He was a runt who liked to play with crayons—or at least that's what his dad said all the time. It didn't matter that Jayce had outgrown crayons a decade before; his dad still saw Jayce as a little kid drawing pictures. Jayce would have stopped drawing by now if it hadn't been for his mom and his favorite uncle, both of whom told him daily how talented he was and what a brilliant artistic career he would have. Their encouragement had been like a bullet-proof vest that protected Jayce from his father's scorn and from the school bullies who frequently stole his sketches and tore them up just to be mean.

Even without his mom's and uncle's reassurance, though, Jayce still would have drawn pictures. He had to. It was a compulsion. No, it was like breathing—it was essential to his existence, so much so that Jayce was sorely tempted to get out his sketchbook right now. His nerve endings had all turned into needles. He didn't know how many nerve endings his body had. Hundreds? Thousands? Millions? It felt like that many pinpricks were assaulting his skin, multiplying every time Jayce heard even the tiniest sound.

After Lucia and Kelly had run down the hall, Jayce had hurried into the storage room, preparing for his escape. Thankfully, the small storage space was lit by one weak overhead light bulb. The bulb revealed a space packed with boxes and toys—or at least Jayce thought they were toys. Small plush, mechanical animals and floppy dolls lay among the boxes. One of the dolls had red pigtails and big, round green eyes that seemed to look right at Jayce. He'd shuddered and put his back to it.

Shoving boxes aside, Jayce had searched for the vent cover he'd spotted when he was in the ductwork. He found it quickly. He'd thought he was going to have to unscrew the vent cover, and for that purpose, Lucia had given him a screwdriver she'd taken from a toolbox in the dining room. But Jayce didn't need it. The vent cover was rusted and bent; all Jayce had to do was give it a kick and it popped away from the wall. Jayce moved a couple other boxes to be sure his way was clear, and then he returned to the hallway.

Then, because he didn't have the guts to wait until the Mimic happened to find him, Jayce decided to make sure the Mimic knew he was here. He took a deep breath, opened his mouth, and bellowed, "Ouch! Stop that! You stepped on my foot!"

Grabbing the end of the tabletop, Jayce pulled it away from the wall and slammed it back again. The bang echoed down the hall.

Come and get me, Jayce had thought.

Jayce didn't know how artificial intelligence worked, but he decided the programming that drove the Mimic's slaughter might be advanced enough to suspect a trap if it spotted a human loitering in a hallway, doing absolutely nothing. Jayce, therefore, had spent the next three minutes pretending to fiddle with the storage room doorknob. Now, his shoulders and back ached from being in the hunched position, and from holding his terror at bay. He was about to give up on the subterfuge when he heard a creak.

Jayce went still. He put all his concentration into his

ability to hear. The creak sounded again. And then he heard what he'd been waiting for. *Tap-hiss-rasp.*

The Mimic was coming.

The pinpricks turned into a gazillion stiletto knives impaling Jayce's skin. His heart rate quadrupled. Sweat slid down the back of his neck.

Jayce shifted his head infinitesimally, just enough to look down the hallway from the corner of his eye. At first, he saw nothing. Then he spotted a shadow stretching out from the open doorway to the employee's lounge. Another tap-hiss-rasp.

And there it was.

The Mimic, in a frayed yellow cat costume, stepped into view. The cat's head, its pointed ears torn at the ends, its whiskers bent, turned slowly. It looked down the hall, directly at Jayce. The hall lights flickered.

Even though Jayce had been waiting for the Mimic, expecting it, Jayce let out an involuntary yelp. The hypothetical scenario had been one thing. The reality was another. Jayce's adrenaline system went into overdrive. He flung the storage room door open, and he dashed into the room. He slammed the door behind him.

Jayce didn't have to hear the Mimic's tapping footsteps getting closer to know the creature was coming down the hall after him. Even if the Mimic had been silent, Jayce would have been aware of its approach; he could feel the thing's homicidal intent scourging through his body as if the Mimic had already started tearing Jayce apart.

Jayce forced himself to focus. He ran through the small maze of boxes and crouched in front of the exposed vent opening. There, he paused and listened.

The storage room door flew open. It slammed against the wall. The small room went black.

Jayce dropped to his knees. He felt for the sides of the vent. When he was oriented, Jayce pushed his head and shoulders through the small opening. Fighting nausea and full body tremors, struggling to draw enough air into lungs constricted by panic, Jayce wormed his way forward.

Jayce had been funneling all his attention to his ears, so they were working overtime. They provided him with an ongoing accounting of very step the Mimic took. Now that the Mimic was close, only a few feet away, its footfalls weren't taps. They were resounding thuds. The storage room floor shook every time the Mimic took a step.

Once Jayce felt his feet slide through the vent opening, his lungs relaxed just a little. His full body was now in the duct. He'd done it. He'd gotten into the duct before the Mimic got to him. Now, all he had to do was keep crawling, as fast as possible.

That, however, was easier said than done.

Jayce could feel beneath his groping hands that the duct seams in this part of the ductwork were barely holding together. Every time the Mimic took a step, the duct rattled, and the seams groaned and plinked as if giving up their connection inch by inch. Jayce was being thrown around inside the duct as it vibrated in response to the Mimic's pounding advance.

On his stomach, though, Jayce was able to keep moving forward. He just hoped the duct would hold long enough for him to reach a more stable section of the metal labyrinth. The seams in this part of the duct were weak, their rivets coming loose.

As he wriggled forward, Jayce strained to hear what he was waiting for. He listened for the bang of a door slam and the snap of a deadbolt sliding into place.

And he did.

Yes! Jayce thought exultantly. Their plan had worked.

Jayce shifted his elbows and pulled himself another few inches forward.

It was a few inches too far.

As Jayce crawled over the next seam, his shirt sleeve caught on two of the loose rivets. When he pulled himself forward, the fabric popped the rivets completely free. Jayce heard them ping off the vent's metal walls. Suddenly, the duct was filled with the grinding screech of metal sheering away from metal. Two more rivets were torn loose from the seam, and the seam failed. The section of the duct that Jayce was in disconnected from the next section. His portion of the duct shook sideways, and then it canted sharply. Jayce began sliding in reverse.

Scrabbling for purchase, Jayce tried to splay his palms against the metal, begging it to hang on to him. His fingers encountered a sharp edge that sliced into his skin. Jayce suppressed a cry as he realized what was happening: he was falling back toward the storage room.

Jayce fought the pull of gravity. He ignored the pain in his hands. He didn't care how badly he was sliced up. Falling through a break in the ductwork was nothing compared to being returned to the storage room, and the Mimic.

For a few seconds, Jayce was able to hold himself in place. He gasped for breath and grunted, attempting to pull himself upward to the broken end of the duct. He made it one inch . . . two inches.

And then something hard and cold clamped around Jayce's feet. Searing pain encircled his ankles.

Jayce was yanked backward so fast he didn't have time to scream. He didn't scream until he was wrenched free of the vent, and his legs were wrested from his body. Then he screamed. But not for long.

Kelly and Lucia had shared an exultant hug as soon as they'd crammed the small table into place. "We did it!" Lucia breathed as she and Kelly clutched at each other in triumph and whirled each other around.

It had worked!

The storage room door was deadbolted. The tabletop blocked the door, and the small table wedged the tabletop tight so it couldn't be pushed away, even by a superhuman mechanical creature.

Lucia and Kelly had pulled apart. They'd exchanged a look. Lucia had suddenly remembered Jayce; clearly, Kelly had as well.

"Come on, Jayce," Lucia had whispered as she strained to listen beyond the newly constructed barricade.

All manner of *thumps* and *bangs* and cracks had been coming from inside the storage room. It was impossible to separate them into a narrative. Was Jayce getting away?

"He'll probably head back to the office," Kelly had whispered after a couple seconds. Lucia nodded.

She and Kelly had turned to start down the hall so they could go back to the office to meet Jayce. But they only took three steps before they understood that Jayce wasn't going to make it to the office.

Jayce's scream undulated through the entire building. It caromed off the walls and echoed down the hallways.

It rang through every room. It speared through Lucia's skin and rippled through her entire body.

His scream went on and on, sounding and resounding. And then it stopped.

Kelly and Lucia once again fell into each other's arms. This time, they held each other in despair.